NO TRUCE WITH THE VAMPIRES

Book One

Yea, all things live forever, though at times they sleep and are forgotten.

—   H. Rider Haggard

NO TRUCE WITH THE VAMPIRES

Those Who Sleep

Martyn Rhys Vaughan

No Truce With The Vampires
Those Who Sleep

BOOK ONE: THOSE WHO SLEEP

ONE

I was born twenty years after the vampires took over the world. So I don't remember a world in which the vampires did not rule, although I did, of course, read about those days in school. Those days seemed fantastic then and even more fantastic now. Their rule is so natural, so inevitable, so—now here's a big word—inexorable, that a world which They do not control feels impossible; no, not impossible—simply not worth talking about. They were made to rule, and that is the way of the universe.

I am not really a user of big words; I'm only a regular guy, although one who got caught up in some pretty crazy events. My Elite Mistress has said I should write it all down before my human memory starts to falter and splutter, and I start to get things mixed up. It must be wonderful to be able to see things from a viewpoint which encompasses centuries, to view the passing of decades the way we see the passing of weeks. I have asked her if she can explain how it feels, but she just smiles, ruffles my hair and says she can't—there's no real way to explain time to a shadfly. (I like the way she says the full word, and not just "Shad", the way many of Them do.)

OK—that's enough philosophy; what do they call it—meteor physics? Never mind.

So who am I writing this for? Who do I expect to benefit?

Well, I'm assuming you're like me—a shadfly, a harmless, mouthless bug that comes up from the lake, lays a few eggs and then skedaddles to the great Bughouse In The Sky. You've probably heard a lot of dumb things about what happened and gotten completely the wrong idea. Well, that's over now because I'm going to give you the plain, unvarnished truth. (Have you ever tried varnishing truth?—I haven't).

OK. Let's get down to it. My name is Charles Gray and at the time I worked in the Human Division of the State Security Police. I was, and still am, a Sergeant, which is a pretty good position when you realise it's usually the highest a regular human can reach in the Police Service, although I think there are a few human Lieutenants in the North. It's a pity Edward and I never agreed about too much so I could have impressed the lunk! I like the uniform, except all that black gets a bit too warm when you're chasing some low-life. I was about thirty-four/thirty-five at the time and was a reasonably fit, reasonably good-looking guy. (Well, I was under the impression I was a reasonably good-looking guy. A lady Vamp told me that once. And, no, I'm not talking about seductive human women. Or short, introductory passages in Jazz either.) If it wasn't for my recurrent "idiopathic" anaemia, I'd hit all the bells. But my shots take care of that.

When this particular yarn opens, I was stationed in Flurida, south of where SeaWorld used to be. It's built over now, of course; the Mistresses aren't really interested in sea life. Especially octopuses and the like, so I'm told. They don't use haemoglobin, which is a big No-No as far as Vamps are concerned. (Apparently earthworms are OK, but they'd have to eat a lot of them!)Funnily enough, the town that replaced it is called "Marinetown": I guess even the Vamps like a bit of nostalgia.

(By the way, I'm sorry if you find the word "Vamp" offensive; normally, I say "Mistress" like they expect. It's street slang, I know, and They don't like it, but I'm assuming no, ahem—Vamp—is going to be reading this.)

You may not know much about my area of work, so I'll quickly explain we were a body of humans entrusted with dealing with other humans—problem humans, if you know what I mean. There have always been people who don't like the current way of doing things and always will be, I guess. Usually, they're harmless, and the Vamps simply ignore them, but they sometimes cause trouble. And Vamps don't like trouble; They like a nice, orderly world where they can get on with their research and find things out about the Universe. I kind of drifted into the job; there isn't much in the way of interesting work around these days now that all our needs are catered for. And I don't like troublemakers. When you think about how bad things were before the Vamps took over, I just don't see what the problem is. I've read about the wars that used to happen every couple of years and how stupid we Shads were. Killing each other in thousands with bombs and guns and flamethrowers and nearly ending the whole world. That's why They moved in, as every guy with a working brain realises. We were fooling around with building killer robots and artificial diseases with one hundred percent mortality, not to mention a zillion different atomic weapons. So when I hear meat-heads talking about the "Good Old Days", I tell them what kind of world we'd be living in if They hadn't moved in and taken our toys off of us.

There wouldn't be a world—just a big pile of radioactive shit with some killer robots nosing around trying to find a survivor or two.

So that's what They saved us from. Sure, we have to pay for it, but didn't anyone tell you there's no such thing as a free lunch? If you disagree with that, you're not a Noramerican and you can put this book down right now.

(I'll stop capitalising "They" now—I think you get the picture.)

And I'll be telling the events from the point of view of the 34/35-year-old Charles Gray, not the grey-haired wreck I am now, so it will unfold before your eyes like a videodrama, with me knowing no more than you. So I won't be revealing then what I know now. And as you will see, I know a helluva lot more now than I did then. Got it? No? Well hopefully it'll get clearer. So it was yet another hot, sunny, Fluridian day when I was called into my Police Commissioner Mistress's office. There was a small woman with short mousey-brown hair sitting in a corner, but I ignored her, assuming she was some kind of secretary. I stood at a respectful distance from my Mistress. I've seen her name written down, but I'm not sure how to pronounce it; it looks like "Alicia Aiyana." As is usual with High-Status Vamps, she was stunning: Ivory skin, eyes of a deep, cruel blue and raven-black hair cascading down her back. I'm not sure how far it goes down her back as I've never seen her standing up with her back turned. I've also never seen a raven, but from what I've read, the word is used to give the impression of a very dark, glossy, shiny sort of black, and that sums up Mistress Aiyana's hair perfectly. I concentrated on looking at her for three reasons: 1) It's protocol, 2) I enjoy looking at her and 3) it takes my mind off the great mural on the wall behind her. It's of a scene I don't understand. It shows what looks like a ruined church of some kind on top of a hill with a lot of steps going up to it. The whole thing looks slightly sinister. I've seen the same mural in other buildings in Marinetown. I don't know why Vamps like something so simple—but for some reason they do.

I stood to attention, but she smiled and said, 'At ease, Gray. This may take a while by my standards and I don't want you to get varicose veins. I might feel the urge to nibble on them.'

I relaxed and waited for her to continue. Most High-Status Vamps don't have a sense of humour, but

Mistress Aiyana does, and that's one of the many things I like about her.

She leaned back in her cushioned chair and placed slim, vermillion-nailed fingertips together. (I used to wonder then whether the colour was natural. Now I know, of course.)

'What do you know about the Diodati Institute?'

I thought for a few moments, not wanting to appear ignorant. Then I had it.

'Blood,' I said.

She smiled again, with the air of a teacher whose rather slow student had just exceeded expectations.

'Well done, Gray. The Diodati Institute is involved in the blood business.' She leaned forward with a mischievous air. 'Now, for extra credit, tell me exactly how it deals in blood.'

My mind whirled for a moment. The last thing I wanted was to appear dumb in front of Mistress Aiyana. What was the correct phrase?

'It's a bioresearch centre,' I said, feeling just like an eager puppy must feel, 'it's all to do with…'

A carmine-tipped finger was raised to stop me.

'Slow down, Gray. Could you remind Cadet Serafina here,'—she nodded at the silent young woman in the corner—'how things used to be, before the Takeover, that is.'

I gave the woman I now knew to be Serafina a quick glance. She stared back at me with dull cow eyes. I dismissed her. She was unimportant. Pleasing Mistress Aiyana was what mattered.

'Well,' I said, 'as everyone knows, before the Takeover, vamp—I mean Masters and Mistresses—had to rely on taking human blood whenever and wherever they could get it. It was a very demeaning lifestyle and meant the natural rulers were always few compared to us. Finally, when the stupidity of us humans threatened all life on the planet, you were forced to intervene and take over the world's governments. But you needed more blood than the human population of the time could supply in order to support a much larger population of Masters and Mistresses.'

('Just call us the Elite,' Aiyana purred, 'it's much quicker.')

I dipped my head briefly to show I had accepted the admonition and continued, 'So your people devised a way to produce large quantities of human blood on demand. And that's why you have places like the Diodati Institute.'

'That will do for the time being,' Aiyana said briskly. She glanced at Serafina. 'You understand this?'

Serafina gave a quick nod. 'Perfectly. It is like wine used to be in the old days; the *Grand cru* is produced by the Blood Farms, the *Vin ordinaire* by factories like Diodati.'

I began to speak again, but Serafina cut me off.

'I understand why the Diodati Institute is so important, Mistress, but why is this Police Division involved? We Originals have no use for its products.'

I cursed inwardly. Damn! This woman is sharp! Why didn't I ask that?

I sent a hostile glance her way but, if she noticed it, she did not allow it to register. To add to my irritation, Aiyana rewarded her with a broad smile.

I couldn't help but notice her superbly sharp canines as her lips parted and I must confess that even after years of close contact with Vamps it still gives me a brief shudder. (One I hope is not visible from the outside!) It must be what a gerbil feels when it realises it's sharing a room with the family cat.

'An excellent question, Serafina,' she said. 'Looks like Vampire Resources have sent us a promising young Cadet.' She looked at me briefly as if to say *Not like you Old Timers!* and then continued, 'Work on the vats is very mundane and undemanding. Even a human can do it. But of course, much of the work is automatic. In fact, all of the work could be automatic, but we of the Elite have discovered your people must have something to occupy their time, some sense of accomplishment. I believe you call it Making A Difference. And so we deliberately hold back from automating everything in this society of ours. That introduces a degree of unnecessary inefficiency, which in turn requires us to administer the necessary chastisements to those who fall below the expected standards, but in the long run it is to the advantage of both species.'

Serafina nodded again.

'Thank you, Mistress. A most lucid explanation.'

Aiyana immediately shed her air of gentle camaraderie and, leaning back, said, 'So now I want you two to go over to the Institute and see why they have sent me some troubling reports. It appears,' and she smiled, 'they have run into something they don't understand. I'm sure it's too trivial to waste Elite time on, but I think I can spare your rather less precious time on it.'

Eager to wrest the initiative from Serafina, I said, 'And what exactly were in those...'

I stopped. Aiyana had turned away but, at my words, returned to look me in the eye. One immaculately tailored eyebrow lifted itself, slightly furrowing the alabaster forehead.

'Are you still here?'

We went.

Outside of the Police Building, the heat smashed down onto me like a sledgehammer. I turned to comment on that fact to my companion, only to find her several steps behind me and shading her eyes.

'Is it always so goddamn bright here?' she said in a peevish tone.

'Well, this is Flurida,' I began and then I picked up on her accent, which, now I was out of Mistress Aiyana's penetrating gaze, I was enough in control of myself enough to notice. 'Say you're not from around here, are you? Where you from: Somewhere up North?'

'Vancouver,' she said, lowering the palm from her eye level and looking up at me.

I smiled: Something in common at last!

'Hey, I got people in Seattle! That's not far from Vancouver, is it?'

She looked at me pityingly.

'Not Vancouver near Seattle. I'm a smidgeon further north: Vancouver in what used to be called Granada.'

It was my turn to give a pitying look. I may not be the sharpest flesh-piercer in the Killer Robot armoury, but I knew "Granada" wasn't right. I might not know the exact name; I know it ends in "-*ada*", but at least I was aware of my ignorance.

I made another attempt to establish rapport, as befits two officers on the same case.

'I don't even know your full name—I'm Charles Gray.'

'I know,' she said in a flat, uninterested voice. 'Mistress Aiyana told me before you came in.' She made an attempt at a smile and extended a white hand. I held it briefly, surprised by its coldness; it seemed she had brought a little of the Northern climate down with her. 'I'm Serafina—Serafina Ginevra.'

I stopped for a moment on the busy sidewalk, causing pedestrians to flow around me like a river around a rock.

'Serafina Ginevra,' I said in wonderment. 'What a beautiful name. What is it—Mex?'

She managed a real smile at my praise.

'No, Italian. I don't know what "Serafina" means, but "Ginevra" is "White Phantom."'

I was really impressed. How is it foreign names always sound so mysterious while I'm stuck with "Charles Gray"?

I was still puzzling over that issue when Serafina touched me on the shoulder to remind me we were on a mission and not beginning a Three Year Course on Comparative Linguistics.

Anyway, we walked to the Motor Pool, booked a car out and I nosed out into the heavy Marinetown traffic, heading for the Diodati Institute on the other side of town.

TWO

The traffic was as merciless as ever, and the July sun was fierce on the transparent roof. I could see Serafina was screwing up her eyes again and so I darkened it. As her vision adjusted, she noticed my hands on the wheel.

'Are you really driving this thing?' she asked, as if I was doing something illegal.

'Sure. It's a perk of the job. Can't let machines do everything. Isn't that what Mistress Aiyana just said?'

'A perk of the job?' she said, in the tone of someone who has just witnessed a chimp refusing a juicy banana. 'You could be reading the case notes rather than weaving in and out of all this traffic.'

I frowned. Perhaps Serafina was a bit too much of the "*kick-ass woman-in-a-hurry*", as well as having just implicitly criticised a senior officer.

'Look, I can drive this thing, as you call it, as well as any electronic gizmo. Well, almost as well,' I added, as I came within a few micrometres of a very expensive-looking limo. 'And there aren't any case notes as yet. We're the ones who'll be writing them after we get there.'

That shut her up, and she spent several minutes gazing out of the car.

'So many people,' she muttered, as if to herself, 'and so many Elites as well. We don't see so many Originals where I come from.'

'Don't you like Originals?' I said, somewhat sharply. Her "I'm-Better-Than-This" attitude was beginning to grate. 'We were here first.'

She glanced at me and then back to the throng of pedestrians.

'No, we weren't. The Elite have been here as long as we have. They stayed in the shadows, just taking what they wanted, when they wanted it. I suppose back when everything was a blob of slime, we shared a common ancestor, but they developed much faster than we did. They're our superiors in every way. It was only when we were about to fuck everything up that they had to move in and actually run the place.'

I don't like profane language in young women and I told her so. She gave a slight shrug and continued as if I hadn't spoken.

'You know what they call us?—"Shadflies". Just things that flutter around for a few days and then fall to the ground and get stomped on. When you can live for centuries, you have so much time. So much time to understand things until in the end you understand it all.' She turned to me with a triumphant look on her small features. 'Everything!'

I decided I didn't like Serafina Ginevra and also decided I really didn't like this near-worship of the Elite she was revelling in. I have nothing against Vamps, but I don't think they're God. A silence fell in which only the gentle purring of the motor was audible. Finally, I decided to break the silence with my irritating subordinate. I'm a sociable guy and I don't like too much quiet. (I get enough of that in my apartment.)

'The reason we're seeing so many Elites is because this is the Farm Store quarter. This is where the very rich ones get their fix of—what did you call it?—premier cru.'

She straightened in her seat.

'Oh, is it? That's interesting.'

Interesting isn't a word I'd use about the Farm Stores, but at least she no longer looked as if she was doing everyone a favour by riding along with me.

I pointed down the street.

'That's the biggest one in Marinetown. Rousseau's. Only the top Vam—ah—Elite can afford his prices.'

'Yes, I've heard of it,' she said, leaning forward. 'What a pity we can't take a look.'

It was my turn to shrug as we swept past the gleaming plate glass and chrome-bright steel of the huge store. Its great windows were coloured red, for obvious reasons, and they shone bright pink in the blaze of sunlight.

'I. . .' she began, but did not complete her sentence.

Suddenly, it was as if the fist of a tremendous giant had struck the car's rear. The back end went up, and I thought for a dizzying instant we were about to flip completely over. Then the terrible roar of the explosion cut through the car as the roof was torn open like the lid of a pickled-soya can. My eardrums nearly imploded as I fought to control the tumbling vehicle. In the rear-view mirror I saw a great red and black ball of flaring, flaming destruction begin to rise into the bright blue sky.

I lost my battle with the car's trajectory and we smacked into a parked vehicle. I was momentarily blinded as the airbags mushroomed into our faces. A terrible furnace wind blasted above us.

'Wha-wha. . .' I heard Serafina mumble. I gave her a quick once-over. No visible wounds; she seemed OK. Then I was out of the car and running towards what had clearly been the site of an explosion.

The entire front of Rousseau's had gone and the walls of the remaining part had been blown out and torn into twisted shards, jagged and fatally sharp, like the teeth of a terrible predator. Here and there were pieces of wet and slippery flesh: The remains of store workers who had been near the centre of the detonation. And the blood! The part of the valuable product which had survived the blast well enough to remain liquid, was pouring over the sidewalk and pooling on the road. It looked like a million men had been instantly exsanguinated. (Sorry—showing off again, I guess.) That wasn't the case, of course; it was just the stock being released. I became aware Serafina was behind me.

'Gray, what happened here?' I heard her say. Suddenly angry, I whirled around to face the cadet.

'What do you think, you stupid bitch? The whole place's been blasted to Kingdom Come.'

She seemed incapable of comprehending me.

'What—blown up? A bomb? Explosives? But that's impossible!'

'Use your eyes!' I roared and, grabbing her shoulders, shook her like a terrier shakes a rat. 'What do you think—someone farted?' Releasing her, I propelled her towards the centre of the wreckage. 'Look for survivors, people who can be saved! And Ginevra. . .'

'Yes?'

'When we're on duty, you call me "Sarge" or "Sergeant." Never call me "Gray" again or I'll bust you!'

She looked even more shocked, if that were possible, but without reply she moved gingerly into the ruined building. Using my wrist communicator, I called for medical assistance and then followed, picking up sheets of torn and twisted metal to see if life was holding on anywhere.

There was not.

I heard sirens and suddenly First Responders were all around me, pushing me out of the way, surging past. I let them pass; I know basic first aid and that's about it. Eventually, Serafina and I met up with them at the rear of the building. There, the walls were still doing their job of holding up the roof and some doors were still on their hinges. Everything else which could have moved, had moved and lay on top and underneath each other at crazy angles. Here, the dead were still recognisable as people, although with severe burns and lacking most of their clothing. I could see all of them had been human— but then I had known they would be.

The chief medic turned to me and took her mask off. She was also human, but then I had known she would be.

'Any view about what happened?'

I shook my head.

'No. Except that somebody didn't like this place and blew it to Hell.'

'No chance of an accidental explosion?'

'No chance at all. Are you saying the Elite don't know how to wire a place up?'

The woman looked embarrassed.

'No, of course not. Well, it looks like we don't have anything to do here.'

'No, you don't, and as this is obviously a crime scene, it's best we disturb things as little as possible.'

She nodded, and the medics left.

Serafina touched a shoulder, making me start as I hadn't realised she was behind me.

'Sarge, what do we do now?'

'We get out and let forensics examine the place. There're no living things here, not even a cockroach.'

We slowly worked our way out of the wreckage, being careful not to rip ourselves open on the jagged metal. Most modern Vamps have a good deal of self-control, but it's not unknown for them to lose their cool at the sight of human blood; they wouldn't demean themselves by licking it off the ground, but a juicy human or two might be too much of a temptation. By the time we had reached the open air, the sleek vehicles of the forensic boys had arrived and their boss, a Vamp Lieutenant, was approaching me. I don't know how he knew me, but it was soon clear he did.

'Anything to report, Sergeant Gray?'

I shook my head.

'No, sir. A very powerful explosion. No survivors.'

He turned from me, sweeping me out of his consciousness, and waved to the forensic technicians to enter the building. I knew they would be looking for traces of whatever chemical had caused the detonation, using clever techniques I knew nothing about. Most of science is a closed book to humanity these days.

Serafina and I stood some distance away from the explosion site. She was looking up at me, apparently waiting for me to say something important, but I had other things to concern me than Serafina Ginevra—like our original mission. The patrol car was now useless, so I had to report for further instructions. Just as I was about to call HQ, a beautiful limo drew up alongside. It was jet black and so polished highlights could be seen glinting in the bodywork as it slid silently to stop near me. It gave the impression of being a sinuous, powerful Big Cat. The driver's door crashed open and a large man almost flew out of it. I could tell at once from his possession of a thick black beard he was a human.

'You!' he barked, pointing a stubby forefinger at me. 'You in charge here?'

Given that I was a regular cop rather than a lab boy, I supposed I was.

'What happened here?' he bellowed, turning from me to look at the twisted remnants of the store which still had a sheet of coagulating crimson liquid slowly seeping out of it.

'It'll all be in the official report,' I said and started to move away from the man and his ultra-expensive vehicle, but he clutched my shoulder with fingers of steel.

'You'll tell me now!'

I removed the fingers: I'm not a particularly big guy but I'm pretty fit.

'What's it to you, buddy?'

My words looked like they were giving him a heart attack. His face, already ruddy, almost became the same shade as the red tide flowing from the destroyed building.

'What's it to me?' he roared. 'I'll have your badge for this! Don't you know who I am?'

'No, surprise me.'

Well, he did just that.

'I'm Didier Rousseau,' he said. 'I own this place!'

'I'm sorry for your loss…' I started, but then my eyes narrowed. 'What—you're the guy who sells his own people's blood for money?'

I saw his fists clench.

'Yes, I am, and in case you don't know, flatfoot, it's a perfectly legal job in a free-market economy. One which keeps our society nice and healthy and peaceful.' He rammed his face so close to me I could smell the tang of real meat in his stinking breath. 'And one which pays your wages, cretin!'

I pushed him away as gently as I could. I didn't want any "Police Brutality" ticket hung around my neck. I knew I had to backtrack after letting my feelings run away with me; I like to think I'm a professional.

'I apologise, sir. It's been a difficult day, as you can see.'

He turned from me to survey the wreck of his business.

'Difficult day! I'm ruined. Now Berislavic will take the top spot. I'm ruined!'

'You're insured, aren't you, sir?' Serafina said, no doubt thinking she should make her presence felt. He looked at her as if he had just found something unpleasant on his sole.

'Insurance doesn't cover terrorism.' He looked back at the wreckage. 'Terrorism! After all these years!'

I nodded at Serafina to indicate it was time we moved on, but Rousseau had not finished with me. He looked back to see us walking away and called, 'I don't know who you are, buddy, but I'll sure as Hell find out! I have regular lunches with Commissioner Aiyana and I'll make sure you never work in the Police Service again!'

Serafina looked worried, but I said, 'Ignore him. We did nothing wrong.'

'The poor man,' she said, 'losing his business like that.'

At that, I just lost it. 'Poor man!' I exploded, 'He runs Farms where they milk people for their blood to sell on to High-Status Vamps who don't like the taste of the mass-produced stuff! He gets more in a month than you'll get in a lifetime of pounding the beat!'

She stared up at me. 'I'm entitled to my opinion.'

I said no more, cursing the gods who had lumbered me with Serafina Ginevra and went back to trying to contact my boss. However, she beat me to it as my wrist communicator flared into life, revealing the statuesque features of Commissioner Aiyana.

'Gray!' the image barked, 'what are you doing?'

I started to explain about the bomb, but she cut me off.

'I know about that! What about the Diodati Institute—why aren't you there?'

'Our car was damaged in. . .' I began, but once again, she cut me off.

'The Institute is within walking distance for a fit officer. Get there now!'

We went.

THREE

We hurried along the sidewalk, angrily pushing the rubber-neckers aside.

'What was all that about?' Serafina asked. 'It sounded like you don't approve of the trade in premium blood. Are you criticising the Elite?'

I was too annoyed to bother looking at her.

'Of course I'm not criticising the Elite! It's the Middle Men I can't stand. They know they've got a captive audience, and so they charge the highest possible prices!'

'The Elite can afford it. So what's the problem?'

I wanted to stop and shake her, but I couldn't afford any further delay.

'Have you ever seen a Blood Farm? Seen the conditions those poor bastards live under? The bosses cut all the basic costs so they can inflate the profits, making sure the Donors get the cheapest possible food, the most basic living conditions.'

'I still don't see your point, Gr…Sarge. Being a Donor is voluntary. They get a secure life without the pressures of holding a job down. As I said, what's the problem?'

You're the fucking problem! I thought, but I tried sweet reason.

'You say being a Donor is voluntary, but it's always those at the bottom of society that end up as one. And there are rumours about people being kidnapped and forced into Donorship. Once you're in one of those places, you never get out—except in a pine box.'

'Rumours. And I thought you were a police officer.'

I almost hit her then, but we had arrived at the Diodati Institute. Nervous-looking security people let us in after we showed our badges at the top of the steps, although I had to hurry Serafina along as she seemed to dawdle at the very threshold. We found ourselves in a classy atrium, all marble and shiny silvery metal. We were standing on a central plaza lined with huge tree-ferns; in a corner was what looked like a Steinway grand piano, and off to our left, a medium-sized waterfall, cascading down into a pool from which a silvery fountain was jetting. I thought for a moment I'd come into the wrong building, and I was standing in the forum of a high-class hotel. Any moment I expected a *maître'd* to approach and ask what I planned to order that evening. (Or, more likely, ask me to leave—I don't exactly move in those circles.)

Instead, a small, rotund guy hurried up to us. The poor bastard was as bald as a well-polished 8-ball. If the security staff had looked nervous, this man looked like he'd opened a letter and found it contained the time and place of his execution.

'Sergeant Gray? I've been expecting you to arrive a long time ago! Your Lieutenant led me to believe you would be here as soon as possible!'

I stared him down.

'That's right. And we have. We had a little distraction on the way.'

The man clearly didn't recognise sarcasm when he heard it.

'Well! Sergeant Gray, I can't say I'm too impressed with your Department so far.'

I didn't allow myself to get too pissed off by his attitude: Clearly, he was under a great deal of stress. I could tell from his—ahem—*hairstyle,* he was human, and most humans get a little nervous when dealing with Elite members of the Police Service, and Mistress Aiyana can be very intimidating.

'Perhaps it's best we start at the beginning,' I said, as gently as I could. 'I am Sergeant Charles Gray, my companion is Cadet Serafina...Serafina...' I don't know whether I blushed at that point, but I knew, if I had, it would have been hidden under my tan. I had forgotten Serafina's last name, even though I had used it just a short time earlier.

'*Ginevra*. Serafina Ginevra,' came a somewhat peeved voice behind me.

'Yes, Serafina Ginevra.' I repeated, trying to give the impression I had just recalled the name. 'And you are. . .?'

'DeLancey. Graeme DeLancey. I'm in charge here.'

An eyebrow of mine lifted slightly. A human in overall charge? That was unusual—perhaps the nature of the product made here would be a tad too tempting for a Vamp to siphon off a private supply. (Not that I would ever suggest anything of the sort, of course.)

'My boss didn't give me many details other than something was troubling you folks here. So what exactly is your emergency, Mr DeLancey?'

'Chief Scientist DeLancey,' the small man replied, straightening his back in an effort to look taller. At that, I had to smile. The guy didn't look old enough to be a real scientist because the Elite had restricted scientific studies to their own ranks several decades ago. If he was a real scientist, he must be more than a little rusty. But I played along.

'Yes, of course.' I glanced over my shoulder at my Cadet. 'Chief Scientist DeLancey, Ginevra.' 'Of course, Sarge,' came the reply. I could detect the undertone of amusement, but I'm sure DeLancey didn't. I turned back to the harassed official, who was now mopping his considerable brow with a pink handkerchief.

'Now, sir, to business. I'm afraid my superior did not give me much in the way of details before I left. With your permission, we'll be taking audio and video recordings of all we see and hear. What exactly is your emergency?'

DeLancey glanced left and right as if checking for eavesdroppers, and then, in a quieter voice, said, 'There's been a fatality. A High Ranking fatality.'

I picked up on the invisible Capital Letters.

'You don't mean…an Elite, do you?'

His face became even more worried.

'That's precisely what I mean. Now look, I think we should continue this talk in my office. It's shielded against surveillance.'

We took the elevator to the second floor. Its walls were so transparent I had to touch one to check it was really there. And as I did, I could see people motionless below, watching our progress. A few minutes later, DeLancey was ensconced behind a large, genuine wood, desk, and was pouring himself a glass of water. He did not offer Serafina or me a glass as we sat side by side, waiting for some revelation.

'I think we'd better move a little more quickly, Chief Scientist,' I said, pulling out my electronic notebook. 'Are we talking about an industrial accident or…' and I hesitated over my next words, 'a homicide?'

DeLancey took a long draught of his water.

'It is definitely not an industrial accident. So,' and he paused, 'I guess it must be a homicide.'

'How was the Elite killed?' Serafina said, in a surprisingly calm manner.

DeLancey looked back and forth between us, giving the impression of a jackrabbit deciding which coyote was the hungrier.

'I don't know.'

Serafina and I exchanged momentary glances. Then I continued: 'You don't know how the Elite was killed? Was it a firearm, a blade, a blunt instrument? Was it a flammable liquid poured on the victim and ignited? Was the victim crushed by a heavy object? Did the victim fall from a great height? Was…'

DeLancey held up a weary hand.

'Please, Officer. There is no need to go through every possible method of leaving this Earthly realm. Suffice it to say that the death appears to have been—unusual.'

I snapped my notebook shut and stood up.

'I think we should see the victim with no further delay. If you would be so kind, Chief Scientist.'

'Of course.'

We left his room and walked along a featureless, totally white corridor; it was so white I began to think I would develop snow blindness if I didn't get out of it soon. Then there was another elevator ride in an invisible cage, and we had arrived.

A door opened automatically, and I was looking down from a platform onto rows and rows of cylindrical vats; one after the other in each row; one row next to another row, and so on. They stretched so far away from us that eventually I was unable to distinguish individual vats. There was just a metallic sheen in the distance. Each vat had pipes entering and presumably leaving at different levels on their sides. And one of the pipes was transparent and contained a deep red liquid.

I knew what the liquid was.

It was, of course, blood.

This set-up was a product of the genius of the Elite, which had stabilised their relations with humans and allowed both species to coexist in relative harmony. When they took over, there had been insane terror from the humans. It's not easy coming to terms with the realisation you're no longer ruler of the world, that you've gone from being top dog to a type of livestock.

But the Elite in their cleverness had solved that: They had developed stem cells from human bone marrow and cloned those cells so they could produce them by the million; each little cell churning out its portion of human blood. As a result, there was enough blood to support a large vampire population for the first time in their history. Most Vamps prefer the *Grand cru*, of course, but that's a different story.

I had been staring in wonder at the serried ranks of vats for so long that Serafina tapped me on the shoulder and gently said, 'Sarge…'

I turned: DeLancey was standing beside an open doorway.

'If I could have your attention, Sergeant. The victim is in here.'

We entered. The lighting was low, and a very peculiar smell was hanging ominously in the air. It was like the strange sweetish smell we used to get in butcher shops—when there were any. DeLancey was standing with another man next to a black sheet on the floor. There was a large mound of something underneath the sheet.

'Be warned,' he said, 'this will be quite a surprise.'

He nodded to the unnamed man, who slowly pulled the sheet up and away.

I was expecting to see the corpse of a dead vampire. They are so similar to the rest of us in outward appearance that I did not expect to see anything greatly different from previous homicides.

But what I saw made no sense at all. It was just a mound of various forms of meat, covered in the purplish sheen that comes from vampire blood. Serafina and I simply stared at the pile of flesh, bereft of the power of speech. The meat had long rods of a yellowish substance on top of it at varying angles. But then, I began to recognise the shapes of various organs. Vampire organs have different functions to human ones, but I have done enough comparative anatomy to recognise a few. And there they were, piled up higgledy-piggledy.

'It's just a crazy mess of organs,' I finally said, noticing my mouth had quite suddenly gone very dry. 'But where's the skeleton?'

The unnamed man had a pointer and gently prodded one of the long yellow objects. I then could see other, thinner, shorter rods attached to it.

'What is that?' Serafina asked, in a hollow voice.

'This Elite used to be called Janos Estok. You're looking at a part of his skeleton,' DeLancey said, so quietly I could only just hear him.

But then the import of his words hit me.

'His skeleton? It's lying on top of his flesh!'

'Exactly. Elite Estok was not shot or burned or knifed. He was turned inside-out.'

Serafina and I looked at each other, eyes wide and staring. A nameless dread began to gnaw at my own vitals. But DeLancey had not finished.

'And Elite Estok was turned inside-out in this very room. One that was locked at the time.'

Reluctantly, I moved closer to the repugnant mess, bending down to get a closer look. As I did, I thought I heard Serafina murmuring to herself. I thought I heard her say *Could it be that they have...* I decided the shock had gotten to her and didn't ask what she meant. I stopped less than a metre away from the grisly mound of dead flesh and stopped. What was I looking for? I was no forensic expert. I glanced at DeLancey, who was standing nearby, with a look of eager anticipation in his eyes. I straightened up.

'Well?' he said.

I shook my head.

'I don't have anything to say, Chief Scientist, other than—he's obviously dead.'

I regretted the remark almost instantly: It sounded like I was being flippant, and he took it that way.

'Sergeant Gray, is that all you can offer? Am I paying your wages in order to be given vacuous platitudes?'

'I don't know what you want, sir. I've never seen anything like this. In fact, I've never heard of anything like this. It doesn't seem physically possible.' I was going to add it seemed "supernatural", but people don't use that word anymore, at least not in polite company. 'I'll call forensics and hand this over to them. They may have heard of this kind of thing before.'

They'll love me, I thought grimly, *first a terrorist outrage and now a homicide performed outside of the laws of physics.*

However, Serafina had not concluded the interview was over.

'Chief Scientist,' she said, moving slightly past me, 'what was Elite Estok's position in the Diodati Institute?'

'He did not have a position. He was sent here to examine our procedures.'

'And what was the reason for this examination?'

DeLancey suddenly looked simultaneously confused and wary.

'Is that any of your business, madam?'

'This is a police investigation, sir, and so anything which may be relevant is my business.'

Jesus Christ! She's after my job! I thought.

He motioned to the doorway.

'Let's go outside. The air's a little rank in here.'

We gathered at the railing along the edge of the viewing platform. DeLancey began mopping his shining forehead again.

'We have had a few problems here.'

'Namely?' I said, wresting the initiative back from Serafina.

'We have had…unexplained losses here recently.'

'Of blood?' I asked.

'Yes, of course blood! That's all we do here. We tried to discover the reason for the loss, but we could not. So the management Board sent Elite Estok here to do a thorough search.' DeLancey's features twisted to a sour expression. 'Evidently, we Originals hadn't been thorough enough.'

'And did he find anything?'

'I believe he did. He informed me he had found something which might be highly significant, and he was in the process of compiling his report.'

'So he had started a written analysis. May we see the report, Chief Scientist?'

Now DeLancey was definitely looking frightened.

'I'm afraid not. It has disappeared.'

Serafina and I exchanged significant glances. This might be the first appearance of a motive. Perhaps some moonlighting employee had been caught out by the sharp-eyed Elite. Trading in Black Market blood can be a highly lucrative market, even after undercutting the State-regulated price. I asked a few more questions, to prevent Serafina from asking them, but we soon ran out of both questions and answers. Either DeLancey was deliberately not telling us all he knew or we had already established the limits of his knowledge. We bade him good day and were escorted out of the building.

Back on the baking sidewalk, I let the overworked forensic team know they had another case to investigate and then called Mistress Aiyana. At first, she seemed merely professionally interested in the fact of a homicide at the prestigious Diodati Institute, but when I stated the unusual circumstances of the death, her expression changed so rapidly I did not see the transition. One moment she was her usual, calm, detached, unemotional self and then instantaneously I was looking at a different female vampire. There was an expression on her face I recognised, but one I had not seen those features display before that moment.

And that expression was fear.

FOUR

Eventually, a patrol car picked us up and took us back to HQ. En route, we received a command to go straight to Mistress Aiyana for debriefing. And that lady looked far from her commanding, untroubled self as we stood before her.

We started with our experience of the terrorist explosion, but to my surprise, she did not seem particularly interested in an incident which had resulted in a large loss of life. Perhaps the fact all the casualties had been merely human explained some of her lack of interest, yet somehow I had a feeling it was more than that. In fact, I felt sufficiently puzzled to risk asking my own questions.

'Has any group claimed responsibility, Mistress?' I asked tentatively.

A look of surprise passed fleetingly over her sculptured features, and I thought for a moment I would be reprimanded for my effrontery but, after a moment or two, she replied with a simple negative.

'No, there has been nothing on any of the usual channels.'

'It's still early,' Serafina said. 'Maybe they are still preparing a list of demands.'

'It's definitely too early for empty speculation,' was Aiyana's curt response, and Serafina accepted the rebuke and fell silent, staring at the mural of the ruined church. The Mistress ignored her for the rest of the debriefing and directed a series of rapid-fire questions at me as the in-depth discussion of the Diodati Institute incident got underway. She made me relate what we had observed over and over again. She looked at the videos we had taken and listened to our recordings of DeLancey's statements.

'There is no doubt about the cause of death of Elite Estok?'

'We cannot be certain of the cause of death. We only saw a body in a peculiar mangled state. He might have been killed by whatever force brought about that state, or he might have been killed prior to the event— whatever it was. As I understand it, the condition of the body prevents any degree of precision about the mode of killing. I am not a forensic expert, Mistress.'

Well-manicured nails rat-tatted on her desk, as Aiyana thought over my words.

'Yes, of course you're not. A forensic team is there now, but, so far, they have not added anything to your report.'

Then she looked directly at the two of us, her face still clouded with what I interpreted as doubt and worry.

'Well, I must await their full analysis. Now, Sergeant, a Didier Rousseau has filed a complaint against you but, as he is no longer in the blood supply business, I have ignored it.' She then attempted a smile, but failed. 'You officers have undergone an unusually difficult day. I suggest you take the rest of the day off. I'll transfer other officers into your shift.'

With a nod of the head, we were dismissed, and she returned to staring at a computer monitor.

Although Serafina looked untroubled, I was beat and suggested we get something to eat before clocking out. I'd forgotten how much of a rookie she was until she replied, 'Where is the Dining Room?'

I laughed.

'We call it the Mess Hall here, Serafina.'

She shrugged, and shortly afterwards, we were sitting facing each other at a table made from chipped blue plastic. To my annoyance, she had put both fingers astride her nose in an obvious theatrical gesture.

'What's in that sauce of yours? It's not garlic, is it?'

'Very funny. I know as well as you the Elite can't tolerate allicin. It's an extract of durian fruit, if you must know.'

'Smells like your very oldest socks,' she observed. 'Ones you've been wearing for the past forty years.'

I decided not to react.

'You did well today,' I ventured, hoping to re-establish friendly relations.

My flattery made no impression on her, and she continued to dissect her very-blue steak without looking up. I know the red stuff on the plate isn't actually blood, but it sure looks like it.

'Hey,' I said, 'can we start again? You're obviously a very sharp officer and I doubt you'll stay a cadet for very long.'

She looked up at me.

'Thank you.'

I spread my hands in a placating gesture.

'Now, I suppose you think I'm just an average flatfoot who likes a quiet life.' I waited a few seconds for her to break into a dazzling smile and contradict me, but as nothing happened, I continued: 'Well, you're working with me for the foreseeable future so it's in both our interests to get along.'

She finished the last piece of nearly raw meat and, leaning back in her chair, said, 'OK. So, tell me a few things about yourself, Sarge. What was it like when the Elite took over?'

I nearly choked on my coffee.

'Serafina! You may think I'm Methuselah, but actually I'm hardly middle-aged. I was only a strand of DNA when they came out of the shadows!'

'Came out of the shadows,' she said. 'Yes, that's the kind of language we use about them, isn't it? Making them sound creepy, evil. Our whole relationship with them has been one of misunderstanding; of deliberate misinformation even.'

This wasn't the conversation I wanted, but I didn't want to show any lack of interest while I was trying to build bridges.

'Misinformation? Such as?'

She looked alert, involved. This was obviously something she cared about.

'The whole B-Movie Gothic Horror bit. Sleeping in coffins; being terrified of crucifixes; being able to turn into a dog, or mist, even.'

'I didn't know about the mist thing,' I said, trying to pretend I was interested. I didn't know what a B-Movie was either, but I'd revealed enough of my ignorance for one day.

She leaned toward me, and I seemed to catch a messianic look in her eyes.

'Do you know they're supposed to frizzle up in direct sunlight? Turn into a cinder or dust or some such gibberish.'

'Yes, I had heard that.'

She leaned back and laughed.

'Well, there can't be many in Flurida then, can there? Now,' and she leaned towards me again, 'how many people know that the whole "frizzling-up" thing came from a cheap motion picture in the Twentieth century? It's not even a genuine legend! Sure, the Elite were originally nocturnal, but they can tolerate a lot of sunlight.'

'It sounds like this is something you care a lot about.'

She took a swig of her coffee.

'Exactly right, Gr…Sarge. The Elite are as much part of the natural world as we are. Why, we even shared a common ancestor back in the Pliocene!'

'What's the Pliocene?' I said, but she ignored my ignorance.

'No,' she said, 'evolution has moved on. We had our day, but so did the Neanderthals. But we're luckier than them—the new rulers don't want to exterminate us.'

Although I am not anti-Vamp I was beginning to find this hymn of praise to them a little one-sided. And more than a little irritating. Especially as she kept using strange words. *Neanderthal*, for God's sake!

'Well, yes,' I said, 'you're dead right. They don't want to exterminate us. Now, why would that be?' I leaned back, rested my chin on a hand and looked around with an air of mystification. (Sometimes I think I should have gone on the stage instead of pounding the sidewalks of Marinetown.) Then I smiled and raised a finger in her direction. 'Why, I've got it! They like to drink our blood! Silly me!'

She did not look too happy with my *coup-de-theatre*. (Ha, ha!)

'Very funny. It's not their fault they developed mutations which have altered their haemoglobin metabolism. The same mutations which give them their lifespans, I might add. What would you have done in their place—starved to death when what you needed was all around you, in nice, soft little packages?'

A frosty silence fell. Much like the one which develops in her northern homeland, I imagine. Then she shrugged, gave a half-hearted smile, and said, 'OK. We were supposed to be talking about you. I've been informed you're not Methuselah, which is a start. So is there a Mrs Gray at the moment?'

I was annoyed by her directness, but shook it off and said, 'No. Jane passed some years back. And we didn't have any kids. Jane didn't want them—she said the world had changed too much to bring children into it.'

Serafina pursed her lips as if thinking deeply about my words, and then said, 'And your folks are long gone as well, I suppose.'

'Correct. I never knew them as I was brought up in an orphanage.'

'Oh, sorry to hear that.'

'Not as sorry as I was to be there. I've blocked most of it out. It was very *Dickensian*.'

I could see she hadn't picked up on the reference. But I've read a lot of books since I've been on my own. I regard myself as a cultured man—not some slob.

'I mean, strict. Very strict. But I wasn't alone. I have a brother, a twin brother—Edward.'

'That's nice. It means you have someone. I guess you guys share a few beers together after the game?'

'No, we don't. He disappeared four years ago.'

'Oh. *Disappeared*. That sounds a bit final. I didn't think people could'—and she actually did the "Air Quotes" gesture—'disappear in our super-efficient, regulated society.'

'Well, they can. Edward was—is—a very effective operator, and, apparently, he found a way.'

'How efficient is "efficient"?'

I put my fork down on my empty plate.

'I think you're taking this "Keen Cadet" business a little too seriously, Serafina. I don't appreciate being interrogated.'

She grimaced.

'Sorry. My bad. I don't have any folks back home, so I tend to compensate by over-analysing everybody else's family.'

I relaxed. It seemed she was human, after all.

'Edward is a physicist.'

Her eyebrows arched.

'A physicist? Now, that is unusual. I thought humans were barred from higher education.'

'Not all of them. Not if it appears they can make a genuine contribution to how the Elite run the world. And Edward was—is—very clever.'

'And his field?'

'Now, stop right there. I said Edward was very clever—not me. The last time I saw him, he said he was working on something very big. He started telling me about it, but he could tell I was just not getting it, so he grinned and we had those few beers instead.

'Then he vanished.'

I tried then to turn the conversation to her background, but it appeared as if she didn't have one—as if she had just popped into existence fully formed. This was one of several things which bugged me about Serafina.

So we called time, and our unusually difficult day was over.

FIVE

Normally, I sleep very well. My apartment is quiet, and I rarely hear much through the walls. There was the time I had two young lovebirds next door and—well, you can guess the rest.

I have learned to cook pretty well, too. I had to after Jane passed. I went through a TV Dinner and TexMex phase, but now I'm pretty good. If ever I had a dinner guest, I'm sure he or she would be quite impressed.

So I don't get a bad stomach or anything like that, and usually when my head hits the pillow, it's lights out until it's time to get out onto the streets and start giving low-lives a lousy day.

But that night, after the experience at the Diodati Institute, things were a little different. First of all, I couldn't get to sleep. I kept looking at the clock, unable to believe the numbers it insisted on showing. I did eventually get off, but instead of my normal deep, dreamless slumber, I became aware in a confused, restless way that all was not right. There was much I could not remember, or chose not to remember, but I do recall one particular incident. I was on a bare, black plain, stretching out forever in all directions. There was nothing to see all the way up to the encircling horizon. Then I felt coldness on my legs and, looking down, I saw a thin, greenish mist rising up from the black soil. As it rose, it became thicker until it wrapped itself around me like an icy green shroud. I felt the coldness invade my nostrils and sink into my lungs, chilling every part of me, inside and out. I knew my heart was slowing; getting slower and fainter, until I was certain it had stopped. I could see nothing but swirling green curtains of clinging fog. And I remember realising this was just a dream and that I struggled to break back into consciousness, like a free swimmer who has gone too deep and can see the faint light of the surface, so far away. You see, I have seen corruption and decay, and I recognise that particular shade of green that accompanies those states—and the enclosing fog was the very same green. And I somehow knew there were unknown shapes out there out in the putrescent fog and that, although I could not see them, they could definitely see me. Strange, misshapen forms there were, moving fluidly in the coils of those intertwining streamers. A sharp wind was blowing, although it did not stir the fog, and it was as if it was whispering one word repeatedly; one word meant as an insult, a mocking insult: 'Shadfly. Shadfly...'

And then: 'Shadfly, you are not our prey. There is no honour in you. But the others, tell them. Tell the others. Tell them we will be amongst all of you soon.'

And I knew then those shapes were evil and were waiting for the moment when they could do harm. Maybe to me; maybe to somebody else.

And then I awoke, covered in cold sweat and shaking.

I was glad to get back to work, and no kidding. Dreams don't usually shake me—even if I do remember them—but that one did. Even Serafina asked me if I was alright when she saw me. My face must have looked different or something.

'I'm OK,' I said. 'Didn't get much sleep. Bad stomach, I guess.' I tried a joke. 'Too many doughnuts, maybe.'

Instead of grinning, she shook her head and said in the tones of a disappointed schoolmarm, 'Too bad. Maybe you should give them up.'

I was searching around for a witty reply when she jerked her head toward Mistress Aiyana's office and said, 'Boss wants to see us. Something's up.'

'What more than already...?' I began, but she had already turned her back on me.

Mistress Aiyana looked up as we came in and stood to attention. She didn't tell us to relax but, in her clipped This-is-Business voice, said, 'I want you to go into the Farm Quarter. Several of the businesses there have received threats recently.'

'Only threats?' Serafina asked.

'Threats at the moment. But after the Rousseau incident, we must follow every potential lead. It may well be someone has begun a concerted attack on the whole supply chain. First the retail outlets, then the primary producers.' She pushed a sheet across the table toward us. 'Here's a list of the Farms which have reported being threatened. Start at the top and work your way down. See if there's a common thread linking them. Something's going badly wrong and I don't like it.'

'Any update on the Diodati affair?' Serafina said—to my horror. It certainly looked like the girl had—what's the word?—*cojones*.

The Commissioner glared at her.

'If there had been, you can rest assured that I would have apprised you of it, Cadet.'

I could almost see the icicles hanging down from her words, but Serafina seemed unabashed.

'Thank you, Ma'am.'

Serafina reached for the list, but I beat her to it. I glanced down at the names: All well-known, well-regarded establishments. All seemed legit, but I must confess I didn't know that much about them. The Farm Quarter is one I try to avoid, if possible.

But it appeared avoidance was no longer possible.

We soon were driving along the sweltering streets of Marinetown. The sun had moved closer to us by several million kilometres; well, it felt like it had. Serafina's face was almost hidden by a pair of huge cheaters.

I was irritated by her get-up; I don't know why.

'What is it with you?' I said. 'You an albino or something?'

'I'm from the north,' she said, staring out at the passers-by. 'I thought I'd told you that.'

'Yeah, you did. I didn't think you meant the North Pole.'

A silence fell, one in different circumstances I might have described as frosty. (I try to avoid clichés.) I couldn't grasp what it was about this young woman—but she had a truly remarkable talent for getting under my skin. So I just ignored her for a while, leaving her to gaze at the sweltering streets and sweating inhabitants of Our Fair City. (That's a joke, BTW.)

She broke the silence.

'You know before I joined, I didn't think Vamps could be cops.'

Despite my inclination to ignore her, I was intrigued. 'Oh, why?'

'Well, that stupid business about not being able to enter a building before being invited. Can you imagine a load of Vamp cops waiting patiently to be invited into some place, while there's a murder going on inside?'

I pursed my lips; she had a point. I hadn't given it much thought until that moment.

'So what's the answer?'

'Well, it's only a custom, it's not like there's some mystical forcefield around buildings. And it only applies to residential properties, in any case. "Residential" means there's people living there.'

'Well,' I said, ignoring the jibe and affecting an air of complete lack of interest, 'you've sorted that out. Thanks a lot.'

Silence returned.

But gradually the blocks became few and far between; the streets meaner. Many buildings had fire damage and displayed black openings in their walls like the eyeholes in a fleshless skull. It had begun to look like what it really was: A region of town left to the humans, and where Vamps rarely trod.

'Doesn't look too pleasant around here,' she observed. 'Looks kind of abandoned.'

'That's because it is,' I said. 'Vamps like the merchandise these people produce, but they don't care too much about the condition of the people.'

She pursed her lips and made no attempt to look at me when she spoke. 'Careful, Sarge. You're sounding like you disapprove of the way things are.'

I didn't reply: Maybe she had figured out the real me. But no point in sticking my neck out.

And then we were out of the city and were travelling through the lush green vegetation of Flurida, away from the Gulf and further into the sticky subtropical interior. Up ahead, I could see a series of low-rise, rectangular buildings which were painted a lurid red to advertise what was produced there.

'Jackson's Farm,' I said, glancing down at the SatNav to confirm my identification.

Serafina was not impressed.

'It beats me why you don't let the car drive itself. Are you trying to prove something?'

'Yeah, I am,' I said. 'Proving I'm still a human being and I can think for myself.'

We pulled up just shy of ornate wrought-iron gates. I saw a camera swivel towards us, and an electronic voice said: 'State your name and purpose of visit.'

I held up my badge so the camera could see it.

'Sergeant Charles Gray and Cadet Serafina... Serafina...'

I'd done it again.

'Ginevra,' came a peeved voice next to me.

'I have an appointment with Carlos Jackson,' I added, without acknowledging Serafina's assistance.

There was no reply, but the heavy gates swung open. I noticed there was a stylised heart logo at the centre of the gates, which split into halves as they opened. I tried to avoid crass thoughts about "Broken Hearts", etcetera.

Jackson was a solidly built man with a craggy, well-used face topped by a white crewcut, and with a handshake like a hydraulic press. Fortunately, he toned it down for Serafina—or she didn't feel the pressure, as if she was tougher than me: In either case, she showed no discomfort..

'I believe you've been receiving threatening messages, Mr Jackson,' I said after introducing ourselves.

He waved a massive hand.

'Call me Carlos. Yes, I have—and here it is.'

He pushed a piece of paper across the desk to me. Picking it up, I held it so Serafina could read it as well. Not that it said much. All that was on the paper was

YOU ARE A TRAITOR TO THE HUMAN RACE. WE WILL DESTROY YOU.

THE SONS OF MAN

'The Sons Of Man?' Serafina said. 'Whoever they are, they seem to be unskilled in logic. That's a tautology.'

Jackson looked at me, and an eyebrow raised slightly. However, Serafina caught the gesture and said, 'What I mean, Mr Jackson, is it's just another way of saying "Men".'

'Yes,' he said, 'I suppose it does.' He looked back at me and no longer seemed quite so friendly. 'So all you sophisticated people have to do is look for someone unskilled in logic and you've got them.'

'I assure you we are taking your complaint seriously, Carlos,' I said, vowing to have a word with Serafina later. I looked down again at the paper. 'They clearly are wary of sending an electronic message, given how easy they are to trace.' I looked up again. 'Where was it found?'

'One of the harvesting rooms. It was pinned to the door.'

'Outside or inside?'

'Outside. Just a simple thumb tack. It would only have taken a second.'

'Could the—uhh—donors have stuck it there?'

'They could have done. But why would they? They're all happy here.

It's an easy life on Jackson's Farm compared with living on the streets in Marinetown. They get good food, security, entertainment—why we've even had a coupla people get hitched here. You see, Charles,' and he leaned forward as if about to impart some sensitive information, 'none of the people in Jackson's have that much up-top. Let's just say they only need a small hat size. What we do here is really a type of Social Security—if you know what that was. They love it here. Whoever wrote the note is not one of my people. They couldn't possibly be.'

'Your place is gated. Any holes in the fence?'

'I've had the security staff check that as soon as I saw the note. If they came in that way, they knew how to make it look like they didn't.'

'And you were on the premises?'

'Of course. All Farm owners live on their Farms; I thought you knew that.'

'Fine,' I said, ignoring the (justified) criticism. 'If it's OK with you, I'll get a team down to review your security.'

He shrugged.

'If you must. They won't find anything. My team know their stuff.'

'Well,' I said, as I rose from the chair, 'we won't get anywhere by staring at a piece of paper. Could we take a look at the particular harvesting room in question, Carlos?'

'Sure,' he said, 'we have nothing to hide here. It's a well-run, clean establishment, completely in accordance with all Elite Federal regulations. We only need to check for bugs and viruses a couple of times a month. I'll be only too pleased to show you round.'

We followed him to the second nearest building. The sun blazed down on the back of my neck, bringing me out in prickly heat. I wondered briefly how Serafina was coping but, being annoyed with her, did not ask.

Jackson allowed a small camera to check his retina, and the door opened immediately and he invited us in. It was a blessed relief to enter, given the coolness of the interior. But after only a few seconds I detected a faint smell which I quickly recognised. It was the sterile, slightly acidic smell of a hospital ward. The room was full of long, low couches with stands holding saline bags next to them. All were unoccupied. Along one wall was a small group of men and women, none of them more than forty, I calculated. Some were reading, some sleeping, some wearing headsets which no doubt had immersed the wearer in some improbable AI adventure. Those who saw Jackson rose to their feet, but he just grinned and waved them back into relaxation.

'It's OK, folks. These people are from the police; they've come to investigate that threatening letter.'

I glanced at him.

'Is it possible for me to talk with them, Carlos?'

'Sure! I'll bring one over. We can all have a good chin-wag.'

'No, I mean just Cadet Gin—*Ginevra*—and me, alone, if you don't mind, Carlos.'

Jackson looked at first surprised and then a little irritated. Then he shrugged.

'Sure. Nothing to hide here.' He waved at the nearest man. 'Bill, come over here. These people would like a little talk.'

A tall, distinctly skinny man detached himself from his chair and came towards us; rather nervously, I thought. I gave Jackson a quick glance, and he frowned, but moved out of earshot.

'Hello, Bill,' I said, giving Serafina a warning look to keep her trap shut. 'How are you today?'

He looked over my shoulder at Jackson and then back at me.

'OK, I guess. I got no complaints.'

Maybe I was letting my dislike of the Farms get the better of me, but I continued, 'You're well treated? Not too much blood taken?'

'No, no, it's fine here, not like some of them places I heard about. We only give twice a week, and we get good rations. We soon make it up.'

'So you wouldn't have written that note?'

He grimaced, puckering his lips as if about to spit.

'Hell, no! Why would we cut our own throats?'

I smiled as best I could and said, 'That's fine, Bill. You get back to your magazine now.'

Although Jackson was getting increasingly irritated, I interviewed a few more, even letting Serafina talk to the one woman who volunteered to be questioned. It was soon obvious they were all telling exactly the same story and, despite feeling Jackson's stare on the back of my head, I came to my own conclusion there was nothing they could tell me.

I thanked them. On the way out, we looked at where the note had been pinned. But there was nothing really to see; just a hole, so small to be almost invisible.

We wrapped it up back in Jackson's office. He had the air of a man who has been vindicated after being unjustly doubted.

'So you see, it could not have been any of my people. They're as happy as they could be.'

'Giving blood, so that others can drink it?' I said, instantly regretting my words and my tone.

He said nothing for a while, and then: 'I think we're finished here, Sergeant. I must say, I find your obvious prejudice more than a little offensive, not to mention old-fashioned. There are maniacs out there who appear to want to destroy a legitimate part of our free-market economy and put a lot of people out of work. Rousseau's was one of the primary outlets for my product and the loss is already impacting the bottom line. I want you people to keep a vital part of the Noramerican lifestyle free and safe. I believe that's why I pay your wages. If you don't like working for a living, I'd gladly take the tax cut and do my own vigilante work.' He glared at the two of us in succession. 'Anything else?'

I shook my head and stood. The last thing I needed was another citizen reporting me to Mistress Aiyana. I have a pension to consider.

'No, thank you for your time, Carlos. If I have offended a hard-working man like you, then I apologise.'

That mollified him a little. He nodded and said, 'OK. I'll see you to your car.'

As we drove away, Serafina said, 'You really shouldn't let your opinions influence your police work like that.'

'You want to button your lip, Cadet!' I snapped. 'Lecturing that guy like he was a kid in Grade School got us off to a real good start! And may I remind you, you're still on probation, so you'd better not lecture me either!'

She did not reply, merely adjusting her glasses and looking out over the lush vegetation as it swept past.

SIX

We were heading for the next Farm on Mistress Aiyana's list when I abruptly stopped the car.

'What's wrong?' Serafina asked, suddenly alarmed.

I got out of the car and crossed to the passenger side.

'You drive for a while,' I said, looking down at her. For a moment, she looked vulnerable, almost childlike.

'I don't know how!'

I pulled the door open.

'I'll tell you what to do. It's a straight road. You'll be alright.'

Reluctantly, she moved over and placed her small hands on the wheel.

After a few cursory instructions, we moved off, very jerkily at first, but I was impressed at how quickly she mastered it. I leaned back and closed my eyes; I needed to think. Nothing made sense; this was not like any case in my—admittedly limited—experience. Life had been predictable, boring even, and now, for no apparent reason, everything had been turned upside down. Or, in the case of Elite Estok, inside out. And there appeared to be two separate problems; why would bad guys, who could turn people inside out, need to resort to old-fashioned explosives? Why didn't they just do the same to the people in Rousseau's as they had done in the Diodati Institute? But then I was jerked out of my reverie: Serafina was speaking.

'We're here. Gilroy's Farm.'

I looked up and saw a block of low rectangular buildings, very similar to those we had seen at the previous establishment. But these were subtly different; Jackson's had been in good shape and freshly painted in bright scarlet. Here, the buildings seemed older, less cared for, shabbier. The paint had probably once been as bright and bold as at the previous Farm, but here it was dull and faded, almost brown in places. And there were patches where it was entirely missing, revealing bare wood. Serafina had stopped just before the gate to the Farm, but here there was none of the intricate metalwork that had been so pleasing to the eye at Jackson's.

A microphone on a pillar on one side of the gate hissed and spluttered, and eventually a crackling human voice could be made out. A voice that was definitely belligerent and unwelcoming.

'Yes? Whadya want?'

'We're police officers Mr Gilroy, Sergeant Gray and Cadet Ginevra,' I said, leaning over Serafina to make sure I could be heard. 'The Commissioner must have told you we were coming.'

There was a few seconds' silence, then: 'Yeah. She did. I wasn't expecting you so soon. You'd better come on in. Park outside the nearest building.'

The gate began jerkily to open, with metal grinding against rusting metal. For a moment, it became stuck and just sat there, quivering. Then it seemed to regain its strength and fully opened. We glanced at each other, and then Serafina put the car in motion again and drew up to the nearest building, which was also the largest. As we exited the vehicle, the door opposite us opened, revealing a man dressed in faded jeans, a grubby T-shirt, and very little else. A black spliff hung from his lower lip. Attached to the building was a large wire cage inside which were four massive black dogs. I did not recognise the breed but they were like Dobermans on steroids. Oddly enough, they showed no interest or excitement at the sight of two strangers and merely looked at us with their languid brown eyes.

'OK,' the man we assumed to be Gilroy himself finally said, 'I suppose I gotta do this.' And with that, he retreated into the building. I walked up the steps and blinked to adjust my eyes to the dimness of the interior. I turned to check if Serafina had removed her ridiculous shades, and was surprised to see her still at the bottom of the steps.

'Come on,' I said. 'We haven't got all day!'

She looked up at me, still wearing her deep black shades.

'It's rude to enter a building without being invited.'

I swore under my breath at her peculiar ways. *Is this what they're like in the North?* I thought.

Gilroy, obviously in a hurry to have done with us, came back to the doorway and snapped, 'Come on in, for God's sake! Let's get this over with!'

We both finally entered and seated ourselves in front of his desk, this time without being invited. The place stank of weed. Gilroy glared at us with red-rimmed eyes.

'Look, I ain't got time to waste on this crap. I want just one thing from you goons—find the bastard who's trying to put me out of business and waste him.'

'Well,' I said, 'I don't think we will be proceeding exactly in that fashion, but we are as eager as you are to put him away, Mr Gilroy.'

'Are you now?' he said, in what was a very badly disguised sneer. 'I'm glad to hear it. Here, take a look at this.'

Once again, I held up the grubby piece of paper so we could both read it.

'Well, there's more than one of them,' I said.

Serafina nodded.

'It's in capitals, but the writing style is quite distinct.' She gave a wry smile. 'Well, we've learned something at last: There are at least two people involved.'

The message was similar in tone to the first one, although a little more explicit. It read:

YOU TRAITOR HELPING THE VAMPS STOP
IT NOW OR DIE FIRST WARNING LAST
WARNING

I knew the routine by now.

'Pinned to the outside of a door?'

'Yes.'

'Any sign of forced entry to the premises?'

'No.'

'We'd like to look inside one of your Farm buildings,
Mr Gilroy.'

He looked hesitant.

'Why?'

'Just routine. We'd like to check that there's no
dissatisfaction amongst your Donors.'

'Would you now? My word ain't good enough for
you?'

I tried an ingratiating smile.

'It's not that we don't trust you, Mr Gilroy. It's
standard procedure. You know what those bureaucrats
in City Hall are like.'

He shrugged.

'Don't I just. All those damned inspections they keep
making. Checking up on me all the fucking...' He
glanced at Serafina. 'Pardon my French.'

Her smile was much sunnier than mine.

'It's fine, Mr Gilroy. I don't speak French.'

That seemed enough for Gilroy, as Serafina's scorn
had obviously gone over his head, and he stood and
indicated the door.

'Follow me.'

I rose from the chair, but suddenly a wave of
blackness flooded my vision. I had to grip the edge of
the desk to keep from falling. I felt Serafina grasp my
arm.

'Sarge, what's wrong?'

I couldn't reply until the blackness faded, and I was
able to see Gilroy's cheap and stained desk below me. I

turned slowly to her, careful not to move too fast in case it started another attack. I smiled weakly.

'I'm OK, it's my anaemia. I get little blackouts if I stand too quickly, that's all.'

'You should get it checked out.'

I sighed. The innocence of youth!

'Yes, Serafina. I had thought of that. I'm a little behind on my injections, that's all.'

'Are you two coming or not?' Gilroy called from the open door, his patience evidently exhausted. 'I've got a business to run!'

We walked through a curtain of heat into the cruel blaze of the sun. Fortunately, the walk to the first Farm building was not very far across the parched yellow grass.

'Come on in,' Gilroy grunted, as he did the security checks. The door swung inwards, and an uninviting smell hit us instantly. It was the stench of an old-fashioned cow shed: The smell of urine, faeces and sweat; the sure sign of poorly-maintained sanitation facilities. We moved slowly into the fetid gloom. It had the same basic layout as at Jackson's: Low couches, blood storage racks. But this time there were distinctly shrivelled-looking individuals on two of the couches, with tubes rising from their arms into the collecting machines. Even in the dim room, we could see the deep red colour of the liquid contained in those tubes. Six other people were sitting dispiritedly in battered easy chairs, all of which had patches where the stuffing was emerging. They stared blankly at us as we came in. There was no flicker of interest or alarm in those eyes. Just blank stares such as a plastic mannikin could produce.

'I'd like to speak with one of the Donors, Mr Gilroy.'

'Would you now?' He hesitated, then 'But if that's procedure, I guess I gotta do it.' He crooked a finger at the nearest of the six, a woman. 'Rosario! Come here! These nice people want to speak to you!'

The woman pushed herself out of the tattered easy chair and came hesitantly towards us. As she approached, I could see the filthy state of her ragged clothing and the dirt on her bare feet. The eyes seemed dead, as if there were no mind behind them.

I glanced at Gilroy.

'We'd like a little privacy, Mr Gilroy.'

'Would you now? Well, you ain't getting it. I'm staying right here so I can make sure no one's telling lies about me. I got nothing to hide.'

Serafina began to protest, but I gave her a momentary touch to warn her off. It was Gilroy's way or the highway. So, I went through the motions of discussing the matter of the threatening note, but all I got was a series of No's. It was soon apparent that either there was absolutely nothing she could tell me, or Gilroy's presence was intimidating her. I risked asking Rosario if everyone was content in Gilroy's Farm, and was assured everyone was. However, I did not miss the quick flick of her gaze in Gilroy's direction. It didn't take me long to decide there was no point in proceeding, and I told Gilroy we had finished. He grinned and, placing his hand perilously close to Serafina's buttocks, propelled her towards the doorway, bending down to say something to her.

For a few brief instants I watched them turn into silhouettes as they walked into the sun blaze, and then started after them, angry with myself for letting Gilroy control the meeting. But as I did, I felt a hesitant hand on my arm and, turning, looked down into Rosario's face. But it was no longer impassive. It was twisted with some strong emotion.

'Señor,' she gasped, 'you must get us out of here! Two months since I was taken. Two months since I see my little Arturo. *Sangre de Jesus*—get me out!'

SEVEN

We visited one more Farm before I used my discretion and decided we weren't getting anyplace. It was beyond belief that all the Farms were sabotaging their own businesses, and we had found the Donors were either reasonably happy with their terms of employment or, if unhappy, unable to do anything about them. I was also increasingly annoyed with Serafina counting every pothole we fell into. How many annoying traits can one person have? Nevertheless, I was calm enough to report the state of Gilroy's Farm to Mistress Aiyana as soon as I checked in. She didn't seem too interested and simply said she'd look into it. However, she took no note of the name or location.

In turn, I was more interested in the person sitting opposite her. He hadn't turned to look at me while I'd been reporting, but now he did. From his confident, aloof expression, I knew at once he was a Vamp. There was no need to ask him to open his mouth. (Joke.)

'Gray, this is Lieutenant Dracul Ardelean. He will be leading the investigation from henceforth.'

Being a Vamp, Lieutenant Ardelean did none of: 1) Rising to meet me, 2) Offering to shake my hand, 3) Saying he was pleased to meet me and was glad we'd be working together. However, I was not upset, as I would have been more than a little surprised if he had done any of the above. Instead, he said, 'Yes, I expect to wrap this up very quickly, Sergeant. I was not surprised when I listened to your report and heard your conclusion that it is not the Donors who are threatening to disrupt the

Farms. It would have been incredible if they had been, and, in any case, they could not have caused any significant trouble. It is quite possible these Farm issues are quite simply some human idiot trying to annoy us. It is very likely these ridiculous threats are nothing to do with the real problem—namely, that there is someone out there with the power to cause genuine trouble. I am, of course, referring to the destruction of Rousseau's retail outlet. That atrocity has resulted in a not insignificant disruption to the supply of premium blood, and simply cannot be allowed to recur.'

'Lieutenant Ardelean has a theory which explains how the criminals destroyed Rousseau's shop. Please explain, Dracul.'

At this point, Ardelean stood and looked down at Serafina and me. (Like most Vamps, he was pretty tall.)

'The solution is exceedingly simple. The explosion at Rousseau's was extremely powerful; powerful enough to demolish the building, almost totally. There are, of course, military and industrial explosives, but they would be difficult for a gang of humans to obtain. There is only one feasible substance to which they could be expected to have access, and that is ammonium nitrate. It is a common ingredient of fertilisers and has—before we took over, of course—caused a number of very destructive explosions. All we have to do is locate the establishments producing that substance, and it is there we will be able to root out this rats' nest.'

I had nothing to say or ask, but Serafina suddenly spoke up.

'How does that explain the Diodati incident, sir?'

Ardelean looked at her as if he had just noticed a slug in his salad.

'Cadet Ginevra, isn't it? Well, you should have realised the Diodati problem is a completely separate investigation. It remains a possibility that Elite Estok's unfortunate demise was due to an extremely rare malfunction in the highly complex machinery employed at the Institute. It is very difficult to see how ammonium nitrate could have been involved. Surely that's obvious.'

Serafina opened her mouth, and I thought for a dreadful moment she was going to continue the debate, but very fortunately she changed her mind at the last second, and simply said, 'Of course, sir.'

Mistress Aiyana then said, 'I said I would apprise you of any development in the Diodati affair, and there is one. I don't believe it is significant but I always carry out my statements: Elite Estok, as you know, was terribly mangled, but the forensic team did discover one thing you did not detect—his heart was missing.

'But as I said, I don't see how that changes anything. Now, to return to the matter in hand: Your involvement in this case, Cadet, is now complete. I will inform you of your next assignment shortly. Dismissed.'

For some reason, Serafina gave me a lingering look and then was gone. Strangely enough, I found myself missing her almost at once. And so I was left under the daunting gaze of two high-status Vamps, wondering what their plans were for me.

Mistress Aiyana looked at Ardelean and said, 'Please inform Sergeant Gray of his new duties, Dracul.'

'Certainly, Commissioner,' was his smooth reply as he turned his attention back to me. 'Gray, I have found the names and addresses of two companies which produce agricultural fertilisers. Of the two, one is a long way from Marinetown and produces only small amounts of ammonium nitrate. The other is just outside the city limits and specialises in that compound. It is the obvious candidate for further investigation. I have already established that they are taking on labour at the moment. You will join the workforce and find out if there are any unauthorised shipments of the compound in question, or any other types of questionable behaviour. There are officers more suitable for the job than you, of course, but obviously the applicant must be human.'

'But sir,' I said, 'I don't know anything about chemicals.'

'Irrelevant,' came the steely reply. 'It is very low-grade work. We will give you a list of terms to memorise to make it look as if you have worked in the industry before, and that should be sufficient. Your interview is in three days' time. Make sure you pass it.'

***

Grogan looked up at me from the paper I had given him. I had arrived at the McKinley Fertiliser Corp bright and early, and had already answered a few basic questions. Moreover, I had slipped a few words into the conversation like "magnetite" and "Bosch-Haber", which appeared to have greatly impressed him.

The Force's Infiltration Unit had worked their usual magic on me: My skin tone was much darker, my face wider, and my whole body looked stronger and more supple—bait for a Sons Of Man scout. Unfortunately, for I had always been proud of my chestnut curls, they had made me balder than a hard-boiled egg.

'Your resumé looks fine, Andrews.' (My cover—*John Andrews*) 'You have a good amount of experience in the industry.' He leaned back in his chair and placed his arms behind his head. 'Strange, I haven't come across you before.'

'I was working up North,' I said, trying to exude a confidence I didn't feel. 'Up in Granada.'

'Granada?' he said. 'That's a long way up. You sound like a Fluridian, though.'

'I was only there for a few years. I'm a Fluridian at heart. You can't beat the Sunshine State, I always say!'

Grogan nodded his approval at my use of such an old-fashioned phrase and returned to studying my resumé. Fortunately, it doesn't have to be very detailed if you're only offering a broad back, and he soon pushed it back to me.

'OK. As long as you believe in hard work, there's a job for you here. We're a local outfit and the owner prides himself in giving employment to local people. Sure, we're a bit behind the times here; Mr McKinley doesn't use ruthenium.' (I nodded wisely.) 'Start Monday. Report to Bixby at Oh Six Thirty.'

The following day found me in the Mess Hall staring glumly at my vegan corned-pseudobeef hash. Sometimes I get a craving for real meat, but I can't afford much of it on my salary. I was wondering how Serafina had been able to afford her steak, when a shadow fell across my plate and, looking up, I discerned the lady herself.

'Morning, Sarge,' she said, in an annoyingly breezy tone. 'With a face like that, it looks like you've been given the latrine patrol. Still, I must admit it's a whole lot better than the one you used to have.'

I was not particularly pleased to see her.

'Cut the over-familiarity.' I said, 'I may not be your Sergeant anymore, but I'm still a Sergeant.'

She was unabashed and, without asking, sat opposite me.

'I hear you've been given a hush-hush job.'

I glared at her.

'The important phrase is *hush-hush*. How do you know about it?'

She waved a hand.

'Oh, just scuttlebutt. You know you can't keep a secret in this place. And I didn't think you were vain enough to pay for that makeover you're wearing out of your own pay.' She leaned forward and, with a grin, whispered, 'It's so kind of you to turn the top of your head into a mirror I can check my hairstyle in!'

I carefully placed a forkful of pseudo-meat in my mouth and chewed silently for a while before saying, 'You're very chipper. Glad to get rid of me, I suppose.'

'Oh no, you weren't that bad. A bit disrespectful to the Elite, but we've all been there, I guess.'

Seeing she had no intention of moving on any time soon, I decided to make conversation.

'So are you working on anything—uhh—hush-hush?'

She frowned.

'Unfortunately not. They've got me on office work. Personnel files. I hate it, it's so boring! I want to get back out on the streets so I can get my promotion.'

I nodded, feeling genuine sympathy.

'I can understand that. I'm sure it's only temporary.'

And then a conspiratorial expression came into her features.

'I can tell you something, though.'

I looked around, suddenly wary.

'Careful. You don't want to get busted.'

She waved the hand again.

'Nah, it's not that confidential. I'm not going to name names.' She leaned in, fractionally closer. 'I can tell they're worried. Really worried—about this Diodati business.'

I shrugged.

'So am I.'

'Sure, but they think something is directed at them and them alone. We're not in the firing line, thank God. But they are.'

'And who's doing the firing?'

'Somebody, some *entity* from the past. Specifically, their past, before they took over.'

'That's not very specific, Serafina. I'm only a human—spell it out.'

'I know. But I've overheard Mistress Aiyana talking to someone I couldn't see about people called *Guardians*.'

'And they are? A burned-out rock band?'

'I don't know. I didn't want to get caught listening in on them. She would have skinned me alive. But I got the feeling these Guardians are only called upon if there's a real big crisis of some kind.'

'And Diodati isn't a malfunction in the machinery, but something real big.'

She looked triumphant.

'Yes! Seems like! I also saw a reference to something called *Zee-Zero-Zee*.'

I gazed stolidly at her.

'I know why you're telling me this.'

She looked startled.

'You do? Why am I doing this?'

I finished the last of my pseudo-meat and pushed the greasy plate toward her.

'You're trying to get me to say something anti-Vamp. Probably Mistress Aiyana has put you up to it as part of your office duties. Some kind of test. Am I right?'

Her face went as still and as cold as stone. Then she slowly rose from her chair.

'No. I was just trying to be friendly. Which is more than you ever did. Goodbye—Gray.'

She leapt to her feet, and gave my shiny pate a none-too gentle slap. And with that, she was gone into the throng of the crowded Mess Hall. I looked after her as she merged into the crowd and wondered if I had messed up. I didn't want to be on bad terms with anyone in the Force, and I had started to like Serafina, once I'd gotten used to her eager-beaver approach to policing.

But why tell me about these mysterious "Guardians"? What importance could they hold for her?

Or me, for that matter.

And, more to the point, how did she know the big bald guy sitting there was *me*?

***

I felt more nervous than I had for many years when I parked the old, battered vehicle the Force had given me. I had already noticed it was in about the same condition as all the other vehicles in the employees' parking lot. It would appear I was not about to enter a particularly high-paid profession. Not that my real job is, of course, but I am used to working on the streets, not undercover work. But times had changed, it seemed. Instead of the usual Rent-A-Lowlife I'd been used to dealing with, there was something much more deadly on the loose. I took a deep breath—here we go!

Ahead stretched a large industrial unit with many low-rise buildings behind a wire fence topped with curling tongues of jagged metal. But farther into it, tall, rust-streaked towers rose into the sky. I knew from my briefing that these were the reactors where the ammonia was produced. And I could taste it in the air: A slight sting in the eyes, a slight acrid uneasiness in the mouth. Nasty stuff. And I would be working on making it.

Mentally, I cursed Lieutenant Ardelean and his bright ideas as I walked toward the nearest building. I had already gotten through the first security level by showing my brand new pass, but had to show it again to the big lunk in the reception area.

'You want work here?' he said, as if I had done something beyond the bounds of normal craziness. English was obviously not his first language, so I simply said I did, and made no attempt at further conversation.

'You wait,' he said, picking up a communicator. 'I call Mr Bixby.'

Bixby showed up about ten minutes later; a large, red-complexioned man with what I was soon to learn was a permanent scowl.

'You Andrews?' he said, looking me up and down, and after I confirmed that fact, he snorted and said, 'You must be desperate—wanting to work here.'

'Times are hard, Mr Bixby,' I said, trying to look as desperate as I could—which wasn't hard. I just wished all this could be over and I could get back to my usual dull routine.

'Ain't they just,' Bixby said, 'and for you, my friend, they're just about to get a lot harder.'

And so it proved. I changed into my company boiler suit and was immediately put to work on one of the reactors. The guy I was working with, a small, dark man called Felipe Ramirez, was friendly enough, but like the lunk I'd met on the way in, his English wasn't too clever. He was from some place called Zitácuaro, which I gather is down south somewhere. Anyway, it sure sounds like it's nowhere near here. (I learned how to spell it later.)

The reactors hadn't looked too bulky from the parking lot, but now I was next to one of the beasts, I could see it was enormous and permanently surrounded by a shimmer of heat. As the day was already hot to start with, it felt like I was being slowly cooked. Pipes as thick as my thigh were going in at various levels, some at ground level, some higher up. I had been put onto the hydrogen shift, which is the first stage in making ammonia. Don't ask me for too much detail, but we split the hydrogen from natural gas, making carbon monoxide along with the hydrogen. It's called steam reforming. Do we reform steam?—I don't know.

'Is it always this hot?' I said to Felipe as a way of introducing myself.

He smiled, his teeth startlingly white in his dark face.

'Oh no, Juan, she usually much hotter!'

I figured he was hazing me, so I just grinned and said, 'Just what I was hoping!'

After that, we got on pretty well, and I learned a lot about him and his family. As I expected, they were dirt poor and lived in a run-down part of town, not very far from the ammonia plant. His car was even more ramshackle than mine, and sometimes he was forced to walk, meaning he had to get up shortly after going to bed. He had one child, scarcely more than a baby.

'It is hard, amigo,' he told me as we periodically monitored the hydrogen flow. 'My Marisol, she want a better life for our little one but there is only this work for men like me.'

I nodded.

'Times are hard. That's why I'm here.'

He looked away from the controls, and a wave of sadness passed fleetingly over his features.

'One day, she say to me: Felipe, why don't you go and work on the Farm and bring in some real money.'

I was puzzled for a moment. There is very little call for manual labour on farms. We ordinary folk don't eat much meat, but we still need stuff grown in the dirt, although I know the Elite have a long-term plan to move us to hydroponically grown crops. Then I realised.

'Oh, you mean—the *Farms*. You don't want to go there.'

'No, Juan, never. My father—he make me swear that I never do that. Sell my blood so that *they* can enjoy it. No, never. But Marisol , she say…'

But I didn't get to learn what Marisol said, at least on that occasion, because Bixby suddenly appeared around a corner, and his features were even redder than usual.

'You lazy bastards! You've been chewing the fat instead of working, haven't you! Look at the pressure!'

Felipe and I turned simultaneously to the pressure controls. Eighteen atmospheres. Too low. We rushed to correct it, getting in each other's way in our haste.

'Ramirez!' he roared, looking at Felipe, 'Your pay will be docked. You'll need a magnifying glass to see it, after I'm through. And you'—he spun round to me—'you obviously don't understand simple instructions! I'll tell Grogan to get rid of you!'

A chill shot through me. To be sacked on the first day, after having discovered nothing! I could see Mistress Aiyana and Lieutenant Ardelean slowly feeding me into a meat grinder if I came back empty handed after getting myself let go of quite so abruptly. I had to get him to keep me on, whatever it cost.

'No, please, Mr Bixby! I need this job! I'll shape up, I promise!'

He planted himself right in front of me and his thick lips curved into a gloating smirk.

'You really need this job, huh? What would you do to keep it?'

Visions of my superiors' displeasure swept across my mind. Say anything!

'Anything,' I said.

The smirk became a grin.

'Anything, eh?'

He moved one foot closer to me.

'See this boot? Lick it.'

I looked at him; I suppose I must have given him a pleading look, for he chuckled.

'Lick it now, or you can get your stuff and go back where you came from.'

I went down on one knee and slowly lowered my lips to his steel-capped boot.

If ever I can be the real me again, I thought, I'll make you pay for this.

My tongue flicked over the cap. It tasted of warm fuel oil and was stickily repugnant. I started to get up, but a large hand pushed my head down. The one boot withdrew and was replaced by the other one.

'Now lick this one. And take it more slowly this time. Just imagine it's your wife's pussy. Really enjoy it.'

I hesitated.

'Mr Grogan will be most disappointed in you, Andrews.'

I ran my tongue over the boot while Bixby continued to hold my head down. Only when he lifted his hand did I quit.

I shakily got to my feet to be confronted by his fleshy red face, now showing broken teeth behind a vast grin.

'You really enjoyed that, didn't you, Andrews? Why, I bet you've got a hard-on now.'

I said nothing but thought: *One day you'll feel something really hard!*

He turned to Felipe.

'OK, show's over. You two morons get back to work.' He looked back at me. 'And I'll be watching you, Andrews. There's something about you that doesn't add up. You've got too much fight in you for a down and out. I saw the way you looked at me.' A stubby forefinger came within a few millimetres of my eyes. 'Remember, loser, I'll be watching you.'

And he was gone.

EIGHT

My first report back to my superiors began in the manner I had expected it would. Mistress Aiyana fixed me with her usual laser stare, but one that was not any more unsettling than usual. Lieutenant Ardelean, however, looked at me as if he were itching to call in an exterminator. He switched his gaze to my Mistress, and said, 'I still think we should simply go in and tear that factory apart and make certain we've crushed the nest. May I ask exactly what is stopping us?'

Mistress Aiyana returned his gaze with a disdainful look of her own.

'The same reasons as I gave you when you arrived, Lieutenant. Tensions are running high at present. I don't wish to apply a match to a pile of dry kindling; we have enough problems, without casually inflaming an at-present docile populace. The human agronomists have informed us even a short interruption in the supply of fertilisers would negatively impact on their food crop production. And that would negatively impact on the, shall we say, mood of our subject population.'

(I noticed that, as usual, they were discussing things as if I were not present. Holding it below their vision, I started fingering the plastic tube they'd given me, as if it were some kind of comfort toy.)

'I don't trouble my head about peasants,' Ardelean said, flicking some dust off his jacket.

She frowned.

'You misunderstand me, Lieutenant. I am not speaking out of bleeding-heart sentimentality. I am simply making sure my officers are not stretched further than they are at the moment.' She raised a slim, sharp-nailed finger. 'The matter is closed. Do not attempt to open it again.'

Ardelean tried to hide his feelings at having been corrected in front of a human but did not quite succeed. Obviously having some tension to release, he directed a piercing stare at me.

'It might interest you to know my people have been to the two Farms you and that female visited, and it is clear the exterior fences were penetrated. Someone—no doubt a member of that group with the ridiculous name—entered and placed those threatening notes on the Farm buildings.'

'Not just threats,' Mistress Aiyana murmured.

I looked at her.

She picked up a print-out from her desk, folded it effortlessly in four, and pointed it at the Lieutenant as if it were a dagger.

'Late last night and early this morning, three Farms were hit. The offices of the owners were totally destroyed. High explosive. This was after your people were supposedly watching the Farms.'

Ardelean tried to endure her stare but could not.

'They cannot be everywhere.'

'Apparently not.'

'May I ask which Farms?' I asked.

'Certainly. Gilroy, Jackson and Lebedinsky.'

'And the casualties?'

'Jackson and Lebedinsky were both killed. Gilroy was not in his office at the time and was unhurt.'

'No loss,' Ardelean said. 'The Donors have mostly survived.'

She gave him a quick glance and then returned to me. 'So, Sergeant, you have nothing to report at present from your new employment? You saw nothing that required taking a sample?'

'Nothing,' I said, feeling nervous that I was not offering them some words of great significance. 'The

McKinley plant is not particularly efficient, and much of the machinery is nearing the end of its working life. There seems to have been a lack of investment in recent years. Grogan rarely leaves his office, leaving shop floor management to people like Bixby.' (If I had been expecting sympathy, I didn't get it. They had heard about the boot-licking episode without a flicker of concern.)

Once again, Mistress Aiyana's fingers drummed on her desk for a few seconds.

'Disappointing. Perhaps your position on the hydrogen reactor is too distant from the area where the putative explosives are being manufactured. Is there any way you can get yourself transferred to a post further along the production line?'

I thought of just saying "No", because that decision was in Bixby's hands, but decided that might be unwise, so I simply said, 'I'll do my best.'

'Make sure you do,' Ardelean said, and there was cold steel in his voice.

I nodded to show I accepted the debriefing was over, and my Mistress left the room. I looked up at the Lieutenant.

'Is there anything else, sir?'

'The debrief is over.'

'Thank you, sir.'

I was heading for the door when cold powerful hands descended on my upper arms. I was whirled around, picked up as if I were made of cellophane, and slammed against the wall. The Lieutenant held me pinioned and leaned in so his face was only centimetres away. As he spoke, his lips curled back, revealing two terrifying fangs.

'Something you should know about me, Gray: I am a vampire of the old ways. I don't believe in taking blood from those pitiful wretches on the Farms, and least of all drinking soulless blood made in vats from human tissue. I may as well drink milk! No, I prefer the old way, as it was before you forced us to intervene. The thrill of the chase, the joy of the hunt. The ecstasy of following some terrified young human in the darkness, closing in on them as they try to run, try to hide, seeing their horror as they finally discover what had been stalking them. I've done it several times, and once you have done it, you want to do it over and over again until you have left behind a pyramid of white, drained bodies reaching into the night. I want to hunt, and, Gray, I want to hunt you.'

I was forced to look deep into his red-rimmed eyes, so characteristic of the aroused Vamp. I felt the strength of the fabled vampire grip, and knew I could not escape. I don't know why I didn't kowtow, beg for mercy, but I didn't.

'Not all hunts end with victory for the hunter,' I heard myself say.

Ardelean threw back his head and gave a deep-throated laugh. Then he released me and I slid helplessly down the wall, ending up in an undignified heap. He laughed again, and, without a word, left me.

I was alone. Truly alone.

***

'So what's it like in—uhh—Zittabongo?' I said, as I sat with Felipe at the start of our all-too-short break.

The skin around his lips and eyes wrinkled with harmless amusement, and he replaced his tortilla on its plate.

'You mean Zitácuaro, don't you?' He leaned back, and his expression took on a far-away look. 'Ah, amigo, she is beautiful. We have the wintering grounds of the Monarch butterfly, which flies down from north of here. Sometimes they make clouds of black and orange against our clear skies. We have the rivers and the Sierra Madre mountains. I used to love how they look so blue in the mornings, so beautiful it makes your heart ache.'

'But you came here.'

He shrugged.

'There is no work. What can a man with a little one do?'

'There is not much here. All the good jobs are taken by Vamps.'

He laughed.

'Amigo, I do not do the things with electric machines that clever people do. I just use my hands and my back. I am a simple man.' He smiled. 'Lucky for me, my Marisol—she likes simple men!'

'But would you like to go back one day?'

Suddenly his face slumped into seriousness.

'No. Not now. Things down there are not what they were.'

'Like what?'

'Amigo, what do you know of the history of this Noramerica of ours?'

'Not much: I know July fourth is important, but I'm not sure why.'

'This I understand; here, you do not think much about the way things were. But in Zitácuaro and villages around her, we are different. We remember our past. There was a time when a foreign people invaded our lands.'

'What—the Vamps? Careful, you mustn't call them foreign.'

'No, no, this was before they came out of the darkness to take control. It was a people called Los conquistadores. They did many bad things; killed many, many people. But there is something they did that was good.'

I raised an eyebrow to indicate *Go on.*

He turned away as if not wanting to see my reaction.

'At that time, the people believed in things called Gods. Gods who controlled the sun; Gods who controlled the rains. And these Old Gods wanted something; something in return for stopping the world from going into darkness without end. They wanted blood.'

66

I shrugged.

'That's not exactly unknown these days, Felipe.'

He did not turn back to me, and his voice was soft and quiet.

'No, not like those we have now; who take the blood and let us live. No, no, these Old Gods, they wanted hearts. Living hearts torn from the chests of the people, the people who were—what is your word?—sacrificed.'

I must admit I felt sickened.

'Living hearts? Good God.'

'And they took not one or two, from bad people, from murderers or thieves, but people they had captured. Hundreds of people.'

I'd had enough and reached for my own tortilla, indicating that this talk was over.

But it was not. Felipe finally turned back to me.

'No, amigo. I talk to people I left behind; my own people who would not come to this strange place. And they tell me things I do not want to hear.'

Back went my tortilla to the plate.

'Like what?'

His face became stricken.

'Juan, they say to me—the Old Gods are coming back!'

I stared at Felipe, momentarily unsure if he had cracked some kind of peculiar joke. But why would anybody joke about people having their hearts torn out? A second look at his expression assured me that this was no joke.

'What are you talking about?' I said. I could hear the angry tone in my own voice: I did not want to believe a horror of that sort could possibly be real. 'Are there people lacking hearts lying around?'

'No, no, Juan. It has not come to so far, as yet. But in my homeland, we still have—I do not know your word—*adivinos*. Those who can look beyond the way things seem to be, to what they truly are. And my people in the south, they tell me that the adivinos, they say the

Old Gods are near again. And they are hungry again; they need our worship. They need our lifeforce.'

My anger burst out in an eruption which surprised even me.

'Stop this nonsense, Felipe! If you want us to stay friends, stop it and never mention that crap again, do you hear!'

He looked strangely shamefaced. Instantly, I regretted my outburst. I'm not sure why I reacted so badly.

'*Lo Siento*. I had forgotten you people of the North— you are not like us. You do not hear the spirits talking when the wind howls beneath the door. You do not see the demons in the thunderclouds, playing with the lightning. Lo Siento. I will not talk of this thing again.' He extended a hand toward me. 'Amigo.'

I smiled and shook the proffered hand. I even tried a few words in his peculiar lingo.

'Está Bien, amigo.'

To this day, I am not certain of what I said.

***

But Felipe's words had scared me; they had disturbed something deep down in the foundations of my subconscious, something that did not want to be awakened. At least, not then. When I got home that evening, I just lay on the bed with my eyes tight shut, and even so, it was as if there were images of terrible things trying to break into my vision. I was too shaken even to fix supper. When I finally drifted into sleep, I found myself dreaming about my childhood, about my time in the orphanage.

I remember I was crying in the dream, and there were stern men and hard-faced women shaking me, telling me I had to do something I didn't want to do. And I remembered things I had forgotten, of how there had been physical punishments, even pain. I saw the young

Charles Gray strapped to what looked like a hospital bed with a kind of metal cap on my head, although I am sure these must have been just false memories produced by a worried brain. I was writhing, trying to break free, but men and women were standing over me, holding me still. And one held a syringe. I watched the needle approach my arm. I saw the look of terror on my face, the glint of moisture at the corners of the eyes.

And then I woke up. It was 4AM. I was shivering as badly as if I had been thrown through thin ice into a deep, cold lake.

I made some coffee and heated up a waffle. But I couldn't eat it.

Knowing I had a hard day ahead of me, I lay back down and tried to get back to sleep while simultaneously being afraid of what I might see.

But eventually I slept, and there were no more distorted visions of evil things that could not possibly have happened.

NINE

Another working day had arrived at the McKinley factory, and I was no nearer discovering anything to interest my superiors. I was still stuck at the hydrogen reactor with little to do other than maintain the flow of natural gas and water vapour at the correct temperature and pressure. I guess it was a pretty important job, but it was still a long way from the business end of the ammonium nitrate production. My only consolation was my conversations with Felipe, but ever since I had forbidden him to talk about superstitious matters, he seemed a little cagier towards me. But we got by, through days which were otherwise ones of relentless tedium.

I still kept the plastic tube in my overalls, waiting for a chance to scoop up any of the illicit materials I had been instructed to look out for. But stuck where I was, the only unusual substances I ever saw were the various forms of filling in Felipe's tortillas.

I hardly ever saw Grogan, who rarely stirred from his office. On the one time he had passed by, I did manage to attract his attention, and enquired about a job change. But his reply—that I seemed only just able to hold down the one I had—put an end to those hopes. It looked like it would be Lieutenant Ardelean's plan, after all.

Having watched Felipe eagerly devour his lunch, I knew it was time to get back to it. We had wi-fi communicators on us at all times, so we knew if the gas flow had altered in any dangerous direction, and our extremely brief lunch break was the only time we were ever away from the controls. Furthermore, the devices both beeped and vibrated at the slightest cause for concern, so I had no actual need to glance at my monitor.

But, not really knowing why, I did.

And all the readings were 0.00.

I leapt up with my heart racing and screamed, 'Felipe! There's something wrong! We're finished!'

I knew a blunder this big meant instant dismissal, at the very least. But Felipe simply looked up at me with an untroubled expression.

'What is wrong, Juan? All is OK on my monitor.'

He held up his device so I could read it and I saw ranks of numbers slowly changing on the luminous screen. Only the figures after the decimal point were changing, and they were just cycling around one number. Everything was alright!

Relief flooded over me. I showed Felipe my communicator with its terrifying rows of zeroes, and he nodded wisely.

'This happen all the time,' he said. 'Grogan always goes for the cheapest possible machines. You will have to go to Bixby to get a new one. Go now; I will watch the gas flow.'

Our tables were only a few metres from the reactor, and so I checked the main screens to make absolutely certain all was well, and having seen that was the case, I set off in search of Bixby. He was obviously in the midst of telling some off-colour story to his work buddies, as I could hear the laughter from some distance. I knocked on his office door and waited patiently for him to notice me. One series of knocks did not appear to be enough, although I was sure he knew I was there, so I entered his office and waited for him to acknowledge me. I saw his eyes flick in my direction a few times, but he continued with another selection from the seemingly endless library of salacious tales. But finally, he finished.

'What do you want, Andrews?'

I held up my monitoring device.

'This one's bust. I need a new one.'

He pushed his way through his audience, pulled the device from my grasp and held it up so he could study it.

'If I find you bollixed this...' he began in his normal menacing tone.

'I didn't,' I said, matching his stare.

He pushed it back at me, but as he did, his hand came into contact with the sample tube I had stupidly put in the top pocket of my overalls.

'What's this?' he grunted, and before I could reply or move away, he had fished it out. He held up the thin transparent tube, all the time rotating it between his stubby fingers. He looked over his shoulders at his cronies.

'Well, look at this, boys,' he said. 'Look what Andrews here has been hiding. Do you know what it is?'

A couple of the men came closer. My heart sank. Why would I be carrying a sample tube around? But Bixby, it appeared, was not interested in any explanations.

'Do you know what this is, boys?' He looked back at me to gauge my reaction. 'It's an itty-bitty condom! Andrews's been walking round with a condom in his pocket. Looks like we'd better watch out!' He turned away from me again. 'Or maybe not. Have you seen the size of this thing?' He rotated the tube between thumb and forefinger. 'With a dick this size, looks like we ain't got too much to worry about!'

I like to think I am in control of my emotions. There have been many times I could have floored some scumbag or other, but I have always managed to hold back.

But not this time. My fist landed smack in the centre of his fleshy face and sent him spinning. The tube flew out of his grasp; I caught it easily and replaced it. A gasp of astonishment came from his cronies.

And a bull-like bellow came from Bixby. He pulled himself upright and charged me, sending the two of us straight out of his office doorway onto the shop floor. His ham-sized fist collided with the side of my face, loosening a few teeth under the impact. But now my blood was up. I'm no office junior or button pusher. Bixby was heavier than me and a bit wider, but he was not as experienced as me in man-on-man combat. And he soon found that out. I dodged nearly all of his blows, while he failed to dodge most of mine. And it showed. His face rapidly began to resemble a squashed pomegranate. Finally, I hooked an ankle behind one of his and sent him crashing to the concrete floor. I heard a gasp of amazement from his pals.

But as I looked down at him, the bloodlust drained from me. I realised I had ballsed it all up. I would lose my job and be sent back to Mistress Aiyana with my tail between my legs. My cover would have been blown, and I would be sacked from the Force. All because I couldn't keep my temper!

Bixby succeeded in getting to his feet without any help, and stood in front of me, rubbing his jaw. A thin trickle of blood began to run from a split lip. I stood there, silently wondering if he had the authority to let me go there and then, or simply frog-match me to Grogan. I had nothing to say. There was nothing I could say.

He turned to the others.

'You! Get back to work! Now!'

He watched them go and turned back to me, still rubbing his jaw.

And then he spoke.

'Andrews, you're all right. I thought you was some kinda wuss, but I guess I got you wrong.' Then, to my amazement, he extended a hand to me. 'You're all right. I know people who'd like to meet you. We could use a man like you.'

Use a man like me? I thought. For what?

***

'You sure you want to go there?' the taxi driver said, after I had climbed in.

'Yes. Why do you ask?'

The driver turned away but continued to regard me in the mirror.

'Well, let's just say people don't usually like to go there after dark.' He shrugged. 'Hell, they don't usually like to go there in broad daylight!'

'Just take me as far as you want to go,' I said. 'Or I'll tell you when you can drop me off where I can walk the rest of the way.' I remembered Mistress Aiyana's scathing observation and added: 'I'm a fit officer.'

'One who likes a fight by the look of your mug,' he said, but he put the car in motion. I had to go with a human driver as the companies rarely retrieve autonomous vehicles once they venture into this area. Too many useful spare parts. I had already noted the hunting knife on the front passenger seat. It should have made me feel safer, but it had the opposite effect. Bixby had been suspicious of my sample tube, but after I explained it was something to do with suppositories, he hurriedly lost interest. Or so I hoped. But what if this whole get-together was just a set-up by him; a ploy to get me somewhere nice and secluded so he and his pals could really work me over? Or worse.

As we moved off, I fought down the urge to leap out of the car. And soon we were in a part of Marinetown that looked like it had just made it through a wave of saturation bombing. Shards and fangs of derelict buildings were all around me and the road had as many holes as a cheese grater. I was continually thrown from one side to the other as it dipped in and out of them.

'I ain't going much further,' he said, as we climbed out of a particularly deep crater.

'It's OK,' I said. 'I can make it from here.'

A few seconds later, I watched the taxi execute a rapid U-turn and disappear into the dusk. I looked around, seeing half-destroyed buildings outlined in funereal black against a bloody sunset. When the Elite took over, much of the human economy was no longer needed, and many hubs of commerce and industry were just allowed to crumble; the Elite provided everything we needed as our reward for not blowing up the planet.

Of course, we had to give something in return. Well, some of us did.

I walked toward the mighty walls of an ex-meat packing plant. Most of the grim building was still in reasonable condition; it even had a roof. There was a yawning gap in the nearest wall, an entrance where the trucks had come and gone in the old days, and I had been told the door to my meeting room was in the left-hand wall. Once inside the marshalling area, near-absolute blackness enfolded me. I felt my way along the wall, my fingers searching for the door. I found it, pushed against it and discovered it would not open. But almost instantly, after I had reached that conclusion, it opened inwards and powerful hands jerked me inside.

I felt a knife against my ribs and heard a gravelly baritone.

'Alone?'

'Yes.'

'You know if you're lying, you won't get out of here?'

'Yes.' I felt a rising anger. 'Now get your hands off of me. I've done everything right, so let's get this over with.'

I was pushed toward a staircase, whose treads trembled and creaked under my weight as I ascended, with the unseen man close behind. He had taken the hint and I no longer felt the knife.

Suddenly, a door opened on the first floor and a flood of yellow light almost blinded me after the near-total darkness. The unseen man pushed me in and I crashed against a chair. Two more tough-looking men came from either side of me, and before I realised what was happening, they had tied me to it with a rope of some unbreakable synthetic material. Gradually, my eyes could make sense of my surroundings.

I was facing three men who were sitting behind a poorly constructed table. It looked like it had been part of the work furniture when this place was a working establishment, and was just about holding itself together as a rest home for elderly woodworms. All three wore pointed headgear, which entirely covered their faces. The middle guy spoke.

'John Andrews?'

I confirmed they had the right man.

'Currently working at McKinley's?'

'Yes. And you are?'

The man to my left cuffed me across the face.

'Shaddup. We ask questions; you answer questions. That's how it works.'

I couldn't reach my cheek to see if there was any blood and so I returned to looking at the middle of the trio opposite me.

'One of our men there says you're pretty quick with your fists, and you don't like being pushed around.'

'Correct. If you untie me, I'll prove just that.'

He chuckled.

'Don't try too hard to impress us, Andrews. Just answer a few questions, and you'll be just fine.'

And then the questioning began.

I had to identify my place of birth, my parents, my grade schooling, my work experience. Fortunately, Mistress Aiyana had expected I would be grilled on all of this, and I had memorised it well. I explained how I had lost both my parents in the riots up in the Panhandle when I was still very young. They seemed to like the idea of my parents as rebels. As I was telling the story, I wondered about the real parents I never knew. Had they, in fact, been rebels against the new life all we humans now had, or, like the majority, just kept their heads down and got on with their quiet, insignificant lives? I would never know.

They were impressed by my time up in Granada, which, fortunately, was like a foreign country to them. They seemed to believe there were still polar bears on the streets, which, as I'm sure you know, isn't true— even if there still were any polar bears.

Then they paused, and the middle man turned to the one on his right. I am sure if they had not been wearing those cowls, I would have seen meaningful glances exchanged. The new man spoke, in a clear, authoritative voice.

'Now we will ask you some rather more important questions. The rope you are tied up with is, in fact, measuring your heart rate, sweat secretion, and other significant bodily processes. It is not a foolproof method of detecting falsehood, but we err on the side of doubt here. We have several times gotten rid of innocent men who could not control their reactions, but it is better to execute the innocent than let a spy into our midst.'

And then the real questioning began.

And it was all about Vamps. All of them were designed to get me to reveal my genuine feelings about our masters: The Elite. It seemed to go on forever, with them circling around the topics, going back to questions they'd already asked to see if they could trap me in a contradiction or even an ambiguity. I tried to stay calm, knowing if I let them get to me, my body would betray me, and I would not get out of that ruin alive. And staying calm when you are in the power of those who would rather kill you than take a chance is not easy, my friend.

The man on the left of the trio spoke up for the first time.

'Exactly why do you want to join us, Mr Andrews? Think carefully.'

This was my chance to ingratiate myself, I thought, and instantly said, 'Every red-blooded guy wants to join the Sons Of Man.'

All three heads opposite me jerked up simultaneously, and I was fixed in stares that had become wary, alert, suspicious.

'Where did you get that name from?' the middle man said. 'No one here has used that phrase.'

Ice ran down my spine. I had been too eager to show my loyalty, like some puppy licking its master's hand! I had to think fast or accept the certainty my rotting body would wash up on Flurida's Gulf coast in a few months' time. Even a few seconds' hesitation might damn me.

'I know someone whose woman was abducted into a Farm. He told me about your message.'

'What Farm? What woman?'

I spoke without thinking; I had no time to think, to make it obvious I was concocting some story.

I just spoke.

'Gilroy's. Rosario. I don't know the rest of their names, but her man told me you had left a message.'

Nothing was said. I could hear the breathing of the men flanking me. And then, without warning, a hood of some kind was thrust over my head. Instantly, I was in a silent world. They must have been discussing me, determining my fate.

Then the hood was removed. I could feel my heart begin to hammer, and I fought to control it. I thought about blue skies, calm breezes, watching pelicans fly overhead, little fish darting about my toes as I sat on the edge of the boat, rod and line in hand.

The central man spoke.

'OK, Andrews. But some of your answers don't entirely satisfy us. Do you really hate the Vamps enough to put your life on the line? At bottom, don't you want love, peace and understanding with them?'

I tried to straighten myself in the chair to give an air of authority, of strength.

'Oh, I hate them enough. I don't want peace with them. I don't even want a truce with the Vamps.'

'No truce with the vampires.' The leader nodded. 'That's a good phrase, Andrews. Maybe we'll use it. OK.'

Silence fell. I looked at them. They looked at me. Then I felt the detector rope unwind from my torso. The interrogation was over. All three removed their cowls, revealing three middle-aged faces topped with grey or greying hair. Proud faces, resolute faces. I didn't know them. I hadn't seen them at McKinley's.

'So what happens now?' I said, licking my dry lips. I felt confident enough now not to be too worried about showing nervousness.

'Nothing for the moment. You go back to work. Bixby will be your contact when we are ready for you.'

Bixby will be your contact. I already knew that. Still no evidence that McKinley's as a whole was part of this organisation. Still no proof explosives were being made there. It looked like Ardelean's raid would have to go ahead.

'But, in the long term, I mean,' I said, not wishing to display any unexpected interest in that establishment. 'We are going to win, aren't we?'

For the first time, the leader smiled, the kind of a smile a Great White might make, just before it severs a leg. 'We will definitely win. We Shads will reclaim this world, reclaim our rightful place. The Vamps won't know what hit them. You see, we are just the beginning. We have an ally—a very powerful ally.'

TEN

I wasn't sure how to react to this comment. A very powerful ally? Were they implying they had infiltrated the Police Force? What else could that deliberately obscure line mean?

They were studying me again, perhaps waiting to see how I reacted. But I simply shrugged and said, 'Well, that sounds good.' I waited to see if they would reveal more about this new enemy; a hint perhaps of his, or her, identity.

But they did not.

Instead, the leader said, 'Well, that's the preliminaries over. Now I want you to prove yourself in the field.'

This is it, I thought; this is what I came for.

'Our aim,' he continued, 'is to wipe out these Farms where our enslaved people are being treated like domesticated animals, pumping out their lifeblood for the pleasure of those monsters. First, we will eliminate every last Farm, deprive them of their entertainment, deprive them of their food. They will learn we humans may be down, but we are far from out!'

The two flanking him thumped on the table at these stirring words, and I heard growls of appreciation from my erstwhile captors, who were still on station either side of me. Hurriedly, I joined in, doing energetic fist-bumps and crying, 'Yes! Yes!' The leader smiled as he surveyed his comrades and drank in their adulation. His gaze rested on me for a few moments, and I saw only satisfaction in those eyes.

'Then our leader will take control and we will carry the war directly into the centre of their existence. They showed no mercy to us: We will show no mercy to them. They like blood; we will give them blood alright, oceans of blood—their own.'

Our leader? I thought. Aren't you the leader?

Further musings on my part were suddenly cut off when the speaker looked directly at me again.

'Enough of this talk. We will not win by talking a good fight. You, Andrews, must show we have not erred by inviting you into our midst. This particular session is over. You have passed the first test. Not by much, but you passed. But now comes the final test. Bixby will shortly give you some instructions, and you will join the team that will assassinate the owner of one of their Farms. Not only that, but we will free those wretched slaves who have been forced to feed these Vamp parasites. It will be a long journey before we win back our freedom and our world, but we will have taken the first step!'

'Which Farm will I be attacking?' I asked, eager to demonstrate my loyalty.

'You will be told that when the instructions are given you. But until you need to know, you will not be allowed to know. We understand the concept of security, which, Andrews, apparently you do not.' He waved a hand. 'No matter. You will be under close supervision when the time comes.' He looked left and right. 'Well, gentlemen, do you have any further questions for our eager young slaphead recruit?'

There were none. The leader stood.

'That's it, Andrews. I will arrange a vehicle to take you to where you picked up the taxi. Oh yes, we have been watching you. We take nothing for granted here. We know only too well our adversary is clever and devious. There is still a small possibility you are a tool of these creatures. And so, it will be some time before we trust you completely.'

'Do I get to know your names?'

The trio exchanged amused glances before the leader turned back to me.

'You get to know our names when you join the top command. And, guess what, you will never know our names.'

***

The following day I awaited the details of my assignment. I saw Bixby on several occasions, but he appeared to only want to chat, man to man. However, one good thing had come out of my improved status with him: He looked more favourably on my petition to get moved farther down the production line.

But at first, he was suspicious.

'Why do you want to move? What's it to you where you work in this shit-hole?'

'I don't like that Felipe guy; he gives me the creeps. And the work is crap: Just staring at a monitor screen all fucking day.'

He shrugged.

'It ain't much different anywhere else, but I don't mind moving you, if that's what you want. I don't like the queer little squirt either.' Then he laid a considerate hand on my shoulder. 'How're those damn piles, John?'

I shrugged manfully.

'They still hurt, but I put the ointment in, most days. They'll get better in time. Meantime, I just get on with it.'

He grinned and nodded with a new-found respect for my fortitude. Christ! I thought, I think I preferred him when he was a bastard!

And when I started my new job, it turned out he had been telling the truth. It was at least as mind-numbingly tedious as the first one. Felipe had been sorry to see me go because work breaks were so short there was no chance of us meeting up, even in a place as small as

McKinley's. But I hadn't been entirely untruthful to Bixby; Felipe's talk about "Old Gods" really had spooked me.

At least in the new job, I wasn't chained to a computer monitor, staring at numbers that hardly ever moved. Instead, I had a slightly more varied career, stacking boxes of ammonium nitrate onto heavy goods trucks. They even let me loose on little yellow forklift trucks to move the really big consignments. But I noticed one peculiarity, not long after I went on the night shift. To one side of the main delivery chutes was a big, low-roofed building that occasionally disgorged different-sized and shaped crates. I soon realised they were not, in fact, crates but drums, metal drums. Although they did not look particularly massive, these were always moved by forklift truck rather than by hand, and placed very carefully on a different type of transporter. And there were always at least two, and more often three, men supervising the transportation. I asked my foreman once about what was happening over there, but a suspicious look told me I had overstepped a line, and I never asked again.

I realised that if I wanted to know more, I would have to find out for myself. And so, I progressed well with my new responsibilities, always making sure I was first in line for new jobs, however onerous. I became quite the hot shot on the forklift truck, until the foreman told me to stop my crazy stunts and concentrate on work. And all the time I was keeping one eye on that big warehouse and the drums coming out of it. Due to my shift pattern and the need to keep my cover watertight, I no longer visited the Force HQ but made contact via a tight, highly shielded beam. I knew my superiors were unhappy with the lack of progress, and my Mistress was about to agree to a full-scale assault on the McKinley chemical plant. Time was running out—and fast.

Then it happened. Bixby was walking past me when we briefly collided. But as he did, I felt something pressed into my palm. A piece of paper. I knew better than to read it in front of everybody else, so I waited until I was in the john. And an electric thrill ran down my spine as I read the message. It was crudely written in capital letters, but the instructions were clear. In a few seconds I knew when I was to begin my assignment. I also knew I would be doing it without backup from the Force: The vital location of the hit had not been specified.

The following day, as I clocked on for my shift, I suddenly noticed that two men I didn't recognise had taken up positions on either side of me. Perhaps the main reason I didn't recognise them was the fact that both were wearing black balaclava helmets, with only their eyes showing. But I didn't recognise their voices either.

One pushed another hood at me, growling, 'Put this on.' Then we slipped out of the premises and into a van. I was thrown backwards as the vehicle took off at speed. Looking at my fellow assassins, I could see they were observing me very closely. And suddenly they moved, pinning me to the floor of the bouncing van.

'We don't know you, Andrews, so forgive us for being a little suspicious.'

With that, one of them ran a detector wand over my prone form. I could see his eyes as he studied the read-out: They were cold, hard, calculating eyes, the eyes of someone on the lookout for trouble and with the resources to deal with it. I knew if I triggered their suspicions, my time on this Earth would be measured in seconds.

The man with the detector wand straightened up and looked at the other.

'He's clean. No wire.'

Silently, I blessed Mistress Aiyana's decision to overrule Ardelean's instruction to have me wired up. She had saved my life.

Feeling more confident, I steadied myself against the bucking motions of the van as it seemingly tried to turn turtle and looked at my co-conspirators.

'You know me. What do I call you?'

The man with the wand tapped his chest. I realised he had been one of the hard-cases who had tied me up in the ruined packing-plant.

'You can call me "Bernie".' He indicated the other. 'You can call him "Fred".' Then he pointed over my shoulder. 'And "Bill" is driving the van.'

I grinned weakly. I was still on probation.

The van hurtled on into the night, taking me to my first assignment.

And somehow I had to ensure it failed, without getting killed in the process.

ELEVEN

Despite the driver's apparent aim of throwing us off the road, we somehow stayed on it and made rapid progress out of the city. We were heading southwest, in the direction of the old city of Tampa; that's all I knew. I also knew Farms were particularly numerous in that area, so our target could be one of dozens. And I decided I had had enough of being treated like unwanted baggage.

'So where's the hit?'

Bernie appeared to be in charge as he was the one who answered, without looking at Fred.

'Harker's.'

I'd heard of it, a large trouble-free establishment, north of Lake Saint Charles. It would not be a long journey. Then a worrying thought struck me.

'The explosive—is it shock sensitive? The way Bill is driving, we might not get there in one piece.'

Both my fellow passengers chortled at the witticism.

'You're the new boy, Andrews,' Bernie said, 'so you wouldn't know. We're not carrying explosives, just in case the cops pull us over.'

I looked at them—two hard, confident, determined men, entirely in control of themselves despite the tension of the journey. No explosives. That meant we would have to deal with Harker on a more personal basis. What would it be—knife, pistol? Surely not hand-to-hand? My mouth was even drier than it had been at the start of the journey.

'Then how will we do it? I mean, how do we kill him?'

'We blow him up in his bed. Then we get the slaves out. Then we blow the whole fucking place up. Don't shit yourself, Andrews; you won't even get to see Harker. One second, he'll be dreaming sweet dreams about all the money he's getting from the Vamps for our people's blood; the next, he'll be waking up in Hell with a pitchfork up his ass. He won't feel a thing when he goes, unfortunately.'

I shook my head.

'How do we blow him up with no explosives? I don't get it.'

They laughed.

'It's OK, Andrews. We've all been the new boy. You'll soon see how we operate. And the good thing is, we can't be stopped. We are going to rid our world of Vamp filth, forever. They haven't got a goddamn clue what's coming their way!'

There it was again, this assurance of absolute superiority, of inevitable victory. But how would any war with the Elite differ from the Takeover, when they had swept humans out of control with no more difficulty than we would have in stepping on a bug?

I realised it would be no good to quiz them further; they were obviously enjoying my bafflement. Then, unfortunately, I realised something else, as Bernie's indifference to my personal welfare came back to torment me.

'Hey, I gotta pee.'

Bernie, as expected, was not a sympathetic kind of guy.

And then we arrived.

I followed Bernie and Fred out of the van and met Bill as he climbed out of the driver's seat. Bill gave me a quick glance and then focused on the other two. We were parked by the high fence surrounding Harker's Farm. Bernie congratulated Bill for his driving, and then studied me.

'We know you don't have any explosive experience, Andrews, but it's very straightforward. We're using a type of ammonal that can be moulded like soft plastic. It's adhesive so you can just stick it on a door or wall. We're not wasting a high nitro shit on this one: It's too small. But don't worry about Harker: The explosive power will be quite enough to reduce his hut to matchwood. And him to little shreds of raw meat.'

I realised he'd left out a key element in his very brief training speech.

'How do I, uh, detonate it?'

'You stick a timer in it. It's calibrated in seconds and minutes. Just turn the pointer to the time you need to get away and you'll be fine. We'll be busy freeing the slaves, so you just wait for us at the van.'

'And when do I get the timer?'

He laughed.

'Same time as you get the ammonal.' He turned to the others. 'OK, let's go. They may have the area under surveillance, but he will be able to confuse their devices.'

Once again, I noticed the mysterious *he.*

I watched Bernie and Fred as they kneeled at the base of the fence. I heard the crackle of snapping metal, and they stood up, pulling an entire sheet of the fence with them. A hole big enough for a man to get through was revealed.

Bernie looked at the others, said, 'Let's go!' and he was through the gap and standing on the other side of the fence in less time than it takes to say it. Bill and Fred followed at once, but as I watched them, I was seized with a sudden urge to turn around and run away. Run anywhere but towards Harker's Farm. But Bernie was watching me, and I saw him make the *Come On!* gesture. So I ducked down and through the gap, and stood next to them. The desire to urinate was starting to own me, but I told myself it was just nerves and fought it down.

'The explosive,' I said, despite a dry mouth and lips that seemed to have turned to stiff rubber. 'Where is it?'

'Hey, we got a keen one here!' Bill said; the first time I'd heard him speak.

The others laughed and the three set off deeper into the compound, without bothering to reply. I caught up with them, but decided not to ask about the explosives again: It seemed to annoy them. Soon the Farm buildings came into view. All these places have the same basic layout: Two or more low shed-like buildings where the Donors are housed, and standing apart, the cottage-like structure where the owner lives. Bernie put out a hand and we all stopped.

'This is it,' he said in a semi-whisper. 'Fred, Bill—do it!'

The other two then removed identical looking-objects from their jackets. I stared at them in the near darkness. Each was simply a transparent tube attached to a cubical base. And a pale light of a weird purple-violet shade was pulsing rhythmically in the tube.

'Do it,' Bernie ordered, and, looking at me, added, 'Move back, Andrews. And turn around or you might get blinded.'

At those alarming words, I obeyed both parts of his order. I kept my back turned to the trio after I had increased the distance between us and waited; for what, I knew not. And then there was a flash of harsh violet light and I saw my shadow leap across the purple-stained grass. And then it was gone.

I turned back to my co-conspirators. A large box was now sitting in the centre of the triangle they had created. They swiftly opened it and passed the contents between themselves, Bernie giving me my share. I saw a luminous dial with numbers on it, and a ball of what looked like putty in the dim light of the Fluridian stars. This had to be the ammonal.

'What do I do?' I whispered, feeling like a drowning man going down for the last time. I was way over my head by now, but I knew there was no way out. I either completed my mission, or they killed me. Those were the only alternatives.

'I told you already,' Bernie hissed. He pointed at the cottage. 'There's Harker. Kill him.'

'Or we kill you,' Fred added. His grin was only visible by the sudden flash of teeth.

With that ominous promise, they left me, heading toward the Donor accommodation. I watched them go, cursing everything and everybody who had gotten me into this situation. Hell, I even blamed Mistress Aiyana. My mission was to abort their mission, but I now knew that task was beyond me. These men were professionals, far more than I was, and far more deadly than me, because they had learned to survive in a world where every hand was against them, where a single slip-up would deliver them into the hands of the Elite. I was just an average Flatfoot, and could not stop men like them.

But neither could I kill Harker.

I knew then there was only one thing I could do to save both his life and mine.

I ran towards his residence, knowing that every second counted; that what happened now would either let me live or kill me. As I approached, I passed a cage where three powerful black dogs were lying. I expected them to leap up and start baying, clawing at their cage so they could get at me and tear me into bloody ribbons. But, strangely, as before, they showed no interest in me.

I reached the door and hammered at it.

Nothing stirred.

I hammered again, glancing at the Donor huts, wondering when my companions would strike.

And then a sensor above the door activated and a beam of light hit me full in the face. Screwing up my eyes, I said in a voice just below a scream, 'Harker! You've got to get out! They're going to blow you up! I'm a police officer!'

I heard movements within; the door opened a crack and the muzzle of a semi-automatic rifle emerged. I could just make out Harker in the gap as the muzzle zeroed in on my abdomen.

'Get the hell away, or I'll kill you where you stand!'

I moved so I was directly opposite him.

'Harker, I am Charles Gray of the Flurida Police Force. I am with a determined group of people about to blow your place apart and you with it. If you don't come with me now, I will leave you here and they will assuredly kill you.'

A few seconds passed. Then Harker, a tall, grey shape in the gloom, came slowly out, the rifle still trained unwaveringly upon me. I pointed away from the complex of buildings, showing the direction he should flee.

'Run, Harker, run and hide until we are gone. You can't stop them. I can't stop them. This is your one and only chance. Go!'

Even in the dimness, I could see his puzzled face.

'But the Farm. It's my livelihood.'

'No, Harker, it's your tomb if you don't move now. Get out of here and stay hidden for as long as you can! If they find you, they will kill you!' I took a chance and leaned over and shook him. 'For Chrissake, go now, or I will leave you to them!'

Finally, he moved, slowly and with many glances over his shoulder to see if I was taking a bead on him. I turned back to his cottage and slammed the door shut. I patted the ammonal putty onto it and then stuck the timer in it. For a terrifying second or so I could not work out how to set the time before detonation, before I noticed the little crown on the side of the device.

How long? How long to get away? Should I go back to the van, or hide from them? No, if I hid and then simply returned to McKinley's, they would know something was wrong with my story.

I turned the dial to a value and moved away, ready to run. Then, I realised in my panic that I was not sure of what time I had set. I moved to return to it and then understood there was no time.

I whirled around. Harker had vanished. I put one foot in front of the other. Then there was a terrific flash and the sound of a thousand thunders. I had just enough time before the shockwave hit me to see remnants of the Donor accommodation leap into the sky atop a roaring cloud of flame.

It was that delay which almost killed me.

Just as I had begun to run, I felt a fiery blast of heat on my back as I was tossed like thistledown across the grass. Burning planks from Harker's demolished dwelling showered down all around me. My straining bladder lost its battle for continence as I crashed into unconsciousness.

***

Sensations.

I was not dead.

I could feel shuddering vibrations shaking my spine.

Opening my eyes, I saw the grey metal roof of the van. I groaned, turned my head and saw a pair of legs in corduroy trousers. Strong arms pulled me into a sitting position on the van floor. They belonged to Bernie. He grinned as he looked down at me.

'Well, Andrews, I don't know whether to kick your butt or congratulate you.'

I said nothing, concentrating on wondering if there were any parts of me that weren't sore. As my mind slowly reassembled itself, I understood that, for the first time in my life, I was living on borrowed time, having succeeded in getting myself onto the top of the Sons Of Man's kill list. I would stay alive for slightly longer than Harker stayed hidden. Shortly after they discovered he had escaped, it would be a one-way ticket to the bottom of the Gulf of Mexica.

'There are two ways of looking at it,' Bernie continued. 'Firstly, you almost got yourself killed by not getting away from the hut in time. So that's a minus. But secondly, you blew Harker to Kingdom Come. That's a big plus. So, all in all, I think you're in credit.' He looked over his shoulder. 'What do you say, Bill?'

'Yeah,' Bill replied. 'I think we can let the schmuck off this time.'

I rose groggily to my feet, guessing Fred was now driving the van. His driving was no better than Bill's. But Bernie hadn't finished praising me.

'You see, we deliberately didn't give you precise instructions, to see if you could finish the job on your own initiative. And you did. So I'm going to recommend you be fully inducted into the Sons Of Man.'

Great! I thought. *One promotion I really didn't need!*

'You passed the test. True, you nearly got yourself killed, but—you didn't.' Bernie offered a large, calloused hand and I shook it, limply.

I managed to make it to my usual seat, and returned his gaze.

'Thanks for the vote of thanks. What happens now?'

'We take you back to McKinley's. You can drive yourself back to your place.'

I hope that means they don't know where I live. But I still don't know if McKinley's is the source of the explosive.

'Thanks. Hey—that was a neat trick you did with ammonal. How'd ya do it?'

To my surprise, Bernie just shrugged.

'Beats the shit out of me. We just do what we are told and—bingo!—there it is.'

'But where does it come from in the first place?'

Bernie's eyes narrowed slightly, and, once again, I knew I'd pushed too hard.

'Never mind about that, Andrews. You don't learn everything on your first day on the job. You're still the bottom mug on the totem pole.'

I gave a curt nod to show I accepted my inferior status.

Shortly after, we stopped outside the compound of the fertiliser factory. I was ordered out, and the van drove off into the morning mist. I looked around: There was an orange glow in the east, showing to my grateful eyes my tumultuous night was over.

The security guard waved me in, apparently unfazed by the direction I was coming from. That might mean he was one of the Sons Of Man, or just someone bribed, or threatened, to look the other way.

And then I headed home, driving considerably faster than the permitted limit. The cops did not stop me.

My battered old wreck of a car had top level security clearance.

TWELVE

L ieutenant Ardelean did not look too happy with me as I studied his image coming from the other end of the beam.

'So, Gray, you were unable to prevent the destruction of Harker's Farm, and the loss of many litres of premium blood. Not to mention the trouble we are having in rounding up the escapees.'

'That is correct, sir. However, I must point out that complete success was always going to be an unlikely outcome. I could not possibly have taken a weapon with me. If I had, I would not be talking to you now.'

'A minor loss,' the Lieutenant growled. Then the field of view widened to include Mistress Aiyana.

'There is no need to be quite so dismissive of Gray's activities. He prevented the death of one of our most productive Farmers. And there is the matter of how the explosive arrived.'

I could have imagined it, but I am pretty sure I saw Ardelean tense slightly, and a momentary look of concern flash briefly over his chiselled features. My Mistress's words had shaken him, although he had hidden it well. I understood that the way the explosive had seemed to just—appear—was impressive, but it must just have been some sort of conjuring trick, designed to impress a rookie. After all, I had been looking in the other direction when it had happened, and all I'd actually seen was a brief flash of light. But his transient expression reminded me of how Mistress Aiyana had looked when she heard the details of the

Diodati affair. Then I saw the Lieutenant give his head a quick shake, as if to remove unwelcome thoughts.

'All you have said is true, Commissioner. I suppose there are some acceptable features of the incident, but I contend we have wasted valuable time by not moving against McKinley's. I do not deny the loss of the nitrogenous fertiliser will cause hardship for the humans, before we can switch production to another site, but we have already waited too long. But if it turns out the manager, what's the name?—Grogan—is innocent, then things will return to normal.' His smile was sardonic. 'And he can hardly launch a lawsuit against us, can he? If he is not innocent, we will stop the Sons Of Man terrorists in their tracks. We must act—now.'

A silence fell, and I sat patiently, knowing to speak would be a severe breach of protocol.

Finally, Mistress Aiyana spoke, addressing me directly.

'Gray, the Lieutenant is correct. We have lost valuable time. The packing plant you were interrogated in was completely empty, with no sign anyone had been there for decades. We may have been too considerate of human feelings by delaying so long. Yesterday's events prove the Sons Of Man snake must be crushed under foot.' Although she was only an electronic image, I felt her eyes boring into me. 'You have one more day to bring us proof of their complicity. Then, either way, we go in.'

***

And then came the night. The pattern I had recognised came again: The heavy-duty truck drew up to the open gate under the blue-white arc lights, and at once, the forklifts came buzzing out like ants defending a nest. I carried on with my normal work; I could drive my little vehicle blindfold by now, and I watched them carefully as I drove back and forth. All was unfolding as it had many times before, when I realised one guy had miscalculated and had not positioned the last drum correctly, leaving it overhanging. I saw it wobble and knew it was going to fall.

And fall it did. The workers pulled back as fast as possible, almost as if they expected venomous snakes to burst out of it. In fact, nothing happened, except it looked like a seam on the drum had sprung open slightly, allowing out a thin trickle of a greyish powder. The workers stood motionless some distance away, but eventually what they feared would happen, evidently had not happened, and they approached the truck again. Two of them picked up the fallen drum and were examining it when disaster struck again. The damaged drum had made the entire stack on the truck unstable, and they began to roll towards the edge of the carrying surface. One tumbled off of it onto the nearest man and he collapsed under the impact. I leapt from my forklift and ran over to help. To my astonishment, the uninjured men whirled around and yelled, 'You! Stay where you are! Don't come any nearer!'

'To hell with that!' I yelled back at them, and rushed to the aid of the prone man. But to my utter amazement, I found myself looking down the muzzle of an automatic pistol, lifted at me by the biggest of the uninjured workers.

'Are you deaf or something, mister?' he said. 'Beat it before I waste you!'

I looked at the man on the ground, who had slipped into unconsciousness. His legs looked pretty beat up. Although they weren't particularly big, the drums must have been heavy. I lifted my hands in the classic gesture of surrender and began to back away.

'OK, OK,' I said, 'only trying to help.'

They didn't reply; some attended to the casualty, others to stabilising the stack. But as I backed away, I saw my chance had come: The warehouse was unattended; all its personnel were busy dealing with the twin crises. I looked around—as far as I could see, all eyes were on the drama with the truck. The entrance to the warehouse yawned huge and black before me. Slipping from shadow to shadow, I entered, fingering my knife to give me confidence to enter the unknown.

At first, I could see nothing; the building was unlit. But eventually my eyes adjusted, there being enough light from the harsh arc lights outside for me to find my way around. All I could see in the front part of the building were the self-same drums I had just seen being loaded. No evidence of anything here. I had to go deeper in.

I had not gone much farther when I realised I could smell the thick, cloying stink of heavy hydrocarbons. In my youth there had still been a few gasoline-powered vehicles shown at fairgrounds, and I had seen some during one of the few days I had been allowed out. The smell was similar but more powerful, in a way that assaulted the nostrils. Deeper into the warehouse I went, and the deeper I went, the farther I was from the lights, and the darker and more malodorous it became. I had been told there were two substances I should look out for, two things, either of which could convert innocent ammonium nitrate into a deadly weapon. Perhaps the unpleasant, heavy odour stinging my eyes and nose was one of them. I did not know; I had been briefed by Mistress Aiyana, but it had not made me a chemist.

I came to an open hopper, and, looking in, I could just make out it was full of small spherical objects. But at least I knew what they were—in the jargon, they were "prills", little balls of ammonium nitrate; perfectly harmless, and a standard end-product of the fertiliser business. I looked up from the hopper and realised I was seeing the end of the warehouse. I was going to come up empty-handed again. And it would not be long before the emergency with the injured man was over. I had to find something! Slightly further on from the hopper, I heard my boots make a sticky, squelching sound and guessed I'd stepped into some viscous liquid. I made a hurried detour and, in the now almost total darkness, crashed into a pile of heavy sacks. I dug my fingers into the material of one and could tell it did not contain prills. Instead, it felt like there was something like sand inside. I slashed the sack and felt a granular, powdery substance pour out. I rubbed some between my fingers and knew it was not an organic compound; it had a rough metallic feel.

I knew I had to take a sample, even if this was yet another harmless product of a totally legit business, and, as the stuff was still pouring out, I held my much-mocked sample tube in the flow until I could feel it was full. Stoppering it, I turned around. Was there a back exit? I didn't want to wind my way through the darkness and come out under the full glare of those arc lights, and the full glare of those unfriendly workers.

I reached the far wall and felt my way along its surface in increasing desperation. Surely, even Grogan's rudimentary health and safety regs would require there to be more than one way out! Then my questing fingers felt a handle. Safety lay beyond!

It was then I saw a dark shape move in the greater darkness of the warehouse.

'Hey! Who are you! What the fuck are you doing in here?'

I did not answer. It was still possible my identity would not have to be revealed in this blackness: I could not distinguish his features, so he could not see mine.

'Cat got your tongue?' he said, and came towards me. 'LeBlanc will want a few words with you. This is a restricted area.'

I still did not speak but measured the decreasing gap between us. Perhaps he was thinking he had cornered an over-inquisitive worker who was just looking around.

Perhaps.

I didn't want any sort of conversation with him, except one delivered by my fists. And that's what he got.

However, I miscalculated in the gloom, and delivered only a glancing blow to his chin. He staggered but did not fall. I had no time for Queensberry Rules and aimed a kick at his crotch, with a heavy industrial boot leading the way. My aim was better this time, although the encounter was far from silent. As he doubled up, his chin came down and toward me, making it much easier to deliver a KO.

Which I did.

But he had let out a hell of a shout when my boot made contact, and the others would surely have heard it and would now be coming my way. I grasped the handle. *For God's sake don't be locked!*

It was not, and I made my escape into the now raucous night. Having pushed my luck beyond its elastic limits, I decided it was time to bid adieu to the McKinley fertiliser plant. And soon my beat-up junk-pile of a car was travelling surprisingly swiftly away from it.

Once again, I was not stopped.

THIRTEEN

I drove straight to HQ, as had been agreed with my superiors if I had any important updates. I wasn't confident I had one, as the substance I had collected might be Civet Cat Coffee for all I knew. But there again, it might be something much more significant.

Even though it was what our overseas friends call the "wee small hours", I knew that the message I was sending as I drove would be received by alert Elite minds. Their sleep is not like ours, and they can do without it for days on end, and snap out of it with razor-sharp alertness in an instant. It is no wonder they are in charge of everything and hold our lives in the palms of their hands.

I screeched to a halt as near to the entrance as I could, burst in, ignoring the security guards, and, forgoing the elevator, leapt up the stairs like a jackrabbit. I wondered why they were following me, bellowing at me to stop, and then I realised they didn't recognise me in my infiltration persona. Unfortunately, as it had taken several hours to change me, it would take several hours to un-change me.

A slug blasted a hole in the wall next to me, and I realised the guards weren't pussyfooting around, but I knew I couldn't let my masters down and rushed on. Fortunately, Mistress Aiyana's room is on the first floor and around a corner, and the next shot came nowhere near me. And then I was there!

And so were they. Mistress Aiyana and Lieutenant Ardelean were both standing by her desk, awaiting my appearance. I know that old story about them sleeping in coffins is just superstition, but there was something unearthly about their poise and self-assurance which was decidedly unnerving. It was as if they had been standing there, untroubled and self-contained, since I had last seen them, which is clearly impossible.

I had just started my spiel when the door crashed open behind me and a burly guard rammed his pistol into the small of my back, and yelled, 'Down on the floor, mister!'

'Stand down, Ferguson.' Mistress Aiyana said, in a voice which was simultaneously quiet, calm and authoritative. 'We know this human. There is no danger.'

'Yes, Mistress,' I heard behind me. I didn't bother to turn around to watch Ferguson go, but walked toward my superiors, fishing the sample tube out of my blouse as I came. I glanced at it: Thank God, I hadn't spilled it!

Ardelean took it off me, murmured 'With your permission, Mistress,' and poured some of the contents onto her desk. Both Elite bent over and closely examined it. All I could see was a nondescript grey powder. Well, at least it wasn't Civet Cat Coffee.

Ardelean straightened himself.

'Do you know what this is, Gray?'

'No, sir.'

'I didn't think you would. It's very finely powdered aluminium.'

He waited for a reaction from me—but didn't get one.

'It's what turns a harmless fertiliser into ammonal—a highly destructive explosive. One which, by the way, was used to destroy Rousseau's. Do you understand?'

But Mistress Aiyana had an odd expression: One I had never seen before. It was disgust. She was wrinkling her delicate nose.

'What is that smell!'

I felt a flush of embarrassment. Had my love of durian sauces let me down again? I thought it was only garlic that affected them badly.

Ardelean strode toward me and bent down in front of me. Crazy thoughts of being emasculated by those vicious fangs of his flashed briefly through me, but then I could see he was studying my boots. Then he laughed as he straightened up and waved a finger in front of me. It had a blob of a thick black substance on the tip, one which was gradually forming a drop.

He laughed again.

'Oh, how I love you humans! Your stupidity never ceases to amuse and repel me at the same time. Tell me what this is, Gray!'

I stared at the fingertip. The black goo was definitely starting to drop.

I was about to confess my ignorance again, when I heard my Mistress's cool voice say, 'Please don't soil my carpet, Lieutenant. I know what that is, and it's very difficult to remove from fabric.'

I stared at the two of them uncomprehending, feeling like a howler monkey that had wandered into a quantum physics symposium. Ardelean was laughing again.

'It's fuel oil, human, fuel oil! What is needed for ANFO high explosive. You needn't have bothered to risk your life collecting that aluminium. You had all the evidence we needed on your boots, all the time, you poor creature!' He whirled around to stare at the Commissioner, his face aglow with unholy triumph. 'You see! I was right along! All along! The destruction of Harker's Farm and the trouble we had in recapturing the Donors—totally unnecessary! If you had only listened to me!'

I groaned inwardly—they had indeed instructed me to look out for that substance; in the turmoil of recent events, I had forgotten about it. Pushing my regrets aside, I watched Mistress Aiyana as she received the blast of Ardelean's self-satisfied rage. Only one short blink showed her discomfiture, as vampires rarely blink. Then she spoke, tonelessly, unemotionally.

'I accept your conclusion, Lieutenant. It would appear I have been too considerate in my dealing with the humans. But now we must act.'

'Indeed we must, Commissioner.' Ardelean returned to me, bearing an expression that was a mixture of amusement and contempt. 'We will now capture Grogan's establishment, slaughter every stale human in it and transfer the young ones to the nearest Farms.'

Nor was that onslaught long in coming.

The eastern horizon had only just been tinged with pink and violet by the time the elements of the Pacification Force had assembled. They had not been activated for quite a long time, not since the riots in the Panhandle, but they had remained on standby ever since, ready to flash into action at the slightest sign of restlessness from the subject population.

And now that time had come.

Despite having no part to play in the operation, as the Pacification Force is Elite-only from Top to Bottom, the Lieutenant had demanded I attend as an observer. He didn't deign to explain his reasons for requiring my presence, but I had already guessed it: He wanted to rub my nose (and, by implication, the olfactory apparatus of all humans) in a demonstration of our utter impotence. Now, there aren't many swells in the Fluridian landscape that can be dignified with the term "hill", but he had found the nearest thing to it, and I was looking down at the factory at a height equivalent to halfway up one of the reactor towers.

And I was thinking about Felipe, as I stood next to the police vehicle, and praying that this was one of his rest days. From Ardelean's description of the operation, I knew my friend would be destined for a worse fate than being made into a Donor.

Don't be there, Felipe! I thought over and over again. *Don't be there!*

Ardelean was not in charge of the attack on McKinley's, as it was a purely military operation, but he was in constant contact with its commander by walkie-talkie radio. Many people believe the Vamps can communicate by sharing thoughts, but I have seen no proof of that. But, of course, I'd have to be one of the Elite to be certain.

Standing right next to him, I heard him say, 'Yes, yes, excellent. I would advise you to attack at once before anyone notices you. We don't want to have to go through the trouble of rounding them up. Such a tedious waste of time.'

Although we were in what used to be called "The Sunshine State", it can get very chilly in the early morning, and this was one of those mornings. Yet I felt much colder than the weather alone could explain; I was about to watch people, most of whom could have no connection to the Sons Of Man, being hunted like frightened deer by a vastly superior power. And what of the regular arable farmers, whose harvests would now fail after being denied the necessary food for their crops? There would be hunger in the Sunshine State.

But as I looked at the factory, I began to realise something was different, something was missing. Something was wrong. Where were the signs of activity, the jets and mists of vapour which were always spurting or hanging around the reactors? Why, at this close distance, could I see no forklifts dashing to and fro with their loads? The place was as deserted as a plague town.

I glanced at Ardelean, expecting to see a look of puzzlement on his sharp features, but all I saw was an eager hunger, a barely concealed lust for battle.

The radio spoke.

'We are going in.'

'Excellent, Commander. Please keep me abreast of all developments. I wish I was with you!'

From my distance, I saw figures in combat gear rise from the brush and run into the compound. I knew that the same scene was being repeated on the other side of the factory, to ensure no-one got away.

And yet I heard nothing. No cries of alarm, or triumph. No small-arms fire.

I could be watching the attackers invading an abandoned monastery.

Nothing.

A military voice came over the radio.

'Lieutenant Ardelean—there's nobody here.'

Watching him, I saw him stiffen, and his expression first go blank and then incredulous.

'No one there? But that's impossible!'

'Don't tell me what I'm seeing—or rather not seeing! There's no one here. It's empty, completely empty. Like a ghost town.'

A wave of relief came over me. Felipe would not be a victim today, at least. But how could the workers have known what was coming? The decision had only been made a few hours earlier!

'We are searching building by building,' the radio voice said. 'If anybody's hiding, we'll find them.' A pause. 'But I don't think there is anything to find.'

It was then I saw something move. Something which sent a blast of fear through my guts. Because what I saw was not a terrified human running desperately from vampire pursuers.

No, what I saw were wisps of smoke—smoke, not vapour—rising in sinister streamers from the warehouse I had recently escaped from, the one full of explosives. I turned to Ardelean and grabbed his arm. He stared at me in total stupefaction at such effrontery. He snarled, displaying terrifying fangs.

But I did not let him speak.

'We've got to pull back!'

'Pull back? And you touched me! You'll...'

I looked up into a face contorted with a mixture of amazement and rage.

'The whole place is going to go up any moment! The explosives warehouse is on fire! Look!'

I pointed at the tendrils of smoke, which had darkened and thickened.

Whatever Ardelean was, he was not a fool. In that instant, he saw what I had seen and reached the same conclusion. We both jumped into the vehicle, and he snapped an order to the driver, even as he was lifting the walkie-talkie to his lips to alert the Pacification Force.

'Commander, get out of there! There's a fire in the explosives area!'

Even before he had begun to speak, the driver had flung the car into a tight curve and we were racing away from McKinley's. One thought kept hammering in my brain: A lump of ammonal as big as my fist had demolished an entire building the day before—what would an entire warehouse of the stuff do? Good God, it would shake the planet!

Every fleeting second took us nearer to safety; every brief metre gave us a better chance of survival. We all heard the Commander speak again, but now in a voice that had lost all authority.

'A fire? I don't…wait, I see it! Soldiers, mission aborted! Get out!'

The car continued to race away, its motor screaming, its crazy motion flinging us up and down like marionettes in the grip of a drunken puppeteer. Why so slow, why so fucking slow!

We hurtled on at the vehicle's very top speed, yet fleeing agonisingly slowly from flaming extinction.

All that ammonal, I thought again, *how big an explosion will it make?*

I found out.

The landscape ahead of me, still in its gentle early morning shades, was suddenly lit up in a lurid yellow blaze. An infinitesimal moment later, a roar like worlds colliding imploded my eardrums. Then the shockwave, as hot as the centre of an industrial furnace, bowled the car over and over. Only our belts and airbags saved us.

Half conscious, I released myself. The car had finished its insane tumbling in the upright position, and I leapt out to see what had happened to McKinley's. And what I saw was beyond belief. A great blinding ball of red and yellow fire was rising into the sky, supported on a roiling pillar of flame-shot black smoke. It looked almost exactly like the explosion of one of those atomic weapons we had been fooling around with just before the Elite rescued us. Then, I wondered why there was no noise. I did not realise at the time that my hearing had been destroyed by the detonation, and I was being buffeted by an immeasurable tumult. My clothing was in tatters, the edges of the holes charred and with reddened, blistering flesh showing through.

Of the McKinley complex there was nothing, absolutely nothing; the explosion had removed all trace of it from the Earth.

And all trace of the Pacification Force.

My knees buckled and silent darkness took me.

FOURTEEN

I don't know how long I was under; I think it was weeks. But my unconsciousness was not empty, was not dreamless. Far from it, for I was back in the orphanage, back in the control of people who I thought should be caring for me, but instead appeared to delight in tormenting me. They wanted me to be something I did not want to be, something that both repelled me and frightened me, some hideous bargain which required me to spurn my true identity, my heritage.

I remembered one occasion when they had allowed me out of the confines of that grim building and its cramped quadrangle, when I had tried to escape. And I nearly succeeded! I slipped under one of the smelly machines I was supposed to be admiring and made a run for it. I didn't know where I was going or what I would do when I got there. I just wanted to be free!

They caught me, of course, and that was the last time I was let out until I was released into the world as a grown man.

Often, I would talk with Edward as we lay next to each other in the dormitory, wondering what wicked thing we had done to deserve such treatment. But we could think of nothing. In fact, we couldn't think of a time before the orphanage in which we could have done anything wicked. But Edward was even more affected by our harsh tutors than I was. I remember one evening when he came back from the treatment room and paced up and down by his bed, shaking a small fist and, with a tear-stained face, swearing vengeance on them.

It wasn't long afterwards that they separated us and a year or two passed before I saw him again. And, if anything, his hatred had grown.

In my dream, I saw him come toward me with a look of triumph on his face and heard him whisper, 'Charlie, I know now what I must do. Would you like to hear what it is?'

And then my eyes flickered open, and I was looking at the plain white ceiling of a hospital ward.

And I could hear again! I realised I must still be of some use to the Elite because, through their incredible cleverness, they had rebuilt my auditory canal. I saw a female face looking down on me and knew, because the face was smiling, that I had a nurse and she was, thankfully, human.

'Mr Gray,' she said, continuing to smile all the time as she spoke, 'you're awake at last! I'm Nurse Kalecki. How are you feeling?'

'Like shit,' I said (and I was not joking). But I could not recall what had brought me there. 'What happened to me?'

'You were very close to a terrible explosion, Sergeant Gray. Do you remember?'

And I did. Once again I saw the horrific fireball climbing evilly into the sky.

'Lieutenant Ardelean, is he…?'

'Oh, he's fine. No problems.'

I nodded, wise after the event. Of course he was; the Elite are virtually indestructible compared to us fragile humans. No doubt he was more afraid of a dose of allicin than a fireball.

She ruffled my pillow as she helped me to sit up.

'There that's better, isn't it, Mr Gray? Can I get you something to eat? You must be ravenous after your long sleep. You're more than a little anaemic, so I'll pop some iron into your order.'

I asked for a frugal dish of soya nuggets and a glass of orange juice, and while she was away getting it I made a pleasant discovery. I rubbed my scalp and was overjoyed to feel coarse stubble where before had been only smooth flesh.

As soon as I had enjoyed my simple meal, I asked for a mirror. She laughed when she heard my request.

'I wondered how long it would take you to realise! I'll be right back!'

A few minutes later, I was staring into the mirror and, joy of joys! Charles Gray was looking back at me! It was my old face, a face I knew as me. I had lost a lot of weight, that was quite obvious, but my features and skin tone were as they had been before my visit to the Infiltration Unit. And although I had not yet gotten my full head of hair back, the dark stubble I had felt earlier was a beautiful promise that, *one day*, I would need a comb again!

I think I spent about a week there while they ran a battery of tests on me. But after a while, I noticed that nurse Kalecki had stopped smiling at me quite so readily, and she was having a number of conversations with senior staff. At first, these discussions happened in the ward, but they could see me straining to hear what they were saying about me, and they stopped, but I guess they continued them somewhere else. At least, I think they carried on talking about me, because I saw a lot less of her. Eventually, I had had enough, and at the start of one of her visits, I came right out and said, 'OK, what is it? What have I got?'

She smiled, but it wasn't her old, spontaneous smile; it was—how shall I put it?—a theatrical smile.

'There's nothing wrong with you, Mr Gray. In fact, you're making splendid progress. Really splendid.'

'Then what are you saying about me?'

'Saying about you? Why, nothing Mr Gray.' She patted my pillow in a clear sign she wanted me to relax and think no more about it. 'I'm afraid a side effect of one of the drugs we're giving you has a tendency to induce mild paranoia. We're not talking about you at all.'

Her actor's smile widened. 'Except to say what a nice man you are, and what exceptional progress you're making. In fact, your progress is so good you'll be pleased to hear we're discharging you at the end of the week.'

I returned her smile with what I hoped was a genuine one of my own.

'That is good news.' I reached up and gently touched her forearm. 'But I'll miss you. I don't suppose…'

But she forestalled me.

'Sorry, Mr Gray. But my dating days are long gone.'

***

Nurse Kalecki was as good as her word, and I was discharged on time. Before leaving, I studied the report on my condition, and it was all good news. I had made a "splendid recovery" and there was no reason I should not resume my duties as soon as I felt well enough. In fact, I spent a few days in my apartment, walking back and forth, feeling my unused muscles complaining at being forced to do something again.

And I was also ignoring the messages piling up on my communicator, asking when I would be back. But it wasn't too long until I began to feel I had swapped one hospital ward for another and so I decided to return to HQ.

Mistress Aiyana did not appear to understand the concept of "convalescence", because she had contacted me many times during my hospital stay, asking me a series of questions—none of which I had been able to answer. So I was not in the least surprised to get the call to see her ten minutes after I checked back in at the office. As I walked in, I saw her sitting behind her desk, with Lieutenant Ardelean standing alongside. In fact, I had gotten used to this particular tableau, and was starting to seriously believe that somehow they could remain in that position for an indefinite amount of time.

Hell, perhaps they did—we don't know the half of what they can do.

'Gray, it is good you have finally decided to rejoin the Force,' she said, in tones that suggested she was dealing with a troublesome schoolboy. 'You have missed a great deal of important work.'

I risked some irony, knowing the Elite do not usually understand the concept.

'Sorry, Mistress. I'll try not to get blown up again.'

She did not catch me out in the irony department; she just nodded and said, 'Good. Now to business.'

I glanced at Ardelean, and decided to offer the hand of friendship.

'It's a relief to see you again, Lieutenant. You've made a good recovery.'

He did not smile, for which I was pretty grateful as Ardelean's smile is a fearsome sight.

'It was not an issue. We of the Elite do not require anyone's assistance to heal ourselves. Unlike you, I did not take any time off work.'

I decided not to risk any more irony; it was wise not to underestimate Ardelean.

'It is unfortunate on many levels that the McKinley factory was so utterly destroyed,' my Mistress said. 'There is no evidence of any illegal activities there. In fact, there is no evidence of anything whatsoever, as all that remains of that establishment is an extremely wide and extremely deep crater. Every single gram of whatever explosive they used was consumed in the detonation. But we cannot even determine if the destruction was deliberate; it is not unknown for ammonium nitrate to explode spontaneously.'

Ardelean spoke.

'If that was the only evidence, then it might just conceivably be the case we were dealing with an industrial accident. But there is a great problem with that interpretation. What is that problem, Gray?'

I was determined to show I was an effective officer again, and parried Ardelean's thrust.

'There was no one there.'

'Precisely. We assembled the Pacification Force and surrounded the factory within a few hours of deciding to do so. It is just possible a warning was sent from this building to a terrorist in the factory, giving them all time to disperse.' He smiled with a dental display reminiscent of a tiger shark. 'If there was such a message, it could only be from someone who was party to the decision.

'There were three such people. The Commissioner, myself, and you, Gray.' He moved menacingly toward me. 'Did you send that message, Gray?'

I stood my ground. I discovered that after nearly being blown to shreds on two separate occasions, I was not so easily scared as I had been.

'I did not. I was with you for most of the time. In fact, we were not separated until we left to go to the transport vehicle, and then it was only for a few minutes. I am not telepathic, so if I had sent the message, it would have been by some type of radio wave, and this building and its immediate surroundings are shielded against unauthorised transmissions.'

He was now only centimetres away and towered over me, a great pillar of terrible power, a strength able to rip me apart and not even notice my passing.

'If it was you, Gray, I will most certainly drain every last drop of your vital bodily fluids. And, I will ensure it will be done as slowly and carefully as is possible.'

'That is enough!' Mistress Aiyana broke into his reverie of revenge with a whiplash of scorn. 'I agree with Gray—he could not have been complicit. Control yourself, Lieutenant. He may be only a human, but he has some rights while working for me!'

Ardelean gave a perfunctory nod to show he accepted the reprimand and returned to his customary station next to the Commissioner's desk.

'It is a pity it was not Gray,' my Mistress continued. 'The situation would be much simpler than it actually is. We are faced with a conundrum. Even if the terrorists had received a warning about our decision the same instant we made it, they still could not have totally evacuated the entire area. There would have been some stragglers. But there were none.' She looked at me and I knew some bad news was coming my way. 'This is where a human will be useful. Your job is to go into Marinetown and find as many of those escapees as you can. Find out how they knew we were coming.'

I straightened my back, after realising I had cowered slightly during the confrontation with Ardelean.

'Of course, Commissioner. But Marinetown is not a small area. I would be grateful for an assistant.'

'Of course. I already have someone in mind.'

FIFTEEN

I leaned back into the softness of my new chair, feeling quite pleased with myself. Because of my work with the Sons Of Man, I had been given my own office, a rare privilege, given that humans normally did not rise high enough to earn such a status symbol.

My pay remained the same, however. Clearly, there were limits to my elevation. And in any case, I wasn't entirely sure I liked it; I felt confined in what was still a very small room, and I missed the badinage with my fellow officers.

But my Mistress had assured me I would soon be back out on the streets, once my new assistant was in post. So while waiting for him or her to arrive, I tried to make sense of the figures on my monitor screen, which were supposedly an analysis of disruptive activities in the Greater Marinetown area. But for the third or fourth time, I could not get the program to reach any conclusion as it did not understand my instructions. That was no great surprise, of course, because I didn't understand them either. I sighed. Street work I understood: Machines that were cleverer than me, I didn't.

Then there was a surprisingly firm knock at the door, which jolted me out of my glum reverie. I waited for a few seconds until realisation dawned that the unknown person was awaiting my permission to enter. (Obviously, I am unsuited for a high rank.) I said, 'Come In' and awaited the appearance of this person with the loud knocking style.

The door opened, and Serafina Ginevra walked in, looking like it was her room and *What-The-Hell-Was I-Doing-In-It?*

I stared blankly at her.

'And what do you want?'

She grinned, and without asking, took a seat.

'Sarge, is that any way to treat your new Deputy?'

If my stare had been able to become even more blank, I'm sure it would have. But I did manage to say, 'New Deputy? You? You were a cadet when I last saw you, filing documents.'

She shrugged.

'I was fast-tracked. They know how to reward talent here, it seems.'

I carried on staring at her, being unable to recall much in the way of talent in our previous liaisons. I had found her more than a little insubordinate, and still remembered how she'd annoyed the owner of Jackson's Farm with her air of superiority.

'This is on the level? You're not doing this for a bet?'

Her grin got wider, revealing surprisingly healthy teeth for a human.

'Would I lie to you? Now, let's stop dragging this out; could you bring me up to speed? I hear you've had a pretty exciting life recently.'

Reluctantly accepting the situation, while also wondering if Mistress Aiyana's famed sense of humour extended to humiliating Sergeants, I related all that had happened since we parted, and what was expected of us now. She gave a loud whistle when I detailed the disappearance of the entire workforce of McKinley Fertiliser Corp.

'Now, there's a strange one.'

'No shit,' I said, slipping back into the slang she seemed to prefer. 'Anyway, we're out on the town tonight.'

'Sarge,' she said, with a twinkle in her eyes, 'I didn't know you cared.'

I stood and crossed to her side of the desk; for some reason, I needed to be looking down on her.

'Let's keep it professional, shall we? If we don't come up with some leads, some kind of breakthrough, Mistress Aiyana will have our guts for Christmas decorations.' (Not that Vamps celebrate Christmas, of course, in case you thought I didn't know that.)

She also stood. I was crazily relieved to observe she hadn't increased in stature since her promotion.

'Well, thanks for the warm welcome, Sarge. I guess you haven't changed. Shouldn't we put a seal of approval on our newfound relationship?'

For an alarming few seconds, I thought she wanted me to kiss her, and I've always hated that *mwah-mwah* stuff, finding it more than a little insanitary. But she just sticks her hand out. I grasped it and winced under the sudden pressure.

'Take it easy,' I said. 'I know I have two hands, but I'd like to keep it that way!'

She looked a little flustered.

'Sorry, Sarge. I've been working out. I'd forgotten how old you are.'

***

It felt strange to be out on the beat as a regular cop again. And it felt even stranger to be back with Serafina Ginevra again, someone I thought I'd said a final goodbye to. I decided to make the best of it; recently, I'd spent too much time alone or with people who'd murder me without a second thought. It was good to have company, especially of the non-murderous kind.

But where to start? How do you find a couple of hundred people who have literally vanished off of the face of the Earth? It is one thing to be a Commissioner and order: "Find them!" and quite another to actually do it. Serafina and I weren't the only ones doing the looking, of course, but somehow the overall responsibility had landed squarely on my shoulders. Sometimes I wondered about the fairness of it all: Could we humans have saved ourselves at the crisis point, was their takeover the only solution? I shuddered suddenly: Maybe it was for the best the Elite don't have the power of telepathy. Some of my thoughts could get me into trouble.

We walked into the bar, the smell of stale beer insulting our nostrils, and saw suspicious faces turn to examine us. Perhaps the regulars didn't like strangers in uniform. Any attempt at disguise would have been pointless; it doesn't take a genius to work out that people who go around asking lots of questions are cops.

The pot-bellied barkeep certainly had it all worked out.

'Whadya want, Cop?' he said, looking up occasionally from polishing a beer glass.

'Just asking a few questions,' I replied, after introducing ourselves.

'Yeah? Who's in trouble?'

'No one's in trouble, citizen. We are looking for some missing people, is all.'

He pointed at Serafina and spread his arms wide.

'Hey! Look no further, lady—you found me!'

She clapped her hands—silently.

'Thanks. I should be so lucky.'

Realising my pugnacious colleague had annoyed another male, I swiftly took charge of the discussion.

'You've heard about McKinley's, I guess.'

He cast Serafina a poisonous glance and turned to me.

'Yeah. What's it got to do with me?'

'We're looking for people who used to work there. Mind if we check your customers out?'

He shrugged and went back to polishing.

'If you want. But ain't you looking in the wrong place? They're all up there,' he glanced briefly at the ceiling, but I assumed he was pretending to look much higher, 'sitting on clouds, practising their harp playing.'

Could it be, I wondered, that the disappearance of hundreds of people was not common knowledge yet?

'You don't know of any of those people, sir?' I said, feeling a wave of futility wash coldly over me.

'No.' He put the glass down with a gesture of finality. 'You drinking?'

'No. We're on duty.'

He picked up another foam-smeared glass.

'Then keep it short. If they're talking, they ain't drinking.'

I nodded and indicated to Serafina we should move to the nearest table. A wizened man was sitting there, staring into an empty glass. I toyed with the idea of buying him a drink, but I knew the budget wouldn't stretch to that. And in any case, the Elite don't approve of alcohol. They don't use or need it themselves, and don't like the possibility a drunken mob of humans might do very foolish things, like objecting to being ruled by vampires. So spirits are banned, and all beers are three percent or less. You'd pass out from overloaded kidneys before you'd get even a little merry. He looked up as I asked if it was OK to join him. Red-rimmed eyes looked us over. He spent no more time looking at Serafina than he did me, which told me a lot about the state he was in.

'I don't talk to cops,' he mumbled, looking into the empty depths of his glass.

'You're not in any trouble, sir,' I said. 'We're looking for some missing people. Nothing more.'

He did not look up.

'You work for them, don't you? The Vamps.'

'Yes, we do. They're the lawful authority.'

He snorted.

'Lawful authority? What hole are you living in, copper? What have those bastards done for us?'

I was shocked at his words, and automatically looked around for disguised microphones.

'Careful, sir,' I heard Serafina say. 'You must remember how they've given us peace. Taken our dangerous toys away.'

He continued to stare into his glance.

'They've destroyed us. Turned us into helpless children.'

My peripheral vision told me Serafina had turned to look at me. This stuff was getting dangerous. The customer did not seem to realise the danger he was in. And yet his voice had changed somewhat; it sounded more educated, more fluent.

'My grandfather was an economist in a big international corporation. If you know what "international" means, or "corporations". He was a great man, dealing in millions of dollars. Heads of state listened to him. He changed the world, controlled the lives of hundreds of thousands of people. I don't say it was all good he did, but he was answerable to his own kind. Men! Not unnatural creatures who just see us as walking meals!'

I started to rise; I didn't want any part of this. But to my amazement, Serafina reached for my arm and held me motionless in a grip of steel while she stared at the human.

'But we wouldn't be here,' she said. 'The world would have been destroyed.'

But now he did look at us, and his reddened eyes held me fast.

'And you think it's not destroyed now! They've taken away everything that made life living! We can't decide anything for ourselves, go anywhere we want, do what we want. It's all gone. There's no economy, no work except what they decide we can be allowed to do.' His fist smashed onto the table with a bang that startled both

Serafina and me. 'You know what our so-called economy has been reduced to, where the only real money is? The Farms, those terrible fucking Farms! That's what we are! Beasts of the field!'

I heard a rumble of agreement from the rest of the room; obviously, the man's tirade had been heard by the other customers. And agreed with.

I could feel danger building. A big fellow crossed over to me and planted himself at my side.

'Guys like you make me sick. Working for them. A goddamn lickspittle traitor.'

I stood slowly and carefully; I did not want a brawl to break out, especially with Serafina in the firing line.

'I'm sorry you feel that way, sir,' I said in as mild a tone as I could, also just about managing to smile. 'I see myself as working for the public. Keeping the peace. Isn't that what we're supposed to do?'

I don't know what might have happened next if the barkeep hadn't intervened.

'I think you two'd better leave,' he barked. 'I run a decent quiet place here, and that's the way it's gonna stay.'

I knew he was offering Serafina and me a way out, and I took it. I gave the crowd one quick look, seeing if their features stirred any memories of my time at McKinley's. They did not.

It was a relief to be out in the evening air, stickily humid and laden with the smell of decay as it was.

'Well, that was a bust,' my companion observed.

'Thank you, Serafina,' I snapped. 'I had noticed. But at least you kept your trap shut, so I thank you for doing what I asked for once!'

She showed no reaction, and I cursed myself inwardly for showing the tension I was under. I had resolved to try to improve our working relationship, but she was so damn feisty!

We tried a few more bars, fortunately without a similar confrontation.

'This is pointless,' I finally said, after being asked to quit the latest drinking-hole. 'The only way to be certain is a house-to-house search.'

Just then, I saw a familiar face. Serafina saw my expression and said, 'Have you found a missing person, Sarge?'

'No, it's Sergeant Horowitz. An old buddy of mine.'

Horowitz was with a Deputy I didn't recognise, a nondescript young woman. He called me over.

'Surprised to see you on this crap job,' he said. 'I thought this kind of thing was beneath you, now that the Vamps think so highly of you.'

'They do? News to me. But if that's true, I wish they'd give me a quieter life.'

'Yeah, I heard about your undercover work. That took some balls.'

I just grinned and said nothing about it; we like to think we're all one band of brothers in the Force; no one likes people who think they're something special.

'Found anything?' I asked, after we had chewed the fat awhile and moaned about our superiors—in a guarded, carefully worded way, of course.

'Nah. Just the usual run of unemployed losers. Beats me what these people do all day.'

I didn't challenge him on that; I had seen what kind of work was out there for regular guys, and it wasn't pretty.

Eventually, his Deputy respectfully touched his shoulder and quietly said, 'Sarge…'

Horowitz slapped me on the shoulder, said, 'Great to see you again, Charlie boy', and the two of them continued on their patrol into another of Marinetown's run-down suburbs.

Serafina watched them go.

'Friend of yours, I take it.'

'Yes. Good old…' I glanced at her, having detected her tone. 'Do you have a problem?'

'He ignored me the whole time. Never looked at me once.'

I snorted my exasperation.

'Look, Serafina. You're just the bottom mug on the totem pole.' (Having heard that expression from Bernie, I had decided I liked it and vowed to use it whenever it seemed appropriate.) ' Horowitz is a good cop; he's seen it all, done it all. He's earned his stripes. Now, you know you're wonderful, I know you're wonderful, but other people need to take a little time to take you in; know what I mean?'

She glared.

'Sarcasm doesn't become you, Sergeant.'

I was about to remind her of her lowly position when I saw a movement at the corner of the street and stiffened. Was it… could it be?

Once again, she followed my gaze.

'Seen something this time?'

I did not reply.

It was dark and the face I had seen was also dark, so dark it was almost indistinguishable from the gloom. But I was sure!

It was Felipe.

SIXTEEN

My heart almost skipped a beat: Felipe had neither perished in the annihilation of McKinley's, nor had he been removed from the face of the Earth by an unknown power. He was alive, and I was glad; although I had only known him for a short time, he had been the nearest thing to a friend I had possessed for many a long year. I made a movement toward him, calling 'Felipe! It's me!'

To my amazement, I saw a look of shock on his face, and he turned and ran, disappearing around the nearest corner.

'After him!' I said to Serafina. 'He's one of the missing people!' She simply nodded and immediately broke into a sprint, leaving me gasping like a stranded flounder as I tried to keep up with her. She burst around the angle of that building like a guided bolt of lightning, leaving me behind like a kind of human exhaust. But as I caught up with her, I saw the street was empty of people. Instead, it was littered with broken boxes, discarded rinds and cores of a rotting miscellany of subtropical fruit, shards and fragments of kitchen utensils… I sighed. Even in my short lifetime, I had seen Marinetown continue its unstoppable decline into destitution.

But no Felipe.

But…

'He's here,' she said, turning her head from side to side like a feline searching for a prey item that could be only temporarily hidden.

'How do you know?'

'I just know.'

I followed her; it seemed the roles had been reversed and she was now leading the hunt. For a second, I realised I would not want to be on the receiving end of that hungry gaze. In the short time since I had last seen her, she appeared to have matured from an eager-beaver pain-in-the-ass to something much more significant; formidable even. It was like I had never really known her.

We moved on down the dimly lit street. I heard something rustle in the detritus to my left, leapt over to investigate, and recoiled when I met the stare of a particularly fat brown rat. Some distance ahead of me, seemingly unfazed by close encounters with Marinetown's rodent population, I heard Serafina mutter, 'He's got to be here.'

And so he had to be, for the road was a dead end. He was here, somewhere.

But why was he hiding from me, his work buddy?

Serafina had crossed to the other side, and I was about to investigate a shadowy doorway when a wiry human form erupted from it and crashed into me. I tried to speak, but a hard forearm was suddenly lying over my larynx, threatening to crush the cartilage. And at the end of the other arm was a knife. I gasped for air, unable to prevent the fatal steel from descending.

'Not tonight, my friend,' I heard the owner of the knife hiss. 'Adios asesino.'

And then a look of amazement appeared on his face as he looked up at something. Through a red mist, I dimly saw Serafina's diminutive figure appear alongside him and rip him from me. She effortlessly knocked the knife from his hand while simultaneously throwing him back into the doorway whence he had come. I heard a thump, closely followed by a groan. *Some reunion*, I thought, as she pulled me upright.

'You alright, Sarge?' she said, looking at me as if she actually cared. 'You've got to be more careful; remember you're not a young man anymore.'

I gave a wry smile at that; it's not easy to hear a young woman treat you as if you were an escapee from a euthanasia clinic.

'Yeah, but what the Hell's got into Felipe?'

She reached into the doorway and pulled out a semiconscious Felipe. I looked him over, now he was no longer trying to kill me.

Yes, it was definitely Felipe. And he was coming round.

'What you want with me?' he mumbled. 'I got no money. Just bag of fruit. I never in trouble with police.'

And that was true; there was a brown paper bag in the doorway, torn and with oranges and avocados spilling out. I held his shoulders, forcing him to look at me.

'Felipe, don't you remember me? It's Charles—I mean John Andrews.'

Then it hit me: He had only seen me in my infiltration getup. He simply hadn't recognised me. *Good God*, I thought, *I should have realised! I really am losing it!*

'You not Juan,' Felipe was saying. 'Juan my friend. You crazy cop. I do nothing.'

'Serafina, this is Felipe Ramirez from McKinley's; help him up.' I had to reassert my authority, having just had my life saved by a rookie half my size. As soon as he was standing, albeit supported by Serafina, I said, 'You've got to believe me, Felipe. I am John Andrews—or rather Charles Gray. And I am a cop—but not a crazy one.'

He looked past me.

'I know what my friend look like. You not him.'

It was very strange, standing there in that dim, stinking alley, trying to convince someone I really was his friend, even though I looked nothing like that friend. I had to explain about being undercover at McKinley's, but at the same time not giving away too much about why I had been there. He was not convinced.

'Look,' I said, in growing desperation. 'Let me tell you about some things we talked about. Your wife is called Marisol. And you come from... you come from...' My mind had gone blank as I looked into his disbelieving eyes. Then I had it. 'You come from Zittabongo.'

He looked at me with a totally blank expression, and then his face seemed to split open, so wide was his smile.

'Ah, Zittabongo! I do not know this place. But I know Juan used to call my home that; the beautiful Zitácuaro!' He extended a hand that not long prior had held the implement of my death. 'I believe you, my friend Juan!'

I nodded to Serafina.

'You can let him go now. He's no danger.'

She gave me an Are You Sure? look, but released him.

Turning back to Felipe, I said, 'Felipe! How did you get out of McKinley's? Where did you go?'

'It's strange story, Juan. But let us go to my place. It is not far.'

I helped him gather up his fallen produce, and then we followed him some distance through the reeking streets to a ramshackle building that had not merely seen better days, but better centuries. A smell of boiled cabbage, strangely mingled with cooking oil and fried onions, assaulted us as we followed him in. A slim woman holding a chubby, dark-eyed child greeted us almost immediately.

'Felipe,' she said, staring at us while talking to him, 'why do you bring these officiales into our home!' She backed away, gripping the child more tightly.

'He is my friend,' he said, and, looking over his shoulder at Serafina, added, 'I do not know the señorita, but she is amiga to Juan.'

The young woman looked unconvinced and backed away into a squalid living room, in which used diapers shared space with simple wooden toys. She looked at me, almost accusingly.

'Pardon, señor. I was not expecting company.'

She hurried to remove the soiled diapers, for which I was profoundly glad.

However, Serafina was up to her old tricks again.

'Do you usually assault police officers going about their lawful business, Mr Ramirez? Especially when wielding a knife.'

Felipe shot me a surprised look, but then said, 'Senorita…'

'I am Deputy Serafina Ginevra, Marinetown Police Force. Not "senorita".'

'Pardon, Deputy. I try to understand my friend is not just wearing a different face, but is a policeman. That is dificile. You see, the police are not usually our friends here.'

'Oh?'

Felipe shook his head while staring at interlaced fingers.

'They do not like us. Say we cause trouble. Try to get us to move out, go someplace else.' His face twisted, as if he had suddenly come under a great strain. 'And once, when I was on night shift, a policeman came to the house. There was just Marisol and little Jesús here. And he tried to do bad thing with her. Only when Jesús start crying did he go away.'

My face flushed with anger.

'He couldn't have been a real police officer, Felipe.'

'Oh no, Juan. Marisol remember his name. It was hard name to say for people like me, but I learn it in case he comes again. Horowitz.'

A stunned silence fell. I gazed at Felipe in disbelief, and then I heard Serafina say, 'Your old buddy, Sarge. Looks like he really has seen it all and done it all.'

'Shut up!' I snarled without looking at her. 'I'll take it up with the Commissioner when I get back! Now drop it!' I returned to Felipe. 'I'm sorry about what you told me. I'll make sure it doesn't happen again. But Felipe, there is something I must talk with you about. My super... the people in charge of me, they ordered an attack on McKinley's because they thought that terrorists—bad men—were making explosives there. But when they arrived, all the people were gone. And then the whole place blew up, killing a great many Elite—and nearly me, as well. Were you there on that morning?'

I felt my heart begin to thud as I waited for his answer.

But he merely replied in a quiet, matter-of-fact voice, 'Si, Juan. I was there.'

I leaned closer in my excitement.

'So what happened? How did you get out?'

To my surprise, he stood, and began pacing back and forth in the little malodorous room.

'I do not know, Juan. One second I was looking at the numbers on the screen and the next I was in field many kilometres from the factory. But still close enough to see the flash, hear the thunder and feel the ground shake. It was a terrible thing. I thought it was el Dia del Juicio!'

I shook my head in disbelief as I gazed at the man, striding up and down, his head downcast.

'But... but that's not...'

'That's not possible, Mr Ramirez.' Serafina interjected. 'It's simply not physically possible. Had you been taking anything?'

Abruptly an angry female voice broke in our consternation.

'Out of my house, *puta*! My Felipe does not tell lies! He is a good man!

I whirled around, seeing Marisol standing in the doorway, hands on hips, eyes blazing.

'No, no, my Deputy didn't mean to suggest that Felipe had been using, Marisol. But like me, she cannot understand how this thing could have happened. It is very strange.'

Marisol crossed to Felipe, who had resumed sitting, and placed a protective hand on his shoulder.

'Now you understand why we not like police.'

I tried to move the conversation on.

'Felipe, this story is very hard to understand. Could you come into the Force headquarters and tell the people there? Maybe they could run some tests on you, to see if…'

Marisol shook her head.

'No! No tests! And we not go into that building. People like us go in but they do not come out!'

'That's simply not true, Marisol,' I said, waving Serafina into silence. 'And in any case, I would not let anything happen to my friend.'

They did not speak. And I realised I would get no more from them that night. So I simply said, 'Please think about it, Felipe. Lots of the Elite died on that day, and we must do our best to ensure it does not happen again.'

He did not look at me, glanced at his wife, then went back to studying his hands.

'I think about it.'

With that, I knew the discussion was over. Marisol heard Jesús whimpering and brought him back into the room. Seeking to ingratiate myself with her, I looked closely at the baby and smiled when he held one of my fingers in his little hand. I tried to encourage Serafina to give a similar display of affection, but she did not appear interested.

And then, after a handshake with Felipe, and my attempt to say Good Night in their speech, we were outside again.

We walked a short way in silence, and then I stopped and spun her around to face me.

'Don't you ever act up like that again! Disrespecting one of my friends! You almost got us thrown out!'

She looked up at me, unafraid, unmoved.

'One of your friends? You only knew him for a couple of weeks. Do you think people go around with signs on their chests, reading I AM ONE OF THE SONS OF MAN? PLEASE ARREST ME?'

I shook my head. Dammit, she'd got the better of me again!

'I trust Felipe.'

Now she was almost leering.

'What, are you going to say, "He's a nice guy", or something? Don't you realise the role of a kind-hearted family man is a classic disguise for a terrorist? This is a war, Sergeant Gray, a war with no end in sight, not even a temporary truce. In fact, it's hotting up.'

I found I was unable to answer: Everything she had said was true.

'What about his story?' I said, rapidly changing the subject. 'Could there be any truth in it?'

She looked away.

'It can't be true. If it were true, it would mean...'

Her voice trailed away.

I grabbed her once more.

'There you go again. Hinting at something; always hinting that you know something I don't! What is it you know, Deputy?'

But her answer left me no clearer than I had been.

'I'm not sure. It's too soon.'

SEVENTEEN

Even those who work for the Elite are allowed some rest, and so it was not until the following morning that we had to face the Commissioner. As usual, Ardelean was standing by her desk.

Christ, I thought, *has she got him on an invisible string, or something?*

I had finished relating my encounter with Felipe and also, his accusation against Horowitz. Ardelean was not impressed by either tale, especially the possibility my erstwhile buddy had been abusing his power.

'We are not interested in the mating habits of shadflies,' he said. 'Your species' sexual behaviour is totally irrelevant to this investigation, and of no interest whatsoever to the Elite. What are you, but creatures that mimic the shapes of the Elite, who grub around for a few short decades and then return to the dust from which you came? I...'

His views on the irrelevance of humans were cut short by a rap on the desk from Mistress Aiyana.

'Enough, Lieutenant. Your views on humans are well known, but, for better or worse, we must work with them.

'Of course, Commissioner. I should not have diverted us from the main issue, which is the disappearance of the workforce of the McKinley factory.'

My Mistress held me in her icy gaze of oceanic blue.

'Tell us again what this Felipe person said about that.'

I repeated Felipe's extremely short description of what he had experienced. And yet again, I witnessed the merest hint of alarm in the glance that passed between male and female vampire.

They know something, I thought. *Something that worries them*. For some reason, I remembered Serafina's mysterious mention of something or other about "Guardians."

I pulled my attention back to the here and now: Ardelean was speaking again, in the cold, clipped delivery which meant he was issuing orders.

'... and bring the human in here immediately. I have procedures which have never failed me yet in dragging information out of them.'

I snapped back into full attention.

'You mean arrest Felipe?'

'Was the thing you call your mind somewhere else, Sergeant? Of course I mean this Ramirez person. I intend to question him.' His fangs showed worryingly as he smiled that vampire smile. 'Question him most thoroughly.'

'But his family? He has an infant child!'

Mistress Aiyana intervened.

'Sergeant Gray, I hope sentimentality to your fellow humans is not blinding you to your duty.'

'Of course not, Mistress,' I said, but all the time, one thought was circling in my mind: Warn Felipe! 'When will the arrest take place?'

'Not before 15:00,' Ardelean said, 'but don't be too concerned, Gray. You won't have to dab your eyes as you weep for a fellow creature. My unit will carry out the operation. You can have a little nap.'

My Mistress nodded.

'That's all, Sergeant. I believe I can spare you for a few hours; I am aware humans do not respond well to sleep deprivation and I need you at peak efficiency. Dismissed.'

I saluted and left, being careful not to lock gazes with Ardelean.

But I did not go to the Mess Hall, or the relaxation area where stressed officers could relax with simple sports or videogames.

No, I climbed into my official vehicle and headed away from HQ into the run-down suburbs where the Ramirez family resided. Using an official vehicle for personal reasons is, of course, a disciplinary offence; with Ardelean on my back, it could well be the end of my career.

Many heads looked up as I passed, heading deeper into the shantytown. Several armed robberies were put on hold until I had passed. But I was only fleetingly aware of them. At last, I was outside their house. I carefully put the car on armed lockdown after I had climbed out; it would be nice for it to still be there when I returned.

But would Felipe be there! I knocked violently on the crumbling door and was gratified to see his slight figure revealed as it opened.

'Juan! What is it? What have we done?'

'Nothing, but you've got to get out! Lots of police officers are coming to arrest you, take you away to HQ for questioning!' *And this time,* I thought grimly, *you truly might not come out.*

I heard Marisol calling out, asking what was happening, her voice troubled.

'Quick,' I said, 'don't worry about your possessions! You have to go!'

'I do not have many possessions,' he said sadly. 'But there are things we must take, food for little Jesús, some provisions for Marisol and me.'

'Yes, yes, but hurry, hurry!'

I joined him inside, and we wrapped up a few pitiful family heirlooms in one sack, and an absolute minimum of food and bottled water in another.

'Will you be alright?' I said, as our frantic labours neared their end.

'Si, Juan. I have some people in the countryside. They will take us in.'

'Thank God. Now get a move on!'

A few minutes later, they were standing in the doorway of their hovel, looking back at me. Strangely, Jesús was not crying.

'This is a good thing you do for us, Juan,' Felipe said.

'Yes, yes, I'm a great guy! Now go!'

And then I was alone. Reaction hit me, and I collapsed onto Felipe's one and only easy chair. Unfortunately, as I was somewhat heavier than its previous owner, it also collapsed. I just lay there amid the sad detritus of what had been a family home; a pitiful one, to be sure, but a home, nonetheless. And for a brief, terrible instant, I found myself sympathising with the Sons Of Man. Who is to say that in that Time of Crisis, it was beyond us to pull back from annihilation's brink and save ourselves, by our own efforts? The Vamps would still have been in the world, of course, but confined to the shadows, not controlling every one of our actions, every one of our thoughts.

I don't know how long I lay there, musing over the tragic tale of humanity, but eventually I stood up, and made my way to the open door.

And, of course, Lieutenant Ardelean was there.

'You're under arrest,' he said.

***

I sat in back of the people carrier, in handcuffs, of course.

I had asked earlier on, what the charge was, and had been told there were two, namely: Unauthorised use of an official vehicle, and helping a known felon to escape. My observation that Felipe Ramirez was not a felon, known or otherwise, was ignored.

I knew this was the end of my police career; Ardelean would see to it, and it might even be the end of my life, given Ardelean's professed desire to drink me dry.

The drive back to HQ seemed much shorter than my drive from it, and soon I was being hustled upstairs, as the Lieutenant was eager to display his prize to the Commissioner.

However, when we entered, I was surprised to see Mistress Aiyana looked uncharacteristically flustered and—yes—alarmed.

'I have brought you Sergeant Gray,' Ardelean began, 'I caught him…'

To my amazement, she waved him into silence.

'Another time, Lieutenant. We have a much bigger problem.'

Standing next to him, I saw him sag slightly as his moment of triumph was being ignored. I fixed my gaze upon my Mistress. She was holding up a small black cylinder and displaying it to Ardelean; and to me, of course.

'I left my office in order to check on some findings one of my other officers wanted to show me. When I returned, this object was lying on my desk. My secretary swears no one entered or came out in my absence.'

'Worrying,' Ardelean said. 'I think…'

But once again, he was cut off.

'I have not finished, Lieutenant. I will tell you when and if I am prepared to take questions.' She rolled the cylinder between slim fingers. 'The presence or absence of this object is not the issue. As you see, all one has to do is hold it for approximately two minutes And then this happens.' And, as if on cue, a beam of a strange violet light flashed out of the end furthest from her fingers. I was astounded to see that the light formed a cone with sharply defined edges, as if it were a solid object. A large circle of violet light was thrown on the far wall. And within the circle, words appeared, words spelled out in gleaming white letters.

And the words comprised the message: TODAY I WILL KILL ONE BLOODSUCKER. THIS IS JUST THE START OF OUR WAR UPON YOU.

I goggled at the message, feeling that I had been flung into some waking dream. Ardelean started to speak, but managed even fewer words than the previous time.

'Wait,' she said, 'there is more.'

A voice filled the room. And I mean filled. It was all around me: Behind, in front, left, right; Hell, it even came up through my boots. It was a powerful, resonant voice, the voice of the ultra-masculine leader, the one no one dared challenge. It was the first time Ardelean had heard that voice, and I actually saw him wilt slightly under its power.

This man meant business!

And there was something else…

'You have read my words. Mark them well; I mean exactly what I say. Today I will kill one of you bloodsuckers. Too long you have gloried in your power; rejoiced in your ability to slay at will. You have lusted after the chase, been triumphant in your hunts; shown your teeth in esurient ecstasy as you slew the helpless creatures you feed on. Those days are ending. My war upon you will progress slowly, so that terror will take residence in your hearts. As the end nears, you will run like sheep before the wolf, aghast at the falling of a leaf, thinking it to be my axe.'

And the voice ended, leaving my concussed ears ringing.

Ardelean at last was permitted to speak.

'It is some trick, some sleight of hand. It…'

'Nonsense! In your absence, I've had the cylinder investigated by our Elite technicians. It appears to be a solid cylinder with no internal mechanisms.'

'Impossible!'

She brought the flat of her hand down on the desk with a sharp crack.

'Be silent! Do not dare to tell me I have misunderstood something, mistaken a human child's toy for an existential threat.' Suddenly, she looked at me. 'Release Gray.'

'Commissioner! I…'

She rose slowly, but with implacable fury smouldering in eyes of adamantine crystal.

'One more word, one more second's hesitation, and I will make you my evening repast, Ardelean. The world has changed under us, and now we need every resource we can find. You have no proof Ramirez was one of the Sons Of Man, or that he could have told us more under your torture than he has already told Gray. Now obey me now, or die now; the choice is yours.'

Seconds later I was free, rubbing my wrists after their release from too-tight handcuffs.

'What shall I do now, Mistress?' I said, in the most appeasing voice I could manage now that the tiger had shown her claws.

'I'll find a use for you, Gray.' Her penetrating gaze switched to the Lieutenant, and she pushed the cylinder toward him. 'Take this. I observed that Gray seemed to notice something when the voice was speaking, something we were not aware of. Perhaps you two can listen to it together. And keep your fangs off him, Lieutenant, or you will find mine on you.'

If ever I saw hatred in someone's eyes, I saw it in Ardelean's as he looked down on me.

'Come with me to my office,' he said in a voice which made a simple invitation more like a venomous warning than anything I've ever heard, other than from a snake.

Ardelean's office was down the corridor from my Mistress's. I was intrigued; I had only seen him in the field or standing next to the Commissioner's desk. However, his office looked almost exactly like hers, albeit smaller. He sat down behind his desk, the cylinder between us. I was not invited to sit, however. He looked at me and I knew then what a vole goes through when it realises it's being watched by a cobra, which is at that moment pressed up against a sheet of glass. I knew if there was the smallest hint of permission from my Mistress, I'd be the main course on the menu.

'Gray,' he said. 'Don't think your reprieve is anything other than temporary. I intend to…'

Intended to do what?

I never found out.

At that moment, from nowhere, two scimitars of lurid purple light appeared on either side of him. I will never forget the stricken look on his face as the scimitars sank deep into his sides. His arms reached out to me, imploring help from a pitiful human.

But no help was possible, human or otherwise.

The swords of light lifted him up, out of his seat, and held him writhing, pleading, near the ceiling.

And then they turned him inside out.

It was a sight incredible to watch, impossible to properly describe. All I can say is that I was showered in blood, bombarded by tumbling, pulsating organs as his skeleton came into view—on top of the pitiful shreds of remaining flesh.

The voice had fulfilled its threat.

EIGHTEEN

When a body's interior becomes its exterior, it is not a silent process, irrespective of what sounds may have led up to that incredible moment.

And so it had been with Ardelean.

The entire process had been so loud that people came running from all over the building. And they found me, crimson-purple from head to foot, standing in a pile of flesh and bone that had wetly dropped from the ceiling.

There was no more Lieutenant Ardelean.

Mistress Aiyana was not the first to arrive, but she shouldered her way through the horrified throng to face me.

'Gray, what happened? Where is the Lieutenant?'

I mutely pointed to the mess encircling me. She understood at once. She called up the medics, who stuck me on a trolley and wheeled me to the infirmary. No-one wanted me dribbling vampire ichor all over the nice clean carpet.

I was in shock, of course, and had no understanding of what had happened to me or what was happening to me. I felt a needle go into my arm, and then it was lights-out.

I awoke an unknown time later, completely clean and wearing a hospital gown over fresh underpants. And looking down at me was Mistress Aiyana.

Her air of cool command was utterly gone, and I was struck by how much she resembled a frightened

Original, an ordinary human woman driven to the edge of madness.

'Gray,' she whispered, leaning closer to me now she knew I was awake, 'tell me what happened!'

For some time I could not speak; I felt my lips trembling, but no words came out.

'Breathe, Gray,' she commanded. 'Breathe slowly and deeply.'

Gradually, my spinning mind slowed and quieted, and I was able to relate what I had seen; how the scimitars of light had come from nowhere and impaled the Lieutenant. And the terrible thing that happened afterwards.

She straightened herself and her lips moved. She was not looking directly at me, but oriented well enough so I could attempt to lip read.

And I am reasonably sure I saw her say *And so it begins.*

Then she looked back down at me.

'Take the rest of the week off, Gray. In fact, take several weeks off. I don't have any mission for you at present. I'll call you when I need you.'

And she was gone, bearing the face of a frightened Ordinary woman.

They wouldn't let me drive back to my apartment, so an ambulance took me there, and two orderlies helped me into my room. Then I just lay on the couch, staring at the ceiling, remembering how I had looked at another ceiling and watched something that looked like a man become pinned there and explode.

I won't bore you with what happened in the immediate aftermath—because nothing did. I just sat in my apartment; sometimes sleeping, oftentimes not.

Serafina says she came to see me, but I don't remember.

And then, eventually, I felt strong enough to return to HQ.

Once again, I was standing in Mistress Aiyana's room, but this time there was no Lieutenant Ardelean standing by her side, eyeing me hungrily. She had recovered her poise and air of command in the interval since we had last met, but on her desk lay the fateful cylinder, and I was immediately taken back to the events of that dreadful day.

She saw it and, surprisingly for a member of the Elite, said, 'Take it easy, Sergeant. Sit down.' After I had obeyed, she said, 'Don't worry; I'm not going to interrogate you about what happened. You've told me all you can already. We've investigated his room very carefully while you've been away, but we have not found anything that could even begin to explain what occurred there. The Lieutenant suffered the same fate as Elite Estok, including the disappearance of the heart. All the other organs were there. But there remains this.' She pushed the cylinder across the polished wood of her desk. 'I had heard the message several times before you did, so I was able to study the reactions of those who were hearing it for the first time. And yours intrigued me. You looked as if you were trying to remember something. Or someone. Was that the case?'

I had deliberately not thought about the minutes leading up to the Lieutenant's death, but now she was forcing me to do so. Under her cold blue stare, I tried to remember my feelings. And there was something—there had been something about the voice: Not the words, but the essence of the voice, its intonation, its timbre.

But I could not say what.

'I am sorry, Commissioner, but I can't explain it. There was something about the voice, but—but I can't explain it.'

To my surprise, she was understanding, tolerant.

'That's alright, Sergeant. It may come back to you. Here, pick the cylinder up; it may stir a memory.'

I obeyed. The object was perfectly smooth, without blemish. In fact, it was so smooth and light that if I closed my eyes, it hardly felt as if I were holding anything.

And I did close my eyes; the cylinder felt like it wanted me to do exactly that.

And within the darkness of my closed lids, I heard a faint voice, and it was saying, 'Come to me, Charles. Come to me.'

And that was all.

I opened my eyes, and there was no voice.

My Mistress was looking at me with an expectant, hopeful expression. I had never seen so many emotions in her face before; usually, there was only irritation or scorn.

But something told me not to say anything, because the message had been private, for me alone.

'I'm sorry, Commissioner. I can't detect anything.'

She showed yet another new emotion: Disappointment, this time. Then she smiled, hiding her fangs somehow.

'Never mind. We'll try again later. Go now, Sergeant.'

I went back to my duties, even out on the sidewalks again, but I felt a sense of helplessness, of futility. I could not shake off the feeling that I was caught up in something which was not simply too big for me to handle, but too big for the entire Marinetown Police Force to handle. And I had seen emotions on my Mistresses' face I had never seen before: Doubt, uncertainty and perhaps, yes perhaps, fear.

Serafina caught my mood very early on and enquired about the cause. In another reversal of the normal, she sounded genuinely concerned. I felt too tired, too dispirited to reply at first, but in the end I did. I explained my fears about something happening which was beyond all our experience, perhaps beyond anyone's experience.

'You weren't there,' I said. 'You didn't see those arms of light come from nowhere and lift him up, squirming, wriggling. One of the Elite begging for help from a human! Even without what happened next, that would have been disturbing. And the Sons Of Man—until now it had been easy just to write them off as a load of disaffected losers. Sure, they got hold of powerful explosives, but I solved that issue. They were getting it from McKinley's—case closed. Except it isn't. They didn't take the stuff onto Harker's Farm; it was given to them when they were already in. Given to them in a similar way to how the Lieutenant was torn apart. I didn't actually see the explosive arrive, but there was a flash of light, like in Ardelean's room. And all of a sudden, they had it in their hands; hands that had been empty a few seconds earlier. How could a raggle-taggle bunch of humans do something like that? Tell me!'

'I can't. But perhaps the Sons Of Man have got hold of something the humans were fooling around with just before the Takeover. We know they had plans for some really crazy shit, like diseases capable of exterminating the entire world population, with the exception of the Warlords—who would have been given immunity. And what about bombs that would kill billions but leave the cities untouched? That's why the Elite took over; we all know the bitter truth. What if, in some laboratory hidden in the mountains, some crazy scientist had made this—this weapon of light, just before the Elite stopped all that madness? Even they wouldn't know about such a weapon.'

I thought about it for a while. Then: 'No. The guys I saw were tough men, hard cases who didn't care if they lived or died. But none of them was a science geek. They were terrorists, plain and simple.'

'I don't doubt that, Sarge. But the rank and file wouldn't have to be. Just as the men who dropped the A-Bomb weren't atomic experts. The guy at the top would be the science geek—and he wouldn't get his hands dirty.'

I pursed my lips.

Maybe that was how it worked, but: 'Yeah, but Ordinaries don't have a science education. We just do as we're told.'

That floored her, and we walked on in silence. I knew this malaise of mine wasn't confined to me; the rest of the Force had it as well.

But it was me who had the real dose: I had seen the enemy in action.

Somebody was waging war on the vampires. And using a weapon that could not be countered—because we didn't know what it was.

Nothing out of the ordinary happened in the next few weeks, just the regular routine crap of petty burglaries, domestic disturbances, traffic violations. Hell, a few people had even managed to get drunk on illegal beer and had gone around bad-mouthing the Elite. Bringing peace and harmony to Marinetown with those kinds of threats was so easy I swear I could have done it in my sleep.

I still had regular meetings with the Commissioner, although they had taken on the air of an Am-Dram performance by unskilled actors. Oddly, my Mistress appeared to have taken me into her confidence a little; maybe the presence of the Lieutenant had hampered that approach.

'Our specialists have gone into the circumstances of the incident in great detail,' she said to me one afternoon. I noticed her fingers now had natural-looking nails, and that she was using those fingers to toy nervously with a pen. 'In great detail. And they have found nothing. No unusual chemicals, no residual energies. Nothing. The Lieutenant's remains show no traces of anything he might have ingested. All the organs were separated from each other with surgical precision with sharp, clean cuts. Just like at the Diodati Institute. There is another similarity: The Lieutenant's heart was missing. All the cardiac blood vessels terminate with mathematical precision on emptiness.'

I had nothing to say on the matter, but to show I was still a functioning officer, I asked, 'Is it known why Elite Estok was investigating the Institute?'

'Yes. There had been an unexplained reduction in the output of blood leaving the site.' This time I was no longer surprised to see her features register confusion and bafflement. 'The records showed the vats produced the same amount of blood, but the records also show a smaller amount being supplied to consumers. It seems that an increasing amount of blood was disappearing after it had left the vats. And I mean disappearing. There was no way that quantity of liquid could have been smuggled out of the premises. It would have required a fleet of trucks. The blood just vanished.'

Another awkward silence fell. I was used to receiving clearly defined orders delivered in a crisp, authoritative voice. To sit there, watching my Mistress wrestling with the insoluble made me uneasy. I wanted my old boss back; I didn't want this uncertain, indecisive individual.

She spoke again, in a different, more confidential, tone.

'You didn't like Lieutenant Ardelean, did you, Sergeant?'

I was startled by this intrusion into my personal feelings, but having been asked a direct question I answered it.

'No.'

'Why?'

I looked around the office, hesitant to continue this line of questioning. Then I looked her full in the face.

'He wanted to drain me dry. I was just an item on the menu.'

She smiled weakly, leaned back in the chair and looked at the ceiling for some seconds. Then she resumed holding me in her gaze.

'Sergeant, what is your favourite food item?'

For a moment, I really thought the world had gone crazy. To be asked about what I liked to eat by the Police

Commissioner seemed to be simply *Howling-at-the-Moon* madness. But once again, my training took over and I answered her.

'Well, I would say SewdBeef burgers and fries, Commissioner.'

She nodded, understandingly.

'SewdBeef burgers. Now, come with me on this one, Sergeant. What would life be like for you if you worked in an environment where these burgers of yours walked around, answered the phone, drove cars, held conversations with you? And all you had to do was to reach out, grab one of those walking, talking burgers and ram it into your mouth, enjoying the wonderful taste of all that pseudomeat and fat. What would life be like for you?'

I thought about it for a while.

'It would be tough. I'd have to keep my urges under control.'

She smiled. (Unfortunately revealing her fangs, which always makes vampire smiles a little difficult to appreciate.)

'Exactly. And that was the environment Lieutenant Ardelean had to work in, day in, day out. To him, you were a walking, talking burger. One he simply had to reach out and enjoy. But he did not. Perhaps now you will appreciate him slightly more.'

I was dumbfounded. But her speech didn't entirely convince me: I have never mocked or demeaned a pseudomeat burger.

But she was still speaking.

'You see, Sergeant, evolution has played a cruel trick on us. We need your blood; we cannot stay healthy without it. We would lose all the centuries of life that are our right. It would be so much easier if humans did not look like us, if they could not talk, answer the phone, drive cars. But they do and they can. That is our problem.' Suddenly she sat straighter and her eyes shone with a cold, Polar brilliance. 'But never forget—we saved you. You showed yourself unfit to run this world, one we have shared with you for millennia. You would have turned it into a graveyard, a wasteland of ash. So do not bemoan your fate. The life you lead now is better than the one you could have created for yourselves.'

I felt the iciness of her gaze pour over me, into me.

There was only one thing I could say.

'Yes, Mistress. Thank you.'

NINETEEN

I can't say that my Mistress' little parable had done much for my peace of mind; indeed, in some ways it had made it worse. The idea that I was little more than a walking, talking beef patty was not a pleasant one. It had brought a realisation to the increasingly turbulent surface of my mind that I was working for beings who saw me as little more than an *hors d'oeuvre*. It was something I'd always known, of course, but it was disconcerting to have it dragged into the light like that. When doing my usual Cop duties, it had been easy to imagine I was just another flatfoot doing ordinary things in an ordinary Noramerican city.

Now that was gone.

It was about then I started having those strange dreams again. I have already told you about the alarming one with the mist and the threatening voice, but these new dreams were not like that. They always started in the same way; there would be a voice, a female voice, and it would be calling to me, usually saying exactly the same thing, or very close variations on a theme.

Sometimes I would be walking through a dark forest along a leaf-strewn path, and occasionally I would catch sight of a full moon in the gaps between the branches. And the moon was always blood red. It was very strange, because I have never been in a forest like those in my dreams—after all, there are none like that in Flurida. Nor have I ever seen a Lunar eclipse.

Sometimes I would be floating in a sea of golden light below a cloudless sky. And the sky was not blue—it was a deep, rich red. The colour of blood. And as I floated (which in itself is strange, because I have never been in water and I can't swim) the liquid supporting me would slowly turn a deep ruby colour.

I think I can stop stating the obvious now.

And the voice, the voice of a woman, would call to me saying, 'Charles, remember! You must remember!'

The voice was urgent, insistent, as if it was terribly important that I remembered—or some great disaster would happen.

And I would try to remember, try to grasp the thing I needed to recall. Have you ever dipped your hands in a pool attempting to catch a small fish, and feel it escape you after a brief touch of its scales? It was just like that. Many times I would feel I was on the verge of remembering the thing that had been kept hidden for so long—and then it would dart away again, into crimson obscurity.

I would wake up with clawed hands and moist eyes, screaming that I wanted to remember.

And you know the strangest thing of all: During the dream, I knew who the woman was who was calling to me.

But I couldn't remember!

For most of my recent past, I had been happy in my small apartment; after all, it was my home and had been for many years. I was now spending more time there as my Mistress had temporarily shortened my hours, but that was not what I wanted. I wanted to be out there, making a difference. But I was haunted by the thought that making a difference was a lot harder than I'd thought it would be. Perhaps humans couldn't make a difference, and I'd be better off getting a job as a pseudomeat burger flipper. Now that humans were at the bottom of the food chain, there'd been no really big criminal cases. There were no audacious bank heists because we no longer had much of a money-based economy. Hell, we didn't really have any kind of economy. There were no international financial corporations, no hedge funds, no private equity, no derivatives, no speculators. Financial transactions rarely got above the level of buying an eggplant or two. Maybe, occasionally, some zucchini would be thrown in. What excitement! Most crime rarely got above the level of domestic disturbances or traffic violations. There was the occasional murder, of course. The Elite took more of an interest in that crime, because what herdsmen want their stock killing each other?

It was about then, during my periods of involuntary idleness, that I began to think about how I had gotten into this situation. Why had I chosen the life of a police officer? As I sat in my chair, or lay on my couch, I came to understand why. It was the only activity which humans could do which retained some dignity. There were humans in the Blood Shops; there were even humans in charge of some of the remaining industries, like McKinley's. The zenith (if I am using that word correctly) was running a blood-generating plant, such as the Diodati Institute. But DeLancey was a rare case; most humans no longer had the necessary education. But on the morning that his sweating, rotund figure had crept into my consciousness, I just accepted it as the normal order of things, and spent another shortened day at HQ. Serafina had been reassigned, temporarily I hoped, to a cop who still had all his marbles. Despite her amazing ability to get under my skin, I discovered I missed her.

But there came a day when, slumped in my chair, I once again began reviewing my past; a past which increasingly felt to me as if it had been wasted.

What had Jane said about my career choice?

But even as I discussed that question with myself, I suddenly felt a mental shock as bad as a sudden jolt of electricity. What had she said about—anything?

I realised I had not thought about Jane for a long, long time. What had been her interests? Had she liked crochet, patchwork, embroidery? Pottery? Had she been good at cooking, or had we lived on tacos and burgers?

A sick feeling of horror began to invade my mind. Not being able to remember a voice supposedly heard in a dream was one thing—but not being able to remember your wife!

I leapt to my feet, hands clasped to my temples, and I screamed.

Reality seemed to be swirling around me like a whirlpool; a whirlpool which was pushing me inexorably to its fatal centre.

I knew I had to look into her face again to pull me out of the whirlpool, to save my sanity.

I pulled open drawers, heedlessly tossing their contents to the floor. I opened my one and only closet, pulling out shirts and pants, looking, ever more desperately, for my wife's face in a family album, or even a single photograph.

There were none.

There weren't even any pictures of me. Surely there would be a few pictures of me proudly wearing my police uniform on my first day?

There was nothing.

Jane didn't exist.

I didn't exist.

Perhaps nothing existed, and I was just a software emulation running on some vast computer, and the programmer had forgotten to give me a back-story!

One thing I do remember was sinking to the floor and yelling, 'Who am I?'

The wandering began, shortly after my moment of utter despair.

It started with me simply walking the dirty streets of Marinetown, continually looking left and right, as if there were somebody I desperately needed to meet. And it nearly cost me my life.

One evening, when I had been walking for so long my feet were complaining real bad, I'd had enough and walked into the nearest bar. It was filled with the usual crowd of no-hopers, down-and-outs and ditch-digging labourers. I guessed most of them had been staring at the same empty beer glass all evening. A few of the less comatose ones looked up as I came in, but the others didn't. I was vaguely aware that a better-dressed guy in the corner seemed to be giving me a hard stare, but I did not return the look. I ordered the strongest beer they had, pulled the greasy glass toward me and knocked it back in one go. I immediately ordered another.

That was a mistake.

It meant I had money.

Almost instantly, I had one malodorous low-life on my left, and another on my right. They bent in, crowding me simultaneously.

'Buy me a drink, mister?' the one on the left said.

I ignored him.

'Hey, my friend spoke to you,' the one on the right said.

'Buy me a drink, mister,' Leftie repeated.

I turned to him. I no longer cared about anything, anyone.

'Are you trying to pick me up? What are you, a hooker?'

His face went blank as his befuddled brain processed what I had said and then twisted into fury. His fist flashed toward me.

I had dealt with a lot worse than these wrecks in my time. It was all too easy. I simply dodged inside his arm and sent his head back with an audible click. Mr Right's arms encircled me, trying to pin mine to my sides, but he too joined his buddy on the floor a few seconds later.

'OK, out! Now!' the barkeep shouted. 'I don't have no troublemakers in my joint!'

'What about my beer?'

'Out! Or this.'

He pulled a shotgun from under the counter and pointed it at my face. I couldn't stop laughing. It was obviously a fake, as the Elite don't allow civilians to own guns, but I guessed it impressed the majority of his clients, most of whom didn't seem capable of distinguishing Up from Down.

'OK, OK,' I said, raising my hands above my head and backing away in mock fear. 'I only wanted a beer.'

As I trudged away from the bar, I felt almost exhilarated. For a moment, when facing down that pair, I had felt alive; achieving something—even if they had been no greater threat to me than a pair of kindergarten kids.

Then I realised I was being followed. There was a regular pattern of footsteps behind me, matching mine exactly. When I slowed, they slowed; when I stopped, they stopped. Somebody had come out of the bar, after me. I turned.

'OK, I know you're there. What do you want? Money? You saw how easily I took down those two clowns. Do you want some?'

A man emerged from the shadows. I instantly regretted some of my bravado; this man was no down-and-out: He carried himself with the air of a man who had supreme confidence in his abilities, someone who had come up the hard way. He was even smiling slightly as he approached, clearly unimpressed by my threats.

'I think your offer was unwise, mister. I don't want any of yours, but I'm willing to give you some of mine.'

He came closer. I could not see his face clearly as it lay in the deep shadows of a cloud-filled, moonless night.

But once again, I found I was half-recognising a voice. This was getting crazy!

'So what do you want?' I said, letting my arms hang loosely at my sides. I understood now that I wanted excitement, danger even. I was tired of rotting in my apartment. What did that famous vampire say? Better to live one day as a lion …

'Those two bottom-feeders were no threat to you; we both know that. But you handled yourself pretty good, I'll give you that. Perhaps we could use you.'

My senses went on high alert. The word *We* was a real danger marker. I had come across We before.

'Use me for what?' My blood was up. 'Do you need your ass wiping?'

He shook his head in theatrical disappointment.

'Knock it off, all this tough-guy malarky. You're making yourself sound stupid. I've got a proposition for you.' He came right up to me and grasped an upper arm. His fingers felt like steel. 'There's a better watering hole just over there. Let's talk.'

I fell in beside him, but I knew something was wrong. His voice was familiar, worryingly familiar. There was danger in this encounter. We walked on in silence while my churning mind strove to identify the reason for my growing fear. I fingered my communicator rod as we walked. A few presses on it and my location would be sent to HQ, along with the implication I needed help—fast!

'Cat got your tongue?' he finally said. I just grunted, not knowing what to say. Fortunately, the next bar came into view around a corner and we were soon in its hot, clammy interior. Although the air was full of the cloying odours of stale beer, it was a step up from the previous one. Well, at least the clientele did not appear to have suffered lobotomies. No-one stared at us as we approached the bar.

My drinking companion jerked his head toward an empty table and said, 'Take that one. I'll get the beers.'

I looked at his back view as I sat down. I still hadn't gotten a good sight of his face, due to the place's soft lighting. But I would when he turned to bring the drinks over.

I waited. He turned, a glass in either hand, a confident grin on his strong features.

My heart leapt.

It was Bernie.

TWENTY

I understood then the danger I was in; if he worked out who I was, one suspicion would lead to another. I wasn't in uniform, of course—that would not have been a particularly good idea for a Marinetown bar crawl—but to be the man he had known as Andrews, yet not to look like Andrews, that could only mean one thing. There was only one power on Earth that could change a man's appearance so thoroughly—and it wasn't human. My sudden disappearance from the ranks of the Sons Of Man would simply be the final proof of what I had been.

An infiltrator. And worse—a traitor.

He sat down opposite me and pushed the beer toward me. You could tell at once he was no bum; he was pretty sharply dressed in a smart casual way, wearing a kind of denim shirt with fancy buttons. He smiled, but he wasn't very good at it. Obviously, he didn't smile very often. I lifted the glass and held it before my face, in as natural a way as I could manage.

He sipped his drink and then extended a hand to me. 'Name's Bernie. What's yours, buddy?'

Once again, my mind whirled. I hadn't expected to have to provide an alias and I couldn't immediately think of one.

'Come on,' he said, his brow furrowing. 'You know your own name, don't you?'

'John,' I finally uttered. 'John, John An...Anthony.'

His look became sharper, more alert.

'Sounds like you have a kind of speech impediment there, John. They must have put you through it at school.'

'Yeah,' I said, giving a sickly smile. 'Yeah, they sure did!' I tried to move on from questions about my identity. 'So what do you want, Bernie? Why are we here?'

'Good question.' Then it seemed like he had ignored the question and gone on to a new topic. 'What's life like for you, John? I mean, are you hanging in there, making ends meet, shall we say?'

I shrugged; I didn't want to appear to be well off in my new persona as a bar-fly. 'OK, I guess. I survive.'

'Wife? Kids?'

I decided not to appear too pliant.

'Hey, what is this? Is this the Government census?'

His head went back as he laughed.

'Government! Hell no, John! We don't have anything to do with those ass-lickers.' His gaze returned to bore into my eyes. 'No, they've sold us regular guys down the river. They've sold us to the Vamps. Do you like Vamps, John?'

'I stay out of politics.'

He reached over and grabbed my wrist.

'That's what they all say! But politics doesn't stay out of you! Those blood-suckers—they're draining us dry, really dry, John! They've made us into fucking commodities, walking lunch boxes! We owned this planet. We still own it! It belongs to us!'

I looked around and then back at him.

'Keep your voice down, Bernie. If somebody hears your talk, we're in trouble.'

He surprised me by displaying a big grin.

'Nah, this place is full of people like me. People who've had enough shit shovelled down their throats, people who are going to take this world back, or die trying!'

I knew then I had to get out. I was about to be recruited into the Sons Of Man—again!

'Sorry, Bernie, you've got the wrong man. I like the quiet life.'

'Oh no, you don't. I saw you in the other bar. You've been around. You know how to handle yourself. I know men, and men like you are no Vamp-Lovers.'

And suddenly, my whole view of the situation changed. I was a police officer, for God's sake! Maybe I could get some information which would lead to the Sons Of Man being taken out for good. Of course, it would be risky, but, as they say in the videodramas, risk was my business. All I had to do was not sign up to any actual mission. I wanted nothing more to do with high explosives.

'Maybe you're right,' I said, after a long pause to show I'd been thinking it over. 'So what if I'm not a Vamp-Lover?'

'Then I can help you give it to those bastards where it really hurts.' The light of battle had now filled Bernie's eyes. He looked almost messianic; maybe that was how he saw himself. I decided to get into my role and show I was a convert.

'Yeah,' I said, putting my half-empty glass down with a bang. 'No truce with the vampires, eh!'

I immediately knew I'd made a terrible blunder. Bernie's face stiffened, his eyelids narrowed.

'No truce with the vampires. That's an interesting turn of phrase, John. Where did you hear it?'

I felt my scalp prickle with apprehension.

'It just came to me, Bernie. I like the sound of it. Don't you?'

He didn't answer at once, and I knew I'd blown it. Then he spoke, in a cold, forensic tone.

'You know ever since I laid eyes on you, I've had this crazy feeling I knew you, as if we've already met. With an ugly mug like yours there should be no trouble recognising you, so why am I not sure?' He grabbed my wrist. 'Where do you work! Quickly now!'

To my horror, my mind had gone blank. I couldn't think of a nearby place of employment. Finally, I said, 'A Farm.'

'Bullshit. I know all the Farm owners from here to the Atlantic. You're not a Farmer, and you sure as hell ain't a Donor. Not with that belly.'

I got up to go.

'Thanks for the beer, Bernie.'

Suddenly I saw the end of a metal tube poke up from behind the table and I knew what was at the other end.

'Sit down, John, or whatever your name is—because as sure as Hell it ain't "John". I've said certain things tonight that I don't want anybody else to hear, especially Vamp-Lovers. Or, even worse, real live Vamps.' He cocked his head to one side while he studied me. 'You take one step toward the door and you're dead meat. They all know me here and they'd help dispose of your carcass. Stay still; I want to look at you.' He continued to study me and I watched his eyes flick over my face, side to side and up and down. 'You know, John, my people have discovered that the Vamps know how to change people's appearance overnight. But of course, they can't do much to change a guy's height or his overall size. So it's mainly the face they change, of course, because that's what everybody looks at first.' Then his grin returned, and it was the grin of a shark. 'I think I've got it. I remember now, I first met you in the packing plant and you said something very similar about the Vamps. I liked the sound of it. And I'm pretty damn sure I know who you are. You're Andrews. Except you're not Andrews. No-one could have had that face-change technique without working for the Vamps. So you're not Anthony and you're not Andrews.' The muzzle of the automatic protruded a little higher. 'But I'm certain of one thing about you—you're a Cop. You're the worst kind of slimeball, mister, someone who's sold out his own people to those soulless monsters. You're a fucking Judas and we're going to enjoy taking you apart.'

'And why would you want to do that?' I said, trying to show a bravado I certainly didn't feel.

'Because we're going to turn the tables on you and your stinking friends. You wanted to find out about us, and now you're going to tell us all you know about the Vampire Police Force. We're going to get a tad unpleasant on the softer parts of your anatomy till you start squealing. And boy, will you squeal!'

There was no point in denying what I was.

'You won't learn too much from me.'

'What, because you're a real hard case and you won't talk? They all say that until we strap them down in the cell and start working them over.'

'No. Because I'm the bottom mug on the totem pole.'

He laughed.

'I gotta hand it to you—you think you have a good turn of phrase. But as I recall, that's my phrase.' The muzzle of the automatic jerked. 'Up. Slowly. We're going outside so I can call the boys. Don't make me shoot you; they're running out of sand here to cover up the blood and they don't like it.'

I stood and waited for Bernie to join me. He pushed me toward the door at the same time as jabbing the muzzle of his gun into the small of my back.

'Slowly, Mr Whoever-You-Are. We'll find out your true name real soon; don't you worry about that.'

The air outside felt oddly cool even though I knew it was not much different from the inside. It was just me feeling cold, I guess. Options were hurtling through my mind. Should I just chance a confrontation with Bernie? If he shot me, wasn't that better than what he had planned for me?

We walked on toward a gap in the run of buildings, where one had collapsed a few years earlier, spreading a fan of stone and brick across the road.

'This will do.'

I obeyed but also slowly turned so I could see him. His right hand held the automatic but his left hand was twisting the top button on his open-neck shirt. It was well for me that night Bernie was right-handed because he wasn't used to doing whatever he needed with that button, using only his left, and was forced to look down to check his actions.

I knew that would be my one and only chance, and I took it. I stepped to one side at the same time as my fist slammed onto his chin. He staggered but did not go down. As I had suspected, he was tougher than me.

A lot tougher as it transpired.

Even as I drew back my fist for another blow, a piledriver came from nowhere and sent me flying. A few of my teeth went off in directions of their own choosing. I went down, flat on my back. He strode toward me, rubbing his chin.

'Not bad, not bad at all. But not good enough, Mr Vamp-Lover. I think I'd better take out a kneecap to slow you down.'

However, as he came up to me, he was a little too near and I kicked his feet from under him and, as he crashed to the ground beside me, I was on top of him, raining blows on his upturned face.

Blows which seemed to have no effect because, despite the fall, he still held the gun. He struck back, sending my head back so I was looking at the clouds. But I knew I was fighting for my life as we rolled over and over the fallen rubble of the collapsed building, giving and receiving piledriving blows. Under his fusillade, my eyes began to close until I could hardly see his grinning features.

'Pity,' I heard him say, 'you're not a pushover. We really could have used you. But now, time to say goodbye to your kneecaps.'

He straightened his legs, jumping upright, and I saw the muzzle point downward to my legs.

Just then, a thick drunken voice called out, 'Hey, mister! What about my beer?'

Bernie turned automatically to check out the intruder and I forced myself upright, taking a fallen stone with me. My fists had made little effect on him, but the heavy stone certainly did as I smashed it onto his temples. Just like the old building, he collapsed. I stood over him, swaying as I did so in a desperate attempt to stay upright. I was dimly aware that my saviour was one of the bums from the previous drinking den, who had finally decided to make another claim on the drink I had refused to give him earlier. Through the slits between my eyelids, I saw him stare at me, hesitate, and then make up his mind he didn't want to take any piece of the brawl he'd just witnessed. He skedaddled as fast as his unsure legs could take him!

Breathing great draughts of the humid Marinetown air into my tormented lungs, I found the gun and pushed it into my jeans. I pulled off Bernie's belt and tied his legs together. I then stepped back, pulling my own belt out, so I could tie his arms. But I stopped to activate my communicator: I realised there was no way I could carry Bernie back to HQ, I needed help. But just then, his eyes opened; he touched the side of his head and looked at the dark stain on his fingers.

'You were lucky, mister,' he said. 'You were good, but I would have taken you if it hadn't been for that hobo.'

'Agreed,' I said, through split and swollen lips, 'but that's life. And now you'll be the one doing the talking. My backup will be here in a few minutes.'

'That's nice,' he said, 'but I won't be.'

I saw the fingers of his right hand do something to the top button of his shirt. Suddenly he was enveloped in a violet aura.

And then he was gone.

TWENTY ONE

I guess I should have been astounded by Bernie simply disappearing before my eyes, but I had seen quite a lot of astounding things by then, and my astound-organ was getting worn out. So when my buddies from the Force turned up not long after, I hardly bothered to explain why I was standing there in torn clothes and with blood on my face.

I had to explain to the Commissioner, of course, and by now I was getting used to the look of worry on her perfectly proportioned features. She was particularly interested in the violet aura that had enveloped my opponent, but, other than describing it, I could offer no explanation. There might have been a swoosh of Marinetown air as it rushed to occupy the space which had once held him, but if there was, I hadn't heard it.

So I spent a few days as an outpatient getting the shots I needed to get my teeth back, and for those days I was forced to eat through a straw. I soon discovered that burgers just don't taste the same once you liquefy them. Serafina was back with me on official duties, but fortunately her warped sense of humour did not extend to calling me "Gummy".

Things had gone quiet in town, although I had the terrible feeling it was the calm before the storm. I don't know why I thought that, but I doubted that old-fashioned "Normalcy" would be returning any time soon. However, nothing happened to confirm my doubts: No more Farms or Blood Shops were taken out, and we spent the time cleaning up after minor misdemeanours or booking wayward motorists.

The only thing which really worried me, and the one thing I couldn't share with my Deputy, was my mental state.

Those dreams about me remembering something kept coming back, and they seemed to be the only thing I could dream about. It was as if I were always on the brink of recalling what this Terribly Important Thing was, but I either woke up just as I was about to pull back the curtain or open the casket, or I held the answer and had to watch it slip away like water through my fingers, never to return.

The other thing I could not understand was why there was no record of Jane anywhere in the apartment. And even more troubling: How come I had only just realised that?

My wandering continued too. I seemed to be spiralling about a central point in the city, but there was nothing at that point but the municipal park. I hadn't been there for years, mainly because there was nothing there. Just a few tired flower beds, a fountain that didn't work, and some trees that should have been cut down years prior. And so I had no intention of going there, just to find something else to depress me.

As we drove along on a day indistinguishable from all the other days, I remembered something at last. I remembered Serafina had inquired into my marital state, and I asked her why she had done that. She adjusted her oversized shades and shrugged.

'Just being friendly, Sarge. If there had been a Mrs G, I might have invited the pair of you round for a burger and a slice of pseudo-meatloaf.'

That didn't sound like my work-obsessed companion, but I needed to talk to someone. Horowitz had heard about me reporting him, so I had one less pair of ears I could bend (not that anything had happened to him; the Vamps aren't interested in human squabbles.)

So I tentatively opened the topic with Serafina, ready to pull back at the slightest sign of disinterest, or worse, her usual sarcasm.

'You can't remember your wife?' she said, and I could imagine her eyebrows arching behind those enormous shades. 'A lot of men would say that was a blessing.'

I frowned.

'Thanks. I guess it was stupid of me to expect any interest.'

She took her hand off of the wheel and touched my wrist, almost tenderly.

'Sorry, Sarge, that was a bit glib. So you're telling me you don't have any documents; no marriage certificate?'

'No.'

'No keepsakes, mementoes?'

'No.'

'No photos, videos, of vacations together.'

'No.'

'No yellow, crumbling Valentine's Day cards?'

'No. Look, can you just accept that there is nothing—nothing at all!'

She pursed her lips and gave a low whistle.

'That's funny.'

She suddenly swerved in an attempt to take out a contented-looking rat that was ambling across the road, but it was too nimble for her.

'Well, there is a way,' she said, after she had calmed down from the failure of her attempt to reduce the Marinetown vermin population. 'City Hall. They'll have a record of your marriage.'

I smote my forehead in self-disgust.

'Of course! I really am getting too old for this job.'

Without taking her eyes off of the road, she patted my wrist again.

'Never mind. I still like you.'

***

And so, as soon as I was able to, I was at that venerable building, enquiring about accessing the records. The whole place looked very run-down; if buildings had emotions, I would say it was a clinically depressed building. It still had its Parthenon-style frontage, with elegant columns in a stone that looked like marble but wasn't.

But that was all it had. The Elite had built it just after the Takeover, to make a now subject population feel they were still important, that they had a form of self-government. They hadn't, of course, and year by year each authority, each power, was slowly stripped away, until there was nothing left but the building itself.

The guy giving me the once-over looked like he'd been standing there while they built the Hall around him. He was so decrepit I felt the light would shine through if I put him in front of a window. His surviving hair comprised wispy white strands at the back of his head, while his face looked as if it had been constructed from nothing but various types of wrinkle.

'You want to look at marriage records?' he said, in tones which suggested I'd just asked him to hand over his family fortune. I confirmed I did.

'You don't have copies?'

I confirmed I did not.

'Most irregular,' he said. 'Everybody should keep copies.'

There was no more I could say, so I just spread my arms wide and smiled.

A few minutes later, I was sitting in a booth with a computer monitor before me, having been assured that the records were complete and up to date and that I would surely find what I wanted. However, the machine was playing up, no doubt because the coding had become corrupt and no humans these days knew how to fix it. Although it appeared to be responding correctly, it was agonisingly slow, so slow that several times I thought it had stopped working completely. But eventually, I found the correct section and was soon looking at a long list of "Grays". Surprisingly, given that there were so many, I didn't know any of them. And because the machine's innards seemed to have been coated in quick-setting cement, it took me quite some time to find the right "Gray".

Or had I?

I flipped the display back and forth, cursing its arthritic performance.

But slowly, chillingly, the truth became inescapable.

There was no marriage between a Charles and a Jane.

My wife had never existed.

I sat back and held my head in my hands. I was insane—or the world was insane; one of the two. Or maybe I had been right the first time when I suspected I was a character in a computer simulation: Me, Serafina, Madame Aiyana, Bernie—all just bits and bobs floating around in cyberspace. Perhaps I had been programmed to feel pain when an imaginary fist hit my imaginary chin. Maybe if I stared at something long enough, I would see it dissolve into pixels. Perhaps there'd been a bit of bad coding, or perhaps a momentary power failure. Maybe even as I sat there, huge green, tentacled creatures with two heads were discussing how the situation could be put right without their electronic puppets noticing the fault.

Why was that scenario any less likely than more everyday explanations?

I switched the machine off, feeling as exhausted as if I'd run a marathon. The day was humid but no more than normal, yet beads of sweat had broken out on my forehead. I seriously considered killing myself as a way out of this madhouse. What did I have to lose? I had no wife; I'd never had a wife. I probably didn't have a brother, either. I'd probably never been raised in a hellish orphanage. No, some weird creature had thought it might be fun to design something like me and watch it suffer.

Then a terrible thought almost laid me low: Perhaps I couldn't commit suicide! Perhaps I'd be instantly resurrected to carry out this crazy computer game for as long as the programmer wanted!

The old guy knocked on the door of the cubicle.

'You OK in there? I thought I heard someone cry out. If you need medical assistance, could you wait until you're outside? We're not covered, you see.'

I burst out of the cubicle, almost knocking him over in my hurry to get away. I was on foot, and I staggered along the sidewalks, bumping into people, pushing them aside, and nearly getting into fights several times. I guess my mad stare warned them off. If pain was just a few lines of computer code, I would take anyone on, even Bernie.

Eventually, I was back at my apartment. I looked around. How long had I lived there? Perhaps the apartment and me had been pulled into electronic existence a few hours ago, at the same time as I had been given a portfolio of false memories about people and events that didn't exist and had never happened. The old guy had assured me that the records were complete; nothing lost, nothing deleted. So where was Jane? Eventually, exhaustion brought on by despair overtook me and I fell face down on the bed. And slept.

But as usual, there was no comfort in my dreams; none at all.

At least this one was different. I dreamt Serafina had turned into a vampire, and she had taken me in an erotic embrace, one I eagerly responded to. And then, just at the last moment when I was ready to give my all to my new lover, she displayed her fangs and sank them into my unprotected neck in a crimson shower.

At least this time, I didn't wake up in a cold sweat. I was becoming immune to batshit craziness. Then I did something I'd never done before: I called in sick. I'd had enough. Let them sack me; I'd become a Donor at a Farm like Jackson's, where they were looked after properly. Eventually, the Sons Of Man would blow it up, but, hey! one day at a time, please!

So what to do with my free day? If my Mistress called to check up on me (I'm not so deluded to think she'd be asking after my health) and found me absent, then dismissal would be the least of my worries. If you lie to a Vamp, the punishments can be very cruel. Or so I'm told; there are few survivors to ask about their experiences.

But having convinced myself I was not real, I decided just to go out walking. Maybe a long walk would clear my mind, electronic or otherwise. And so I changed my shoes, wore slacks and a thin T-shirt and off I went. This time my expression was not one of barely suppressed rage, I was starting to see the whole damn thing as just one big joke. With every man I bumped into, I thought You're not real! If I saw a good-looking woman, I thought Just a collection of voltages. Nothing to get excited over.

And so I walked on and on. I lost track of where I was, even though Marinetown is not large. I spent the time in thinking Maybe here is where they had the fish shows; maybe here is where the dolphins did their funny tricks.

And then I finally looked up with a clearer vision and saw where I was: I saw the untidy, weed-strewn flower beds, the dry fountain, the senescent trees.

I was in the park.

As I always knew I would be.

I felt utterly tired, but not through walking. I am a tad flabby, but no cripple, as Bernie found out. Instead, everything seemed frozen in time, waiting for something momentous to happen. It was like a great hand was pressing down from the sky onto me, forcing me to stop, to sit on the tattered park bench, whether or not I wanted to. The whole world seemed to be holding its breath.

I sat, feeling the slats move protestingly under me. I intertwined my fingers and lowered my head. Waiting.

I felt someone sit next to me.

I knew who it was, who it must be.

I did not turn my head, but just spoke quietly.

'Hello, Edward.'

TWENTY TWO

Finally, I turned to see him. It had only been four years since I had last looked upon his face, yet for some reason I could only envisage him as he was when we had been together in the orphanage. He had been a pubescent boy then; now, he was a man, a robust, powerful man.

He was more powerfully built than I, with a square, angular face topped with black hair streaked with grey, as was his clipped moustache. His large hands rested in a relaxed fashion on his upper thighs.

He smiled.

'Charlie, it's so good to see you again. Apart from putting on a lot of weight and going completely to seed, you haven't changed a bit!'

Despite having dropped an octave or two since the orphanage, his voice was recognisably Edward's. My own voice was temporarily mute as my mind tried to make sense of conflicting emotions. Finally, the power of speech was restored.

'Edward, where have you been all these years? Why didn't you keep in touch?'

'All these years? Four years isn't long, Charlie.'

I rubbed my hand over my forehead and looked away.

'Sorry, Edward, I'm all mixed up. I keep thinking of us when we were together all those years ago. Your departure four years ago is difficult to remember; I don't know why.'

'It's the shock of seeing your handsome brother again,' he said with an expansive grin. 'Completely understandable.'

I shook my head.

'Come on, Edward, I'm serious. You just disappeared. No one knew where you were.'

He looked away over the decaying town and then up at the subtropical sky.

'I've been busy, Charlie. Very, very busy.'

'Doing what?'

'Things you wouldn't understand, at the moment. Very challenging, very advanced things.' He paused. 'Yes, very advanced indeed.'

I looked at him intently. This wasn't quite the brotherly reunion I'd been expecting, wanting. Why all the mystery?

'Why all the mystery?' I asked.

'All will be revealed, little brother. All in good time. Let's just enjoy the moment, shall we? I'm back, and this time I'm not going away. I have a lot of very important things to do. I'm here to stay.'

'That's good,' I said, starting to relax. But then I realised why I'd been so confused earlier. 'Wait, Edward. There's something wrong here. I remember now. The voice; the cylinder; Lieutenant Ardelean. It was your voice from the cylinder, threatening the Elite!'

'Not just threatening,' he murmured, half-smiling.

I looked at him in amazement, aghast.

'You killed the Lieutenant!'

He shrugged.

'I believe so. The second of many.'

If my mouth could have opened any wider, it would have dropped off.

'You mustn't say that! You can't say that!'

He looked directly at me for the first time since I started talking about the cylinder and the aftermath of its appearance.

'Don't worry, brother. No one is listening; no one can listen. We are secure here. You will not be arrested.'

'What? How can you say that? How can you know?'

A tolerant smile.

'Charlie, you picked up the cylinder; I know you did. Did anything happen when you held it?'

I thought. Then I spoke—slowly.

'I heard a voice. Calling me. Saying "Come to me".'

'And how did you find me?'

'I don't know. I walked around a lot, always getting closer to this park—now I come to think of it.' Then the realisation hit me like an uppercut from Bernie. 'It was you! Some kind of subliminal message from you!'

'It's slightly more complex than just a subliminal message, but you've got the gist of it. Only you would have felt that message in his mind. Only you would have been called to this park and this meeting of brothers.'

I shook my head in gathering confusion. My whole world had been rocked to its foundations recently, and this surreal conversation wasn't helping.

'But how can you do that? Nobody can do that!'

Once again the confident smile, the confident, tolerant smile of someone who knows for certain his power is greater than his opponents realise.

'I can do that.'

'How?'

He shrugged and looked away.

'Stop this, Charlie, it's getting tedious. You were never one for science, for mathematics, the power of the intellect, and it's rather late for you to start now.' His gaze, the amused look of the tutor for the struggling student, returned to me. 'I have friends, Charlie, powerful friends. Very powerful friends. And I am helping them and they are helping me. The vampires are predators, glorying in their power and strength. But there are *super-predators.*'

I said nothing, knowing nothing would help me understand further until Edward wanted me to understand. He spoke again, and I had the feeling it was a speech intended for a wider audience than his dullard brother.

'A change is coming, a great, wonderful change. The world will be remade, made anew, and humans will be restored to their rightful place.' (I winced.) 'The planet will be ours again, to do with as we wish. Those who have usurped it will be swept away and forgotten.'

I stared at him, eyes boggling, mouth open, feeling like a parent whose infant child had suddenly spouted the vilest obscenities in the language. I could not prevent myself from looking around, expecting to see vengeful members of the Elite descending on this simple park bench. Then I looked back to see Edward standing over me, arms raised like an Old Testament Prophet.

'I want you to join me, Charlie, in my great crusade. Victory is certain, so don't fear for yourself or those you love. My friends and I will sweep the filth away from our world, and then we will rebuild.' He extended a hand to me. 'Come. I am your brother. I would not lie to you. Join me in the great victory.'

I stood and looked at his huge, calloused hand and almost extended my own to clasp it.

But something stopped me.

'No, I can't, Edward. What you're asking is insane, gibbering madness! You're unwell; you must be to say such things!'

He shook his head again, tolerant, understanding, forgiving.

'It is too soon. I see that now. You will join me, but I must be patient a little longer. Perhaps you need a few more signs of my power to be confident it is safe to throw in your lot with me. That is understandable, brother.' His gaze passed over my shoulder at something behind me. 'Ah, here she is.'

I whirled around. My face was already rigid in amazement, so I could not display any more of that emotion. A young woman was approaching.

A woman who looked almost exactly like Serafina, except for raven-black, shoulder-length hair!

'Is he ready yet?' she asked Edward, giving no clue she was talking about me, or had even noticed me. My twin brother walked past me and embraced her. Then, turning back, he said, 'Charles, let me introduce the fragrant Eleonora, my friend and companion in these troubled times.'

I looked at the pair in utter stupefaction. Friend? This was the friend who would enable him to conquer the Elite?

He really was insane.

She smiled at me, and that smile turned my knees to jelly, sent my heart racing. And I saw another difference: She had green, incredibly mesmeric eyes.

'Charles. I have always longed to meet you. Edward thinks so highly of you.'

'He does?' I croaked.

They smiled at each other with looks of love, and then Edward looked at me and said, 'We will talk again soon. Stay safe,'

And with that, the two of them walked away, still locked in their embrace.

I collapsed onto the bench.

This is what insanity feels like! I thought.

As they disappeared, my strange compulsion to be in that park evaporated, and I made my way back to my apartment, where I fell into a deep and—at last!—dreamless sleep.

From which I was roused by insistent knocking on the door. Wearily, I drove my way back into consciousness and opened the door.

To find I was looking at an agitated Serafina. I was so struck by her resemblance to Eleonora that I was struck dumb and stood looking down at her.

'Wake up, Sarge, wake up!' she snapped. 'The boss wants to see us, and she wants to know why you haven't been answering her calls!'

I have my communicator on me at all times, and I fished it out of my pocket and stared at it. Sure enough, three calls from my Mistress were shown as having been received—but I had not heard the message tone, nor had I felt it vibrate.

'Wake up,' Serafina said in the hissing voice of exasperation. 'You'll be let go of for sure if you don't move!'

But I did not move toward the door. Instead, I reached out and held her shoulders, rendering her immobile. I leaned in.

'Serafina, do you have a sister?'

I had never seen the interplay of so many emotions on a human face before: Astonishment, alertness, concern and dismay all rapidly crossed her features. Then, finally, her face became blank, unreadable.

'Why do you ask?' she said in a completely neutral voice. 'You've never asked before.'

'Because I've just seen someone who looked very much like you.'

She gently removed my hands from her shoulders.

'I don't have a twin, and as far as I know, I haven't been cloned.'

'I didn't say she was identical, but there was a family resemblance. Such as sisters of about the same age might have.'

'I don't know. We're living in crazy times. You had a brother you hardly knew; perhaps I had a sister who was separated from me when we were kids. Families don't mean what they used to before the Takeover; the Elite just see us as individuals.'

I could see I wasn't going to get anything else out of her, so I dropped it. If the Commissioner was annoyed with me, I had to get there yesterday! But I was convinced that Serafina knew more than she was letting on. Something was being hid from me and I didn't like it.

Well, I didn't get to HQ the day before, but I did arrive as soon as was physically possible, and I was soon standing in my accustomed position before Mistress Aiyana's desk with Serafina beside me. I was prepared to get my pants burned off by the heat of my Mistress's wrath, but in fact, she was too preoccupied to consider any punishment and accepted my face-saving explanation of a malfunction in the communicator. We soon learned why she was so uninterested in my excuses.

'There has been another incident at the Diodati Institute,' she rapped. 'I'm sending all my spare officers over there at once.'

'May we know the nature of the incident?' Serafina said. I found I was experiencing an odd sensation of detachment from all that was happening around me, as if it were just a play I was watching. None of it seemed to matter, and I no longer cared if my superior considered me a capable officer or a useless lump of human flesh. So I let Serafina do all the talking.

Mistress Aiyana looked uncertain, an expression which now appeared to have permanently replaced her image of brisk efficiency.

'The reports are confusing. DeLancey has called for help, saying that his staff are under attack.'

'And who is doing the attacking?'

'He said something that made no sense.' Suddenly, her old strength and power returned to her features. 'Why am I sitting here, allowing myself to be interrogated by you? Get over there—now!'

We were soon flashing down Marinetown's steamy streets, our siren blaring.

'She's under a lot of pressure,' Serafina said, mainly to herself.

'Aren't we all? Nothing makes sense anymore.' I glanced at her. 'Like those sisters you may or may not have.'

She did not reply.

We roared past the great black scar where Rousseau's had once stood and screeched to a halt outside the Diodati Institute.

'Good God,' my companion muttered, 'the whole freaking Force is here!'

I paused after exiting the vehicle and followed her pointing finger. Not that she needed to point. There was a ring of blue-black uniforms standing beside empty police cars and each blue-black uniform contained an officer whose weapon was trained on the doorway to the Diodati Institute.

TWENTY THREE

'Something big's going down,' I said to her, reaching for my automatic.

Her only reply was something that sounded like *No shit, Sherlock* and she was advancing on the ring of officers, her own weapon on show. Not wanting to be upstaged by my Deputy, I first caught up with her and then moved slightly in front.

The first guy I ran into was Varney O'Rourke, who turned around when he heard us coming up behind him.

'Took your time, didn't you?'

'We're here now. What's happening?' I said, slightly out of breath.

'The head guy reported that some of his superiors had been killed.'

'Terrorists.' I shook my head; the Sons Of Man were getting bolder, attacking people in such an open and blatant way. 'Why aren't we going in? Hostages?'

He gave a short, unconvincing laugh.

'What do you take us for—idiots? We haven't gone in because we can't.'

'You can't? What are you talking about?'

'We can't get in. Is that simple enough for you?' He waved toward the huge, plate-glass door. 'Look, try it. No one's going to take a pot shot.'

I stared at him. He was asking me to stroll up to the front door of a building where a terrorist attack was in full swing as if I was making a social call?

'You serious, Varney?'

He turned away.

'Try it. I ain't got all day.'

Others in the ring of Marinetown Police Officers had heard the conversation and had turned to look at Serafina and me. Some were openly laughing. I holstered my gun and began to push through the throng.

'Sarge…'

'Stay where you are,' I ordered, not looking back at her.

As soon as my fellow officers saw what I was about, they parted to let me through. My heart began to thud as I started to mount the line of steps leading up to the gleaming doors. At any moment, one of the Sons could blow me away; I knew that.

I was halfway up the steps when I stopped.

Or, to be more precise, I was stopped.

It was like I had hit a very thin, invisible rubber sheet, and the more I pushed onto it, the firmer the invisible rubber sheet became until it was actively pushing me back down the steps. I put a hand in front of me to where I thought the invisible barrier began and watched the skin on the tips of my fingers flatten out as they pressed against something.

Something that both wasn't there and was.

I took a few steps back, hearing laughter start to break out behind and below me. I did a crazy thing then: I pointed my automatic at the doorway and fired. There was the flash, the report and the kick-back, but to my amazement, I saw a blurred object appear along the trajectory of my shot. The thing slowed and became recognisable as the slug from my pistol. Stupefied, I watched the bullet rapidly decelerate until it hung absolutely stationary in the air a few metres away!

The laughter behind me had become a roar as I descended the steps and returned to the crowd. O'Rourke was waiting for me.

'You knew?' I said.

'Of course. We haven't been playing with our dicks, waiting for you to turn up to save us. Nothing can get in or out. And when I say "Nothing", what I actually mean is—Nothing!'

I swung back to study the building.

'Mistress Aiyana said the people inside were being attacked. Do you know any more about the attack? How many Sons Of Man are in there?'

'None.'

I jerked around to glare at O'Rourke to see if this was one of his bad taste jokes.

'What the Hell are you talking about? Are the Elite killing each other? Are you shitting me, O'Rourke?'

'No, Officer Gray, I am not. DeLancey said that only members of the Elite are being attacked—and not by human terrorists.'

'What—alligators in combat gear? Very pissed-off snapping turtles? What for Chrissake, is attacking them?'

Serafina had joined me.

'Let him talk, Sarge.'

I glared at her, but shut up. And waited.

O'Rourke looked confused, started to speak, stopped, started again, and this time succeeded.

'What he said didn't make much sense. He said the Elite was being killed by some kind of animal he hadn't seen before. They walked on two legs, but he didn't get a good look at them. He was too busy hiding under his desk.'

'An animal walking on two legs? What, killer kangaroos?'

I thought O'Rourke was about to hit me then, but Serafina stepped between us.

'Talk to me, Officer. He didn't describe them in any clearer terms?'

'No, too much was happening all at once. The line went dead shortly after he said the next thing.'

'Which was?'

'He managed to say how the Elite were being killed.'

I came back into the conversation.

'Is that important, O'Rourke? Knife, gun, blunt instrument. When you're dead, you're dead.'

He looked at me with undisguised contempt and then switched back to Serafina.

'DeLancey said their hearts came out of their bodies—as if being pulled out by invisible tongs. Then the corpses were turned inside out.'

Silence fell.

Serafina and I looked meaningfully at each other. Since the first Diodati Institute atrocity, no officer other than me had seen that kind of death. O'Rourke was now as shocked as we had been by this kind of murder.

Then we heard someone shout, 'They're coming out!'

I whirled around to see the great glass doors wide open and a small file of humans running as fast as they could down the steps. All the other officers seemed paralysed with shock, but Serafina and I rushed to meet them. DeLancey was leading the line. He obviously didn't recognise us as we came up to him. I stopped his headlong flight.

'Mr DeLancey, what's been happening in there?'

He looked at me with blank, unseeing eyes.

'It was horrible. They were all lined up, and one by one, they killed them. Tore their hearts out! They're all dead now, every last one!'

'But who did it, Mr DeLancey? Who killed them?'

'Things, things that walked like men, but weren't men.'

'Can't you describe them, Mr DeLancey?'

He looked up from his trembling hands, but once again he was not seeing me even though he appeared to be looking straight up into my face.

'No, no, they were kind of blurred.'

'Blurred? What does that mean?'

'Like—like a photo not properly focused. I could see two legs, two arms, but everything was smudged, blurred, not quite right. Couldn't see faces clearly, like a video broadcast with a poor signal.' Suddenly, his face twisted, and I realised he could now see me and understand who and what I was. 'That's all I can say! That's the best I can do! What more do you want? Let me get away from this place!'

And with those screamed words, he rushed away, forcing his way through the crowd of burly officers as if they were cardboard cut-outs.

I looked at Serafina and then O'Rourke.

'If they can get out, we can get in! Get your weapons out!'

I had not the slightest idea what we were now facing. Delancey's incoherent ramblings had told me nothing. If this was a Sons Of Man weapon, then once again they had upped the ante. Where were they getting all this power from? From Edward?—he had intimated a great change was coming to the rule of the vampires, but what could one man do?

A problem for another day, I decided. First, we had to go in and clear out whoever these new terrorists were. Maybe they were wearing some kind of disguise. In the hell of an ongoing terrorist outrage, nobody would interpret events calmly and rationally. But one thing was certain—they were still in there, and we were just about to meet them.

'Let's go,' I said, as matter-of-factly as I could muster, and started my second walk to the steps.

I didn't get very far.

All at once, the entire building trembled. But it wasn't the tremble of a quake. Instead, it looked like it was being viewed through a sudden huge heat haze, as its lines shivered and swayed and quivered. Then there was a flash of violet light.

And the Diodati Institute was no more.

It did not explode like Rousseau's. It just wasn't there anymore. Water pipes cut off with mathematical precision fountained water high into the air, meeting blue electric discharges from severed power cables. This time there was a noticeable concussion, as air rushed to fill the vacuum left by the building's instant disappearance.

Because the Diodati Institute was no more.

***

What more was there for us to do? We rounded up the human survivors, many of whom were on the brink of madness after what they had seen, and tended to them as much as we could. None of them had been injured, but the psychological scars were deep. A few were able to relate what had happened, but their stories did not add that much to DeLancey's statement. All agreed there had been a purplish glow in the air, at first no bigger than a football, but which rapidly become a rippling curtain of light from floor to ceiling.

And out of that curtain had come—creatures.

The stories differed at this point, and disagreed on a description of what they had seen. They were consistent on only two things: The invaders had been bipedal, but had been difficult to focus on—even if you were not running from them. There was an unfinished, vague, shimmering look to them.

But when hearts started to be pulled out of Vampire bodies—no one stayed long in that location to witness the full horror.

The refugee humans were then taken to secure locations where they were given medical assistance. Not entirely out of concern for them, but in the hope they would be able to put together a more coherent story.

But as it transpired—it could not.

As I related what I had seen and experienced to Mistress Aiyana, I came to a conclusion both surprising and disturbing: She had no more idea of what to do than I did. It is difficult to explain the effect this realisation had on me. I had lived my life waiting for, and then acting on, instructions from one member or another of the Elite. They had all the answers, all the power.

Nothing could touch them; nothing could challenge them. But as well as her now obvious impotence, I sensed something else in her reactions: She knew more about what was happening than she was prepared to share with a lowly human.

A great sense of helpless futility lay over the Marinetown Police Force. We had been revealed to be hopeless observers of events not only beyond our control, but beyond our very understanding. But Edward's words came back to me, hammering at the base of my mind: Those "super-predators" he had mentioned, almost as an afterthought. Could such things really exist and, if they could, were they now entering our world?

I had no answers.

The Mess Hall was very quiet from that day onward. There were no more off-colour jokes, no more ribald camaraderie between officers, between man and woman, woman and woman, man and man. We were like turkeys who had finally realised what Thanksgiving entailed. (That's *Thanksgiving for the Takeover*, in case you are misunderstanding me.)

But I had unfinished business with Serafina.

'You're holding back on me,' I said to her, eyeing her carefully as I chewed another taste-free mouthful of pseudo-meat.

'Am I?' she said, in an unconcerned voice. 'And how do you work that out?'

'Several times now, I've caught you muttering things to yourself at times of crisis. Words I haven't quite caught, but the things I have heard seem to suggest you were expecting these events to happen.'

She shrugged.

'I talk to myself. It's my way of defusing tension. You pick your nose.'

'I do not! I...' I stopped my protests, realising she'd thrown me off kilter again. I glared at her. 'OK. You're not ready to come clean with your old Sergeant. But when will you?'

She shrugged and then looked at me with a face devoid of all emotion.

'Soon, Charles, soon. We need a little more time.'

TWENTY FOUR

The news of the destruction of the Diodati Institute spread rapidly through the rundown streets of Marinetown. It had an electrifying effect on the normally placid, if not actually supine, inhabitants of our fair city. The result was an awakening in its majority population of resentment against the Elite. For decades no one had considered them as anything less than the natural rulers of the affairs of humans, as natural and unremarkable as the rising of the sun, the coming of night.

It was just the way things were.

But now everyone knew they had been slaughtered like hogs on an old-fashioned farm. The aura of invincibility had been shredded. The old hatreds came flooding back: How dare they confine us to their Blood farms and suck us dry! How had we been demoted to pathetic servants and near-slaves, fetching and carrying: Yes, Mr Vampire, No, Mr Vampire?

Even posters glorifying the Sons Of Man had started appearing on walls. It was my job to tear them down, of course, but there were always more. I had even heard some of my fellow officers muttering complaints about their superiors, words they would never have dared use a few months earlier.

The world was going mad.

Could there be an actual uprising against the Vamps? The thought was horrifying. Other than the Police Force and Farm managers, humans had no weapons, no scientific or technological knowledge. Weapons had been taken from them, and knowledge denied them. An uprising armed with sticks and stones would be a pitiful sight and would lead to terrible reprisals. If humans thought their state was bad now, just wait until their tragicomic uprising had been crushed!

And so it was with an ever-growing feeling of despondency that I returned to my apartment after another pointless day of petty crime and poster ripping. I knew an axe was going to fall; I just didn't know when.

The door swung open, and I tugged at the buttons of my uniform.

And stopped dead, as an electric shock flashed down my spine.

Edward was sitting on my bed. He rose to his feet, every centimetre radiating power, strength, assurance.

'Hi, Charlie. You look beat. Hard day—helping vampires?'

My hand automatically went for my gun. He smiled. I stopped the motion, feeling incredibly stupid. This guy was my brother.

'How did you get in?'

'I have my ways. It doesn't matter. What matters is you and me.'

'Is there a you and me? Four years went by and I haven't seen you, and I hardly saw you before then. Why have you popped up again like a freaking Whack-A-Mole?'

He waved at my easy chair.

'Sit down. We'll talk.'

I obeyed, not knowing why I obeyed. His voice, his demeanour, was hypnotic. There seemed to be a kind of a force of compulsion flowing out of him in an invisible tide. He looked at me, and I wanted to be instructed.

'I have been busy, Charlie, very busy. You know my line of business?'

I nodded like a child on his first day of school, eager to learn.

'You were in some kind of scientific work.'

'Perfectly correct. The Elite rulers recognised that there was something different about me. The complexities of my brain had resulted in something special, giving me abilities even some of them do not have. So they allowed me to study, really study. Things that weren't immediately important to them, not things that would have made me a better servant. And study I did. And I learned. I rediscovered theorems in physics our forefathers had been working on just before the Takeover.'

'What—things like making better bombs?'

His face flashed into anger and he half rose.

'Stop that! Think for yourself, man! Stop swallowing their propaganda! Humans would have found a way out of that mess if they'd been left to it!' His face relaxed. 'Just as we will find our way out of this mess. The one the Vamp masters have forced us into.'

I felt like a student who had just disappointed his tutor. So I just said, 'What did you find?'

A look of hungry anticipation filled his features.

'I found out something about our masters.'

Despite my efforts to resist, I felt myself being dragged into the power of his conviction.

'Yes—what?'

'They are not the top predators. There is something they are afraid of. To us, they are indomitable, invulnerable; we are like fur seals desperately paddling to escape the Carcharodon carcharias—the fearless Great White Shark. But in the great ocean of reality, there are other predators—shall we call them "Orcas"—to whom the Great Whites who control us are simply another meal.'

'I haven't seen any of these Orcas, these super-predators.'

He smiled tolerantly.

'Charlie, we have been apart for too long. You have descended deep into a slave-mentality. But it is not too late; I can save you. And I will save you.' He leaned back against the wall, interlinked his fingers, and closed his eyes, his mind presumably on sights I could neither visualise nor understand. 'I found them, Charlie. They are outside the walls of our reality, kept from their conquest behind a boundary I term the Barrier—but they are out there. Circling, waiting. Because the vampires have met them several times before, most recently in a great war before the first human knapped the first flint tool. The memories of that war echoed down the millennia, moulding the development of our own civilisations. Our people knew of those predators on the vampires, and worshipped them, knowing humans were not their preferred prey. The Elite survived the onslaught—but only by the narrowest of margins. They succeeded in closing the breach in the Barrier their ancestors had created, just in time to save their species, but they were thrown into barbarism, existing only in the shadows while humans grew in power. And every day since, every year, every millennium since, they watch and watch the Barrier, knowing that just beyond it lies their Doom. They feel the tremendous pressure upon it, know their enemies are searching for weaknesses in the great wall; they hear the gnashing of ravenous teeth, feel their enemies' rapacious hunger for Vampire flesh—a hunger-driven lust which is close, so very close.'

I looked at Edward in amazement. His words seemed like bolts of lightning, burning flames, rousing me to become his fanatical servant.

'But what part do you play?' I finally managed to whisper.

He rose from the bed and strode to where I sat, standing above me like a Prophet resurrected from the Pentateuch.

'I have found the wall of our reality, the Barrier, which keeps their annihilation out. And I will open it.'

TWENTY FIVE

I stared at him. Was I trapped in my apartment with a madman? How had he even gotten in? I had to keep him talking, had to humour him. Warily, I watched him sit back on the bed, feeling that somehow I had blundered into the lions' cage, and the door had slammed behind me.

'Well, that sounds pretty dramatic, Edward. But aren't you bigging up the Sons Of Man a tad? I mean, they've got some pretty cool firepower, but they can't be capable of taking out the whole Elite!'

He gave a laugh; the amusement of an adult listening to a small child trying to explain something beyond its abilities and producing harmless comedy instead.

'The Sons Of Man! You've finally made me laugh, Charlie.'

'I did? But aren't you in charge of them? Aren't they your Vampire-Predators?'

'I am, and they are not. Listen to me, Charlie and try to understand. I realise I'm upending your entire world, making you see you have wasted your life, and that's hard, I'll grant you that. I am indeed in charge of the organisation you refer to, but they are just a game, a hobby if you like. I have helped them with a small portion of my abilities, because it makes them feel good, and I like making people feel good. They are fighting back against their oppressors as best they can, and I admire their spirit, but they could never overthrow the so-called Elite in a million years. Without me, they would be reduced to stone throwers and scribblers on walls.

They are not the ones who will destroy the rule of the vampires, believe me.'

'Destroy the vampires. You know that's impossible, Edward.'

'Not in the least. It nearly happened once before, and in the coming conflict, it will finally be accomplished.'

'Edward, you have been on your own too long. This is insanity.'

'Insanity? I think not. I am far from alone, and it is you who is insane, Charlie, and I can prove it.'

'How can you do that? We've only just met up again.'

'Four years is not long. You were insane then.'

'Pardon me? I was?'

'Yes. You saw yourself then, and I guess you do now, as an ordinary Joe. A regular guy who got lucky and was accepted into the Vamp Police Force. You saw yourself as a widower, gradually putting his life back together after a sad bereavement, throwing himself into his job, and rising to the giddy heights of Sergeant.'

'Minus the sarcasm, yes, that is how I see it.'

'And what did you find at City Hall?'

That threw me; had he been watching all the time? I was silent for a few moments, and then, reluctantly, I said, 'Nothing.'

He nodded understandingly.

'Nothing. Because there was nothing to find. You are not a widower, Charlie, because you were never married. Jane was a false memory implanted by your Vampire Overlords.'

That revelation did not shock me as much as he obviously expected it to; after all, I had been groping toward that conclusion for some time. So I just shrugged and said, 'Why would they do such a thing?'

To my surprise, he did not come back at me with some kind of mocking explanation. Instead, he just quietly said, 'I'm not sure. It's as if they wanted to hide you away, pretend you're just a small fish in a small pond, a nobody with a nobody lifestyle.'

'But I am a nobody.'

Once again, he did not come straight back at me, but stayed silent for a short while. Then he said, oddly slowly, 'Yes, you are. I wonder...'

Silence fell. I got the feeling something important had just occurred to him and he was mulling it over. Then he spoke again, having put what was puzzling him to one side, for the time being.

'We lost touch for a long time after the orphanage, didn't we? I did some research on you shortly afterwards and couldn't find you. When I rediscovered you, you were already a Cop. It was like you'd just popped into existence fully formed as a friendly, down-to-earth Keeper of the Peace, complete with an average-guy life story, including a wife who nobody had ever met and nobody had ever heard about. Of course, your buddies accepted it all; why would they pry into your sorrows? But your superiors knew; it was part of their plan.' Once again he paused and his gaze turned from me and focused on nothing. 'But what was their plan?' Then he shook his head and returned to looking at me. 'Never mind, I'll find out. Back to you—so you have already suspected much of what I've told you?'

'Yes. I don't know why I began to doubt my own memories; it only started a very short time ago. But Edward, after that last time we met, I carried on looking for you, but whenever I tracked you down, you'd just moved on to someplace else. I only ever heard about you from people who'd worked with you. About how brilliant you were—are.'

'Yes, I am. Too brilliant for our Lords and Mistresses. They thought they could use me without telling me what they were using me for. So I did what hardly any of my fellow slaves did—I became a scientist, and a damn good one. And I tired of doing things for them, without knowing why. So gradually, I did my own research, going beyond the simple, childish explanations they had given me. At first, I just stumbled in the dark, but slowly the pieces came together, and I understood what my work was actually about.'

'And what was it actually about?'

He leaned forward and his eyes seemed to light up with an inner glow.

'The Barrier, Charlie, the Barrier! I found it! First me alone, and then Eleonora and I together, then sometimes my woman alone, together or singly we probed beyond it. And more importantly, I discovered why there was such a structure in the first place. What is the function of a barrier, brother?'

'To keep two sorts of things apart, I suppose.'

'Precisely. There were—are—entities behind it, entities which want to be on our side of it. So they can feast. I told you our rulers and these creatures have met several times. Initially, the Vamps were in the same position as we are now, a slave race, used for sustenance by their owners. As slaves, they were no danger to the human race, which was just emerging from brutish ignorance. But the Vamps were able to throw off their yoke because a specialised group working in secret created the Barrier to keep themselves safe. But their calculations were not complete, and the creatures found a way back through the Barrier and almost destroyed them in a bitter war of revenge. And this war happened at the same time as our own race was making its first steps toward civilisation. Although we played no part in it, we saw that war, and ever since, our minds have been infected with visions of gods and demons, angels and devils. But there are demons—and they are pressed up against the Barrier, trying to get back in, to re-establish their control over their livestock.'

'The Elite.'

He waved a hand in dismissal.

'Don't call them that; it's insulting, degrading for us to call our slave masters by that undeserved honorific. Those cowardly oppressors are terrified, Charlie, soiling themselves in their terror. They know the Barrier is weakening.'

Suddenly I understood his ideas, even though I couldn't accept them, and didn't believe them.

'All these flashes of purple light, Vamps being turned inside out—that's the work of these things beyond this, this Barrier of yours?'

He smashed a mighty fist onto a thigh in his joy.

'Yes! You are my brother, after all!'

'But you said they are still on the other side, so who's doing all these things?'

'They are on the other side, but let me explain in pictorial terms for you. Imagine a dam, holding back millions of tonnes of water. And that dam is weakening, starting to fail. Little cracks are forming, little holes popping up here and there. And little trickles of water are seeping through those weak spots, only small jets of water so far, but hinting at a vast power just beyond, still controlled by the bulk of the dam. Everything that has happened, the events that puzzled you, and frightened them, has been due to the equivalent of those tiny cracks. Imagine what will happen when the entire dam collapses! Such tremendous slaughter!'

I gazed at my brother, with a growing sense that I was dealing with someone who had lost the last vestige of a hold on reality. The nonsense he was spouting was literally beyond belief. Why was he saying these things: Gibberish about Barriers and unpleasant things beyond them? That there was an organisation, a force, trying to destroy the rule of the vampires was undeniable, but why make up this nonsense? It was now clear the Sons Of Man were a more formidable set-up than we had first believed and somehow they had gotten hold of advanced weaponry, but that was all. Now we knew what we were up against, we would have to redouble our efforts to hunt them down and root them out. End of.

'You don't believe me, do you, Charlie?' came a voice, intruding on my thoughts.

I looked at him as he sat nonchalantly on my bed, a faint smile playing on his lips.

'No. Did you really expect I would? What do you take me for? I may only be a flatfoot, but I'm not Funny Farm material, just yet. This "Barrier" you keep raving about, where is it? Why has no one seen it?'

'Charles, Charles, how can I begin to explain to you? The Barrier isn't down some Marinetown alley, or atop the Rockies. It's not in our three-dimensional continuum, but outside it, around it, like the shell of a nut, protecting the soft centre. That's the best I can explain it.'

'If that's the best, you can forget it. I don't know what you want from me with all this crazy talk.'

'I've already explained. I want you to join me.'

'To overthrow the Elite? Not gonna happen, whether I help you or not. Why exactly do you hate them so much?'

'Two reasons. One for our species, and one for me, personally. I've already explained what they've done to the human race. You worked for them for so long you're blind to the horror of our situation. They've messed with your mind—for reasons I haven't worked out yet—and forced your fellow humans into the worst kind of slavery imaginable. Living in a miserable existence just so other creatures can feed off of them! And that's OK with you?'

I looked away, unable to meet the ferocity of his stare.

'Well, that's not ideal, sure. But at least we're secure; we're not going to blow ourselves up.'

'I've already demolished that argument; if you're too dumb to understand me, it's your fault, not mine. But the other reason is what they did to me, did to us, in that orphanage.'

'It wasn't that bad.'

He threw up his hands.

'Listen to the lamb looking into the slaughterhouse and bleating, "I'm sure it's all for the best." Wake up, man! Grow up, man, grow a pair! They did something to me, did something to you—but your addled brain can't remember it. There were operations, injections, pain, tears. Surely you remember!'

'Well, I remember some happenings. But I try not to remember.'

He groaned theatrically, and then pulled a small device from his jacket, rolled up a sleeve and pressed the object onto his bulging biceps for a minute or two. Catching my gaze, he shrugged and said, 'Vitamin B12. I have a touch of anaemia.'

Well, we really are brothers, I thought.

But apparently, he had gotten enough disappointments from me, for as soon as he had stowed his medical device away, he stood and walked toward the door.

'I've had enough of this.' He turned back to me. 'I sure as hell don't need you, Charlie. It's just that I'd like you to be at my side come the great victory. But I can't make you wake up if you insist on sleeping. But I'm not done with you yet. We'll meet again. But while I await you, I will send you a vision. A vision of our allies.'

He opened the door and walked out without a backward glance.

I realised he hadn't explained something, and called after him, 'Hey! How did you get in?'

He didn't answer.

TWENTY SIX

My encounter with my brother had left me in a whirlwind of conflicting emotions. I had been overjoyed by his reappearance, reconnecting me to a childhood when he had been my only comfort in those terrible days, but the madness that had poured from his mouth! It is not easy to realise your brother is insane.

But as I sat there in my pokey apartment, another unpleasant fact came to me: I now knew who the head of the Sons Of Man was.

My brother.

I was honour-bound to report him to Mistress Aiyana and have him imprisoned; an incarceration that would merely be a prelude to execution. I was sure that once deprived of his charismatic leadership, his organisation would fall apart, and we would be safe again. Could I do such treachery to my brother? Did my loyalty to the Elite trump my loyalty to my kin?

I sat there for a long time, cursing the way things had turned out and putting me in this terrible bind. All I had ever wanted to do was patrol the streets and keep things safe, for humans and Vamps. And now, instead of being called in to defuse domestic quarrels, these dreadful events had pushed me into having to make momentous decisions; way, way above my pay grade. And I could not share this responsibility; it was mine alone.

And here I was, standing before Mistress Aiyana once again. Until recently, she had always given off an air of simultaneous elegance and authority. Now I saw neither; in fact, she looked almost dishevelled, almost ordinary. She had never looked more—human.

'I have nothing to report to you, Gray,' she said, hardly bothering to look up from the desk. 'Have you anything for me?'

This was the moment I had been dreading. I felt my pulse speed up, and my tongue felt like it was stuck to the roof of my mouth. Finally, she raised her eyes and looked me full in the face.

'Well? Have you?'

I could not meet her gaze; I wanted something to happen, something to interrupt this interview, to save me from this decision. Then I spoke.

'No, mistress. Nothing.'

She stared at me silently for a few moments, making me feel like a frog about to be dissected.

'Are you telling me the truth, Gray?'

Then to my horror, she rose from her seat and approached me. I had only on occasion seen her standing, and I had forgotten she was taller than me. Her face came close to mine, closer than ever before, so close I could smell the iron scent of blood on her breath, the death tang of a rich, red liquid which had once belonged to men and women.

'It is said the Elite can read minds. Do you believe that, Gray?'

'I—I don't know, Mistress.'

'Perhaps we can. Or perhaps we are just good at detecting falsehoods from the lesser breeds. Breeds like you, Gray. Maybe we have erred by allowing your kind into areas of genuine responsibility. Maybe it has made us vulnerable. Maybe the Farms are the best place for your entire race.'

I said nothing, but I could feel my right knee beginning to tremble. I was centimetres from a creature who could kill me in an instant, who could tear me open like wet tissue paper and feast on my lifeblood.

'I sense doubt in you, Gray. I sense something is being withheld from me. What is it?' The tip of a right index finger touched my forehead, and I felt the flesh dimple under the pointed fingernail. 'Give me your thoughts, Gray; unburden yourself from this load you are carrying. Share it with me. I will be forgiving, compassionate. But only if you share it now. If I find out later you have lied, your fate will be talked about by your people for decades to come.'

I don't know why I held out. The right thing to have done would have been to confess, go down on my knees, beg for forgiveness, crawl and abase myself. Only that would have guaranteed my survival. Oh, of course, I would be punished, and no doubt the punishment would be terrible. But she would not kill me; surely, she had promised she would not kill me?

But for some reason, I saw Edward's face, and I felt again his calm assurance, his strength.

'There is nothing, Mistress.'

Her face was empty of all emotion other than suspicion. The seconds ticked by, each one perhaps taking me closer to oblivion. Then she withdrew her finger and returned to her desk.

'I sense nothing,' she said, rearranging the papers on her desk. Then she looked back up at me. 'I am confident no simple human could have withheld anything important from me. I do not know what I sensed in you, Gray. I could not read it; perhaps it is simply exhaustion. I can understand that. Even I grow tired of this endless shadowboxing.' Then she waved at the door. 'Go away. I have no further use for you at the moment. Go and arrest a drunk or something.'

Once safely out of sight, I leaned against a wall and took in a great draught of the moist air.

Before we set out on patrol, I shared a light lunch with Serafina.

'Is it true that the Elite can read minds?' I asked.

A piece of extremely rare (in both senses of the word) meat halted its journey to her teeth.

'Why, has a Vamp been trying to read your mind? Did they find anything—other than the football scores, or whether it was time to change your socks, that is?'

'You are wasted here. Surely somewhere there must be some rundown joint still doing stand-up comedy.'

The meat resumed its journey and disappeared. After a few seconds of chewing, she leaned back indifferently and said, 'How the hell do I know anything about mystic powers of mind-reading? I'm not a Vamp.'

'You've lived other places than Marinetown. Do they know more about these things up in Granada?'

'Nope. Too busy hiding from all the rain we get. But you're talking about "telepathy", I guess.'

'I've heard the word, but I don't know anything about it. Do you?'

She pursed her lips.

'It's a very old idea, I believe. An idea people have believed in for centuries, but I don't think its reality has ever been proven. Perhaps human brains can do it, but only sporadically and not to order. But Vamps are not humans, and their brains are quite different. It could be that they can call it up when they need it.'

'Not all the time? (Like an hour or so ago? Was I being toyed with?)

'Perhaps not. It could be that telepathy requires a lot of effort, of energy. If they could do it all the time, surely by now they would have ferreted out who the Sons Of Man are?'

'But it is possible they can do it—for at least some of the time?'

'Yes, of course, it's possible. Vamps are not like us.' Her eyebrows knitted together. 'Why is this so important to you? Has someone actually been reading your mind?'

By now, I had regretted opening the topic with Serafina; her answers had done nothing to reassure me.

Perhaps as soon as I rose from the table, I would feel a heavy hand on my shoulder and know I'd been arrested.

'No, no, of course not,' I said, with what must have been a very unconvincing smile. 'It's just an argument I've been having with some of the boys.'

'You mean the boys actually talk about things other than beer and women? Well, well, I've learned something today!'

Bitterly regretting I had ever raised the subject, I vowed never to raise it again, having failed to get the reassurance I'd been fishing for.

And so we went out on patrol.

Absolutely nothing happened, including not being arrested, when I got back.

***

But that night something happened; something I had hoped would not happen again.

I dreamt of them.

It started the same way, the thin greenish mist, rising up out of the ground, the cold wind coming from all directions and penetrating my body, my being.

And the voices: Dread, inhuman voices.

Once again, I saw figures in the putrescent fog, eldritch figures which seemed human, but were not.

And then there was madness.

They came out of the fog towards me, staring at me as they approached.

How shall I describe them? They were like people, but the proportions were wrong; the heads too big, or the legs too long. The features were likewise distorted, wrong, unnatural, fearsome. As they emerged from the clinging tendrils of mist I could see they were all dressed in very brightly coloured garb, in which long feathers played a significant part.

They formed a circle around me, studying me, looking past the flesh and tendons, the fascia, the bone.

I knew they were searching for something in my inner being. Although they had dismissed me in our first encounter, something had stirred their interest. Now they wanted to know me, even if it required dissection.

The nearest spoke. It was a mocking voice of a being who knows it is infinitely superior to the entity it is addressing, a mockery which is an inevitable consequence of the vast gulf between them.

'We are the Old Gods.'

If I could have been more terrified than I already was, I would have become so at those words. Felipe's warning came back to me—*The Old Gods are returning!*

My knees buckled and I went down on them, almost as if I were worshipping these creatures.

Perhaps I was.

A bony hand pulled me upright and I found I was staring into an inhuman face with eyes like flaming coals, orifices through which the interior of a raging blast furnace could be glimpsed.

'I am Tezcatlipoca, the Smoking Mirror. I am omnipotent and All-Seeing. I am known by my servants as the Lord of the Shadows and Night, a sorcerer of black magic and bringer of evil, death, and destruction to those who defy me by refusing me worship. Do you offer me the worship I demand?'

I struggled to answer; I felt if I said *I did not*, I would be annihilated on the spot, but to say *I did* was a lie and an abomination.

But Tezcatlipoca, or whatever the foul thing was, did not require an answer.

'It matters not to me whether you do or do not: There are other creatures on this Earth who are our prey. They defeated us once and drove us out of our rightful domain, cast us down as if we were nothing. But we are not nothing.' The thing lifted skeletal arms to the black void above us. 'No, they have no comprehension of our true nature: We are the Lords of Creation.' It looked back at me. 'One of the names by which I am known is

Yaotl, The Enemy. Those who make me their enemy shall know many torments before I destroy them utterly. Do not make me your enemy, shadfly.'

The thing retreated slightly, but others pushed forward to take its place. I recoiled involuntarily: They seemed like women, but were a foul twisting of all that was female; instead of compassion I knew they brought hatred, cruelty, rage, joy in pain. They spoke as one.

'We are the Tzitzimime, the Star Demons. We roamed the skies before we were driven out by the usurpers. We were there in the aurorae, in the eclipses, in the lightning. We devour the unwary; those who do not pay us sufficient homage; those who do not abase themselves before our wrath. We have the power to destroy the world if the Sun does not arise again after the completion of its Cycle. Tread warily, shadfly, lest we devour you.'

They in turn withdrew and the arc of the circle opposite me parted. Some deeply unpleasant thing had been waiting in the rotten embrace of the mist for its moment and now it approached.

This time I thought I had literally become insane. I told myself this was not happening, that I was lying safe on my bed in my apartment, and this was only a hideous dream.

But if it was a dream it was a nightmare; no, it was the condensed distillate of every nightmare that had ever been, moulded together into one frenzy of irresistible horror. For the thing approaching had no face above its blood-splattered bones, for it was a walking skeleton. Instead of a face there was only a fleshless skull, but one which bore rolling eyeballs in its sockets. And there were more eyeballs in the vile necklace hanging to the shoulder blades. Where its ears should have been, bony whorls were attached instead, random dry bones from a previous owner. There came a voice, the voice of endless night.

'I am Mictlantecuhtli, Lord of The Land Of Death, god of slaughter, darkness. I am the ruler of the Underworld, into which we shall shortly cast our enemies, where they will serve my pleasure in an endless round of torment as they act and re-enact the rites of worshipful cannibalism.'

Finally, I found the strength to speak. I knew I had to break out of this nightmare or die.

'Why are you telling me this? What do you want with me?'

Mictlantecuhtli opened its mouth as if trying to smile.

'We want nothing of you, shadfly. We were sent by an ally of ours who wished you to make our acquaintance before you meet us in person. I could have said "in the flesh" but obviously that would not be appropriate in my case.'

An ally of theirs? Could this be the vision Edward had promised?

Then the full import of its words struck me like a physical blow.

'In person!'

But my ordeal was over.

Without any more warning they shimmered like figures seen through a heat haze.

And were gone.

***

I woke up; apparently I had kicked off my boots and crashed out on the bed.

I was shivering and covered with a cold, clinging sweat.

I was not alone.

I opened gummed-up eyes, and for a few seconds, I could not focus on what I was seeing, could not identify the human figure I saw.

And then I could.

Eleonora.

'How did you get in?' I said, forcing myself into a sitting position.

She smiled.

'Does that matter? I am here now. Just you and me. I know what you have seen. Do not let the vision trouble you; now is not the time to think about them. Let the memories drift away, Charles. You are safe with me.'

Now I was standing.

'Where's Edward? What do you want?'

Again the smile.

'What do I want? That's an excellent question, Charles—I may call you "Charles", mayn't I?'

Her formal way of speaking threw me for a second, and then I said, 'Yes, of course. And your name is— Eleonora?'

Her smile was radiant, like the sun suddenly breaking free of a cloud.

'Well remembered! I was afraid that I hadn't made an impression on you, that you'd forgotten all about me. I'm so glad you haven't.'

'Well, it's not easy to forget you,' I said, and then realised I'd said the wrong thing. I simply meant she was hard to forget because she looked so much like Serafina, but it had probably sounded like a come-on. Perhaps she took it that way, without offence, because her smile became broader and she came closer.

'It's hard to forget you too, Charles. You're very much like your brother.'

Now it was my turn to smile.

'Hah! I'm nothing like my brother. He's a man of action, a fighter. I'm just the guy who hands out traffic tickets.'

'No, no, you're more than that. Edward knows you're more than that. You have hidden depths.'

I snorted.

'Lady, I've got as much depth as a puddle in the middle of Arisona in July. Tell Edward to find another brother. I'm not his man.'

Now she was close enough to place her hands on my shoulders and exert a slight but noticeable traction toward her.

'You could be my man, Charles. Edward is so busy with all these plans. His head is full of schemes, of wonderful ideas about overthrowing the Elite. He's very busy, Charles, so busy that sometimes I wonder if he knows I'm there. Women like me…why, sometimes we get lonely.'

I looked down into her face, smiling up at me.

She's so like Serafina! I thought. My mind started to whirl as delicious new possibilities began to open up to me. I wondered, not for the first time, if I had feelings for my feisty young Deputy. She was way out of reach; I could not possibly, but…

Eleonora had evidently guessed my turbulent thoughts because her hands reached for mine and slowly pulled them down to her breasts. Her emerald eyes sparkled as she saw my reaction.

'Yes, Charles, it's alright. I want you to. I want you to take me. Edward will never know. Or care. He's a very busy man.'

I leaned in, putting my arms around her, and our lips met, drowning me in a swirling ocean of sweetness.

The same few thoughts hammered over and over in a mind that was losing all control: She wants you. How long have you been without a woman? She wants you. Take her!

I crushed her to me, my arms tightening into bands of steel as I tried to surge into her softness.

And then I called a name.

'Serafina!'

Instantly, she broke free and recoiled.

'Serafina? That's not my name! Why did you say that woman's name and not mine!'

I looked at her helplessly, my passion weakly subsiding. I held out my arms in a vain attempt to pull her back to me.

'I...I don't know.'

'Well, I know,' she spat. 'You're in love with her, aren't you?'

Serafina? I thought. In love? Me? That's crazy!

I slumped back onto the bed, turning my head from side to side in my sudden anguish.

'I'm sorry.'

Suddenly Eleonora was sitting next to me, stroking my cheek.

'It's all right, Charles, it's all right. You passed.'

I jerked my head around.

'Passed? What...? You mean...?'

'Of course. It was a simple test. Edward and I are bound together for all Eternity. He is a great man. At first, I wanted nothing to do with his war with the vampires. I thought it was wrong, wicked even. But he convinced me humans deserved a second chance, a chance to show they are capable of greatness. But he doesn't know much about you. You two have been apart for so long. He needed to be sure you have the necessary strength of will, the iron discipline that will be needed in the war.'

I looked at her, dully at first but with growing anger.

'So all that was just a test, to see if I thought with my dick!'

She gave my cheek a friendly pat.

'I'm sure it's a lovely dick, Charles, but I will never see it. But you and Serafina, Edward and I, what a team we shall make!'

'Me, Serafina, it's just, I...'

I spluttered to a halt.

'Trust me, Charles. I can see that you and Serafina will play a great part in the coming conflict. You particularly. And when you are ready to join Edward, just call out his name. He will hear.'

I stood and turned my back on her.

'You've humiliated me enough. I think you'd better go.'

There was no answer. Angrily, I spun around, raising a fist in my fury.

I was alone.

TWENTY SEVEN

The next day, I tried to shake my thoughts into something bearing a passing resemblance to normalcy. But it was not easy, for I was not alone in thinking that normalcy was a thing of the past: The Good Old Days.

I could sense that all the Marinetown Police Force—well, the humans, at least—had been infected by a feeling of futility. Vampires seem to have fewer emotions than we do, and those they have are usually kept well hidden from their servants.

But we are different; when we emote, it shows.

I ran into O'Rourke as we were standing in front of the automatic dispenser as it dropped unappetising gloop onto our plates.

'Heard about Horowitz?' he said as he reached for a condiment shaker, no doubt in the vain hope it would add flavour to his meal.

'No. What starving peasant has he abused this time? Moved on to rape now?'

'He may have done. But we won't hear about it for a while. He's quit the Force.'

I pulled my plate from out under the nozzle, as it was refusing to dispense any more of today's glutinous meal.

'That's odd,' was all I could think of to say, and moved to the next dispenser.

And it was odd. Opportunities for meaningful employment for humans are not that abundant. There's arable farming, there's hospitality (otherwise known as running drinking dens), some limited forms of entertainment, and precious little else. I have seen a few comedians in my travels, but they have rarely produced more than a weak smirk. Satire is out, of course, in case it upsets the Elite, and in any case, an impoverished, under-employed society is not fertile ground for any other type of humour. One of the best types of employment, if not the best, is the Police Force. It's impossible to rise above Sergeant, but at least we feel we're doing something worthwhile.

Or at least we did.

Curiosity finally got the better of my staged indifference.

'So what's he doing now?'

O'Rourke took his unbelieving gaze from the mess on his plate and shrugged.

'Beats the steaming shit out of me. He's just vanished. Must have gone into the country and gotten himself a job on a farm. That's "farm" with a small "F",' he added, unnecessarily.

'Couldn't happen to a nicer guy,' I said, and with a nod, broke off the conversation. I'd spoken ironically, of course, and I'd meant what I'd left unsaid because incomes on regular farms are picayune, little above subsistence. And the destruction of McKinley's plant had depressed the sector even more. The Vamps don't like the idea of work that doesn't directly benefit themselves, which is why their long-term plan is to move all of us onto hydroponics.

But that was some way off, especially now they had other things on their minds.

Like survival.

I was toying with my food, aimlessly pushing slices of pseudo-meat around in their thin sauce, when I was aware I had a lunch companion.

'Oh, it's you again,' I said, looking up to see Serafina.

'Sarge, you're so gracious. But I love you for it.'

She carried on grinning as she slid her legs under the table.

I looked at her plate and frowned. There was something I'd been meaning to ask for a long time, and now I said it.

'How come you have real meat, and I get these slices of tasteless crap?'

'Well, if it really is crap, you should be grateful it's tasteless.'

I was not, definitely not, in the mood for clever wordplay.

'Give a direct answer for once, will you, for Chrissake?'

She showed no sign of repentance and her lips continued to grin, until she opened her mouth to pop a tasty-looking morsel inside.

'I have a metabolic condition which means I have to have real meat. I can't digest this pseudo stuff. Aren't I one lucky girl?'

'That's funny. I've never heard of anyone else with a "metabolic condition".'

'It's very rare. Which means I'm even more special than you thought I was.'

I forgot my meal and stared at her. How close was the resemblance between Serafina and Eleonora? Did Serafina's breasts feel as firm and inviting as her strange twin's? Was the taste of her lips as wonderful as those other lips? Could I...?

Suddenly I realised she was banging her fork on the table.

'Hello? Hello? Is there anybody there?'

I shook my head, realising my stare had gone beyond the bounds of normal sociability.

'Sorry, I was daydreaming.'

'A very nice daydream by the look of it. If I didn't know better, I'd have said it was a wet daydream.'

I spluttered as I tried to chew a particularly stringy piece of pseudo-meat.

'Ha, ha. Very funny. Does your mother know you say things like that to your superior?' I was struck by another stray thought. 'Do you have a mother? Alive, I mean, up in Granada?'

All traces of her teasing grin had vanished.

'No, I'm an orphan.'

My fork made a scraping noise on the plate as her surprising reply finally sunk in.

'An orphan? That's a coincidence.'

'Hey, why are you suddenly asking me about my family? You've never shown an interest before.'

That threw me. Why indeed? Ever since my encounter with Eleonora, my attitude to Serafina had changed markedly. I had always seen her as a scratchy-itchy, pain-in-the-proverbial before, just a somebody a rung lower than me in the Service. But now I was seeing her as female, a woman, in a way I had not before.

A good-looking woman—just like the woman who was her twin in all but genetics. If Eleonora was telling the truth about the lack of connection, that is; I was discovering that people don't always tell the truth.

I discovered I couldn't think of anything to say, and simply sat there, trying to look at her without actually staring at her.

'Are you OK?' she said, and, leaning over, she touched my forehead with strangely cool fingers. 'My, you're burning up!'

'It's this pseudo-meat,' I managed to say, 'It's burning my throat. I must have a metabolic condition.'

She laughed at that, and the mood lightened, returning to normal. And the danger of me revealing my new feelings receded. I asked if she had heard about Horowitz disappearing, but she had not. However, she knew of one of the woman officers who had gone AWOL.

'There's no work out there. Another mystery,' I said, finally succeeding in clearing my plate.

'Perhaps not. There is something else people can do.'

I raised an eyebrow, waiting patiently for enlightenment.

'The Sons Of Man.'

'Good God, do you really think…'

She had also finished her meal and took a sip of an orange-coloured drink before replying.

'It was always foolish of them to give themselves a non-inclusive name. One which appears to exclude women,' she added, seeing my incomprehension of the unfamiliar word. 'If you are so-called Freedom Fighters' (She made the air-quotes sign) 'then why use a name that seems to restrict yourself to half the population?'

'I hadn't thought of that. On reflection, it seems a clumsy name.'

'Not good propaganda,' she confirmed.

But I was thinking. Edward had said the Sons Of Man were just a side-show, the overture to the main event. If so, then the appropriateness or otherwise of their name didn't rate a fart in a paper bag.

'So, who is the real enemy?'

'Pardon me?'

I hadn't realised I'd spoken out loud.

'Sorry, I have all these crazy ideas banging about in my head, bouncing off of the walls.'

'Well, there's plenty of space in there. Shouldn't cause much damage.'

I glanced up to see her smiling at me, and I found I no longer cared about her little barbs. Instead, I now saw them as they had, presumably, always been intended: Just harmless banter between work colleagues.

And I smiled.

'I'll get you back for all this insubordination one day.'

'Have to get those rusty cogs oiled up first, Sarge.' She stood. 'Time to go, I think.'

I rose as well, and for a few seconds we were standing with only centimetres between us. I was suddenly seized by an aching demand that told me I could simply reach for her, press my lips on hers, and feel her body begin to respond under my exploring hands. You are so close, Serafina, so incredibly close…

I did nothing, of course. I let her walk on before me, thinking, *If only you knew…*

But then, unexpectedly, she turned, looked over her shoulder, and her smile was radiant.

TWENTY EIGHT

'**Y**ou ought to be ashamed of yourself!'

I looked down at the old man, smelling the cheap beer wafting sickly from him, mingling with his body odour, and tried to get neither angry nor nauseous.

'Oh, and why is that, sir?' I said, emphasising the "sir" to make the conversation as unthreatening as possible.

'I'll tell you why, you apology for a real man! I can remember when the cops used to stand for something, when they worked with the people, for the people, not like now when you're all lickspittle cowards, selling your asses to those monsters!'

I quietened my temper, telling myself he was simply an old man who'd drunk too much beer, that he didn't really mean what he was saying. He cut a pathetic figure in cheap, shabby clothes with as many patches as original fabric, where there weren't holes, of course. A few strands of his remaining sandy-coloured hair hung down his scrawny neck to below his collar.

'I think you'd better go home, sir, and sleep it off,' I suggested, and made to move on. But he grabbed me with surprising strength and tried to pull me closer.

'Oh no, you don't! I'm telling the fucking truth, and you're going to listen! Let me tell you, sonny, I remember when we normal folks used to run this place before they moved in and bulldozed everything. Built their stinking town here on top of what they'd destroyed. This was a family place, where little kids like me could run around, safe, having fun. Where men like my father were in charge, real, true men, not these things that look a little bit like us but have no souls! I was there; I saw them come out of the shadows, out of the dark, and enslave us, turn us into farm animals. In my father's day, we were in charge, we were our own masters, we were free. We had freedom! You don't even know what that word means, do you, you sonofabitch traitor!'

I gently removed his fingers from my shoulders, and realising that further discussion was pointless and might easily turn ugly, I smiled and turned away. To be confronted by a group of men of a similar age blocking my way.

'You're going nowhere,' the nearest man said. 'Your days are coming to an end, chum. We're gonna take everything back, bring it back to where it belongs. We're not taking their shit lying down anymore. Your bosses are finished; soon we'll be stringing them up from the lampposts!'

'Or driving a stake through their hearts!' another cackled.

'Yeah, that might work better,' the first said, a wolfish grin on his face, 'just like in them old movies! I can't wait to find out!'

'I'm sorry you feel that way,' I said, as quietly as I could. 'Now, if you could kindly move aside, I must be on my way. I promise I won't report your words, so let's just leave it at that, shall we?'

'Sure, we're all law-abiding citizens here, copper.'

The first indicated to the others they should move aside. Still bearing a fixed smile, I moved carefully between them, looking straight ahead.

And received a staggering blow to the side of the head.

I went down on my knees, holding my head, the pain lancing through it like shards of broken glass. Dimly I heard someone say, 'Get him! Kill the bastard!'

Blows rained down on me as I crashed full length on the ground. Then fists and boots thudded into me, and the world started to grow dim.

Suddenly I heard a shrill female voice yell, 'Police! Move away or I will shoot!'

I heard defiant growls and curses from somewhere above me, but they slowly grew fainter, receding into a background buzzing. Hands grasped me and I realised this unknown person was trying to get me to stand. I did my best to obey and finally managed to get jerkily to my feet, leaning heavily on my saviour.

It was Serafina; she had gone on ahead but had returned to see me minutes away from being kicked and punched into a pulp. I touched the side of my head and my fingers came away bloody.

'One of them hit you with a length of pipe,' she said, looking at me with concern-filled eyes. 'You'd better get checked out.'

My mind was clearing rapidly, however, and I shook my bloodied head.

'I'm OK; I've had worse.'

Looking around, I saw my assailants had only pulled back a little and were still watching me, waiting for an opportunity to finish the job. But Serafina had already pulled out her gun and was waving it at them.

'I'm giving you ten seconds to disperse, and then I start shooting. I'll disable the ugliest of you first, and then work my way down the list.'

'You wouldn't dare!' the sandy-haired oldster yelled. 'You haven't got the guts, you Vamp whore!'

A cloud of dust erupted between his legs as Serafina showed her sharpshooting skills. Mr Sandy Hair looked briefly down at the crater between his feet, looked back at Serafina with alarmed astonishment written plain on his face, and then the whole lot of them went away like Scotch mist on a sunny morning.

'Thanks,' I finally said to my Deputy. 'They could have injured me bad.'

'They could have killed you bad,' she responded, still looking at my bloodied head. 'Those goons were ready to murder you. Their blood was up, right to the boiling point.'

I looked around and sat down on a fragment of wall, more heavily than I intended. As I fully realised how close my brush with death had been, the pain returned, twice as bad.

'Kill a police officer? In broad daylight? Come on.'

She sat beside me and put a hand on my shoulder.

'No, Sarge, they really meant it. I saw the hate in their faces. They were ready to kill you. And they were going to kill you.'

I shook my head in disbelief.

'Murder me? But what's gotten into them to make them think they could get away with it? The Elite would go ape!'

She shook her head as if dealing with a slow child.

'Sarge, Sarge, what do you think's gotten into them?'

I thought for a moment, trying to ignore the scalpels that were busily slicing my brain into bloody sections. Then, of course, I had it.

'The Sons Of Man,' I said. 'It's giving them hope. Hope that the Elite can be defeated, driven back into the night.'

'Precisely. They would never have dared to attack a police officer before the terrorists appeared. Now they can see that the Vamps are not invincible; like all the other conquerors in history, they can be defeated. So, they're getting restless, eager to be on the winning side. And wanting to play their part in the destruction of Elite power.'

I knew she'd gotten her history wrong; many conquerors had never been defeated or driven away. But that was beside the point. Someone had told me the Sons Of Man were just a plaything, a hobby to keep the populace amused, that behind them was something vastly more powerful. Something that had not yet entirely shown its hand, but every day was bringing us closer to a terrible unveiling. Unwisely, I revealed I knew more than she thought.

'Edward told me...'

She was so close I felt her body suddenly tense.

'Edward? Your brother? What's he got to do with anything?'

So I told her as much as I could remember about what he'd said. Even his fantasy of some "Vampire-Predators." I expected her to laugh—but she did not. Instead, an already grave face grew graver, alarmed, perhaps even fearful. Especially when I said...

'A Barrier? And he says he's found a way to open a chink in it?'

'Yes, that's what he says.' Then it was my turn to become tense, alert. 'What, do you believe him? It's just a fantasy, the rantings of a bitter man who thinks life's given him a raw deal.'

'Have you told Mistress Aiyana this?'

'No. I couldn't bring myself to betray my brother.'

She shook her head, looking into the far distance.

'Well, you've sure as fuck betrayed yourself. When she finds out she'll flay you alive. Literally. You fool, you fool.'

This time I felt no urge to reprimand her for insubordination. I was too confused, too mixed up in the madness my entire world was rapidly being sucked into. Already I'd learned I was not the man I'd thought I was. I had no late wife, no past.

And it looked more and more like I had no future. So why not believe in Barriers and terrible things behind them? So I told her about my futile search for Jane. I expected amazement, incredulity in her face but they did not appear. She continued to look calmly and seriously back at me.

'Why aren't you reacting, Serafina?' I shouted. 'Did you know all along, is that it? What haven't you been telling me?'

She turned away, and once again, I heard her mutter things I could not quite catch. Something snapped, and I roughly pulled her back to face me.

'Enough of that, Serafina! No more mutterings, no more asides to people I can't see, no more talking about me like I'm not here! I'm through with all that! You know something, something important, something relevant to my situation and you're not telling me! I don't want to beat it out of you, but unless you start talking, by God, I will!'

She was unmoved, unconcerned. I felt like a child upset enough to issue empty threats to an adult. Had the roles been mysteriously reversed? Was she now the Sergeant and me the Deputy? She spoke.

'Gray, you're right. You've been right all along. I do know things about you, important, perhaps terrible things, and I haven't shared any of them with you. That time is coming to an end. Soon. But there is one more step that must be taken before I can tell you what those things are. And you must take that step, however wrong it may feel, however terrible. And when you have at last taken it, everything will be clear to you. And you will know what you must do.' She stopped speaking, and her face underwent a subtle change. Suddenly she was the old teasing, irrepressible, pain in the ass Serafina again. 'Right, now that's all sorted out, you're going to call for someone to take over your patrol. We're going to get that head looked at. I think you've been having a few hallucinations.'

TWENTY NINE

After they had checked my head for fractures, I was let off the rest of my patrol in the city, so they gave me some office work. I hated it; imagine having nothing to do all day except look at computer screens and shuffle papers! One of the other guys went off with Serafina to finish the patrol; for some reason, I didn't like the idea of her being with another man, but that was stupid as she meant nothing to me. Still, when she came back, she said she'd call in on me at my apartment to see how I was getting on. I had no problem with that as I still had a blinding headache, which unfortunately, all that monitor staring had not helped in the least.

At last, they let me go, and I headed back to my place. For the first time in my career I looked back and forth as I walked along, half expecting some thug to jump out at me from the shadows. Nothing happened, although a few rough-looking individuals studied me as I passed. I'm well known around Marinetown, so being out of uniform was no protection. But my lonely walk was not disturbed.

Back at my apartment, I microwaved some soya strips and sat down to think with a mug of my usual thin, near-tasteless coffee. I felt more than a little dizzy, so I gave myself one of my anti-anaemia shots, even though it wasn't the scheduled time. I had a lot to think about, and that didn't help my head either. Why had someone—presumably one of the Elite—given me a false identity? When had it happened? When did the false memories stop and the real ones begin? I now knew I

224

had never been married, and was all too sure I had not had any encounters since my supposed bereavement— Hell, had I ever been with a woman? I couldn't bring any former lovers to mind; all my probing just resulted in me having images of my fictitious wife served up to me instead. So I gave it up and lay on the bed, staring up at the ceiling with a mind as blank as the ceiling.

I must have fallen asleep because I gave a start at the strong knocking at the door. It was Serafina, of course, and I was gratified to see she looked pleased to see me. I had rarely seen her not in uniform, and she made quite a pleasant sight. She asked me a few polite questions about my head and then sat on the only chair in the room. Looking at her, I could not help recalling how a short time before, a woman almost identical to her had been standing here in my grubby little room, apparently offering me no-strings sex. Had I been a fool to turn her down? Was it likely a chance like that would ever come my way again? My face must have shown my self-pity because Serafina told me to cheer up.

After I had made her a cup of my coffee and watched her try to hide a look of near revulsion as she reluctantly sipped it, we got down to the serious talk I'd known would be coming.

'Tell me about Edward,' she said, in what sounded suspiciously like a command.

'I hadn't seen him for about four years, and then he suddenly came back into my life.'

'How did he contact you?'

I hesitated; did Serafina know about the mysterious cylinder that had produced his commanding voice on the day Lieutenant Ardelean had died?

'I met him in a park. It was by chance.'

She seemed satisfied with my explanation, which was kind of a relief as I did not want to tell her I had been under some kind of compulsion. I don't know why I was unwilling to give up all my secrets to a friendly face; it seemed I had come to distrust everybody.

'But he is behind the Sons Of Man. That is certain?'

'Yes. Although he seems to regard it as a kind of hobby.'

'And there is a woman he associates with, one who looks rather like me.'

'One who looks almost exactly like you, apart from eye and hair colour. If she were here now, I could probably tell you apart, but if I met one of you by chance, out of uniform, wearing a hat, I would not be certain who was who.'

She shook her head at that and looked away into a corner of the room. Then back to me.

'Tell me, Charles, did they seem very—close?'

'Close? I don't understand.'

She made a tutting noise and frowned.

'Do I have to spell it out with alphabet blocks? Did they look like they were—lovers?'

I hadn't thought about such matters, with all the other mayhem occurring around me. But then I remembered Eleonora's speech to me after I had turned her down: "Bound together for all Eternity". That didn't sound like a simple working relationship.

'Yes, I suppose they are,' I finally replied.

She drew in a great draft of the humid air.

'Bad,' she said, 'very bad.'

I was annoyed.

'Serafina!' I snapped. 'Don't be so prissy! Why does Edward's sex-life matter to you? He's not beholden to you or anyone else in this stinking city!'

'It's not that, you fool!' she snapped in return. 'I couldn't care less if he's fucking his cat!' She stood and crossed to me, sat close to me on the bed and, to my amazement, started to stroke my cheek. All vestiges of Sergeant-Deputy relationship looked like it had gone with the wind. 'Charles, Charles, please wake up. Why don't you wake up? The time is close!'

'What time?' I said, jumping to my feet. I couldn't risk being that close to her and humiliating myself with another woman. 'And how do I wake up? And what am I supposed to do when and if I wake up?'

She looked down at her hands, avoiding eye contact with me.

'I can't tell you. You have to come to the realisation by yourself. It can't be forced by an outside influence. That's the way it works. It's the only way it works.'

I clenched my hands in frustration.

'You're not making any sense. Realisation of what? That's the world's going crazy? I've already realised that a long time ago!'

'I can't help you.'

'What—there's this wonderful, incredible thing I've got to realise, and you know what it is, but you can't give me a clue? What is the only way something works? What is this—some kind of intelligence test?'

'I can't help you.'

'You say that one more time, Serafina, and I'll…'

She smiled.

'What, knock me out? Pull my hair? Force me to wear unbecoming clothes? Come on, Charles, you know you wouldn't do any of those things. Especially the last one.'

I sat back down, completely defeated. Now it was my turn to study my hands.

'So, I have to realise something, something that will stop bad things happening.'

'Oh no, I never said that. Bad things are happening, all right. It's a question of how bad.'

I did not look up from my hands, but said in a low, defeated voice, 'I think you'd better go, Serafina. Perhaps it's best we stick to our roles in the Force. I'm not happy with this "Charles" business. It's not like you know me as a person.'

'Well, perhaps you're right,' she said, rising gracefully. 'I know I've annoyed you tonight, but Hell, I've annoyed you every day since we met, haven't I?'

At that whimsical comment, I was forced to laugh.

'Yeah, you sure got that right!'

To my amazement, she leaned in and planted a soft kiss on my cheek. For a trembling moment, I thought of Eleonora's lips on mine, and I almost pulled Serafina on top of me.

But I didn't.

Then she was gone and, once again, I was alone. I now understood that being alone had been my normal state ever since the orphanage. What was I—some kind of human hermit crab? When would I get my chance at happiness?

But perhaps there was someone who could help me make sense of this swirling insanity; someone who had shown himself to be a leader of men.

But what of his avowed aim of overthrowing the vampires?

Was I so far sunk into insanity that I could even think of such a thing?

I decided I could not, but perhaps talking to Edward would help blow away some of the fog that had invaded my mind.

I remembered Eleonora's parting words: *Call out his name and he will hear.*

I felt like a complete fool, but I lifted my aching head and yelled, 'Edward!'

Nothing happened.

THIRTY

I don't know what I had expected to happen; maybe a puff of scarlet smoke and Edward stepping out of it, dressed in a loincloth and wearing a turban, and then offering me three wishes. I waited a minute or two and then gave it up. It was still early, but my head still hurt, so I turned in. Fortunately, I had a dreamless sleep: No green mists or mocking voices referring to my status as a mere shadfly.

I wouldn't go so far as to say I woke refreshed, but at least I didn't feel any worse. Which meant I was well enough to do my regular patrol. Serafina didn't mention anything about the previous evening, and neither did I. She treated me the same as she had always treated me: A little teasingly, a little condescendingly. I was used to it, and after the pressure of recent events, I wouldn't have wanted it any other way. And, praise be! we had nothing out of the ordinary or too difficult to deal with. There were no explosions or people being turned inside out; it almost felt like the events of the past few months had just been a bad dream. It's true we had lots of sour looks from lots of sour people, but no violence. I was glad of that in more ways than one; I really did not want to kill any of my fellow citizens.

And so I felt almost relaxed and at peace with the world when I stretched out on the bed after my humble meal. I finished the last of my coffee, wondering why Serafina had found it so repulsive. After all, it had hardly any taste. But as I stretched out, trying to relax my stiff muscles, my hand hit something. I brought the object into my field of view and then gave a sudden start of alarm.

I was holding a featureless grey cylinder, just like the one I had seen on the day of Lieutenant Ardelean's death. I dropped it as if it was red hot. Did this mean I was about to suffer a death both painful and weird? I jumped off of the bed and just stared at it for several minutes, before plucking up enough courage to slowly approach and warily pick it up. For a few seconds, nothing happened, and then I heard Edward's voice inside my skull: Powerful, strong, masterful.

Come to me, Charles. You know where to find me.

It was then I dropped the cylinder and backed away from the bed. How had it gotten there? I was certain it had not been there when I had woken. Yet there was absolutely no sign of anything having been disturbed. The room was exactly the same as I had seen it that morning—except for a featureless, grey cylinder. Had it implanted another subconscious command in my brain?

It had.

And so, the following afternoon, I finished work early and walked to a quiet neighbourhood where most of the buildings were not only still standing but in reasonable condition, many with regular families inside. Quite a few had windows. I had no reason whatsoever to go to that neighbourhood, but I did not attempt to resist and go someplace else. I knew it was Edward guiding me.

Unlike the park, there was no bench, so I sat on a horizontal section of the remains of a wall and waited.

How long did I wait? I have no idea: It might have been an hour; it might have been ten minutes. It might have been a lifetime. I was cut off from reality; several people passed pretty close to me but did not address me or even look at me. I was just a guy sitting on the remains of a wall, but their total lack of awareness of my presence, my very existence, was strange.

But strange was normal now. Everything was strange. And if everything is strange, then it is normal.

Initially, I had glanced up as people had passed by, but after realising they were not going to disturb me I simply spent the time looking down at my interlinked fingers. Waiting.

Then it happened.

Suddenly two trousered legs came into view beyond my hands; slim legs, the kind belonging to a young woman. I looked up and saw the rest of my visitor. And it was indeed a young woman.

Eleonora.

She smiled.

'It's so good to see you again, Charles. Edward will be very glad you called him; decided to join him.'

I stood.

'Who said I'd decided to join him? I haven't decided anything.'

The tolerant, forgiving smile I'd seen before appeared on features that were simultaneously familiar and unfamiliar—like a facial version of What's His Name's Cat. It was the gentle smile of the mother when explaining a simple but important concept to a confused child.

'Of course you have decided, Charles. There is no point in pretending otherwise. You are his brother. You have always wanted the same as he, but did not want to accept the knowledge of your own desires.'

'And what desires are they?'

With a swift, sinuous movement, she was beside me. She was so like Serafina! And yet there were differences. There was an animalistic quality about her body; the easy, assured, powerful stance and movements of the female predator: The vixen, the tigress. She slowly ran a slim index finger down the cheek nearest her, smiling all the while. I could have pushed her hand away—but I did not.

'To rid our world of the bloodsuckers. To reclaim the Earth for its true owners, the men and women of the abused and enslaved human race. To cast the usurpers down from their thrones. You, me, Edward—we shall destroy them.'

I moved away from this woman, shaking my head as I retreated. She was Serafina, but not my down-to-earth, cheerful, impertinent Serafina, but one reborn as a pitiless huntress. I knew then I was afraid of Eleonora.

'Impossible,' I managed to articulate. 'They can't be defeated.'

A scowl disturbed her captivating features.

'Charles, you're starting to become tedious. I am patient, much more patient than Edward, but this must stop. You must accept what your subconscious already knows: You are Edward's man. You can either serve him as an obedient underling, or you can stand shoulder to shoulder with him and share in his triumph. You can choose between being a footnote or being a chapter in the magnificent volume of humanity's liberation. The choice is yours.

'But play your part, you assuredly will.' She glanced behind her. 'This has gone on long enough. Edward will be impatient, and he prefers to mould events, not wait on them. We must go.'

I followed her glance and was surprised to see a sleek open-top motor vehicle nearby. Oddly, I had not heard it arrive. Modern cars are quiet but not silent. A quick toss of her head made it very clear I was meant to get on board. She slid into the driver's seat and grasped the wheel with long, red-nailed fingers. That was another difference: Serafina's nails were always short, and ever-so slightly bitten, and she never wore cosmetics, even when off duty.

'Where are we going?' I asked, feeling a slight shock at how weak my voice sounded.

She did not look at me, but shook her head with evident disbelief.

'Please don't be foolish, Charles. You know exactly where we're going.'

I leaned back into the soft covering of my seat. Of course, I knew.

We soon left the crumbling mass of masonry known as Marinetown behind and sped out into the Fluridian countryside. The car was travelling faster than I was used to, and I expected at any moment to hear the whine of a speed cop's siren behind us and have to accept a ticket from one of my buddies from the force.

But just as everyone had ignored me as I had sat morosely on the wall, so no speed cops appeared. Indeed, there was unusually little traffic of any kind. Unsurprisingly, Eleonora was actually driving the car. I knew she was not the kind of woman who would accept being passive in the face of events. She liked to be in charge.

And also to drive very fast.

'Where are we going?' I finally asked.

She did not take her eyes off of the turning, twisting, pot-holed road.

'South.'

'That doesn't help much.'

Still staring at the road, she shrugged.

'What does the name of the place matter? It's what's there that is important.'

Silence fell, a silence I could not tolerate. I was alone in a car with an exotic, highly attractive female, heading I knew not where. I tried again.

'You know about Serafina, but how much do you know? I take it you realise how much you two resemble each other; you could be sisters.' I waited for my courage to build before I asked the next question. 'Are you sisters?'

She laughed; a laugh without joy, without musicality.

'Superficial, Charles, superficial! Surely you don't judge people by their appearance!'

'So you're not sisters.'

'Now, Charles, are you so easily fooled by a few millimetres of epidermis? How could two people so very different in character be sisters? Now close your eyes and try and sleep. It will be a long journey. Your understanding will be sorely tested when we get there, so you will need your wits about you.'

'How long a journey?'

'About six hours.'

I had a sudden idea of how to ingratiate myself with this alluring woman, whose closeness had definitely aroused me.

'We could share the driving.'

She laughed again, and this time there was humour in the sound.

'Yes, we could, Charles. If we wanted the journey to take twelve hours!'

'What about you taking a rest?'

'Me? I don't need much sleep, Charles.'

Having been reminded so forcefully of my inadequacies, I decided to take her advice. Eleonora clearly had no intention of unburdening her soul to me, no intention of revealing any secrets. I was a passenger in more ways than one, that was obvious.

The car was bouncing around quite badly due to the combination of the poor road surface and the vehicle's speed, but I took her advice and, to my surprise, fell asleep quite soon.

When I awoke, nothing seemed to have changed; the landscape was still a green blur without observable detail, and the car was still maintaining its insane speed.

'Well, you certainly took my advice, Charles. You've been asleep for an hour.'

An hour. That was a surprise. But I had a suspicion my encounter with the strange cylinder had something to do with my lack of energy. I felt like I had been on an all-night bender and was now trying to sit an important examination. (Not that I have a great deal of experience of all-night benders, of course.)

'So another five hours, I guess.'

'No, four, I made up some time while you slept as I could make my normal speed without frightening you.'

Frightening me! I was annoyed at the implication I was a fuzznut until I realised she was right: I had been frightened.

Then I realised I had another problem, apart from being seen as ineffectual by a woman I was finding increasingly captivating.

'Sorry about this, but…'

'You need to go to the john,' she said, smiling as she negotiated a particularly sharp turn. 'That's OK, we're stopping for something to eat soon. Hang on.'

True to her word, we pulled up at a run-down looking diner shortly afterwards. Most such places are run-down these days, of course, as we shadflies don't do much travelling, neither for work nor pleasure.

I attended to my need and returned to find her looking out through the large window by the entrance. There was a plate of soya and beans opposite her, which I correctly assumed was mine. Halfway through the first mouthful, I noticed there was no plate in front of her.

'What finished already? I didn't think I'd been that long.'

Again the tolerant smile.

'You weren't. I don't need…'

'Much food,' I finished for her. I studied her as I slowly chewed the unpleasantly tough soya strip. She sat poised, as if she were in a fashion shoot (in the old days when such things were possible.) Her hair was cut exactly right for her features, and so black it was almost unnaturally glossy as it lay softly on her shoulders. Her lips were a soft scarlet bow, and curved in the slightly amused expression she nearly always adopted when looking at me. She knew I was staring at her but did not show any annoyance or look away. And then a very peculiar thought rose to the surface.

'Eleonora—are you human?'

She laughed, a full-throated laugh that tossed her hair and revealed amazingly white teeth behind the red lips.

'What a strange question, Charles! What do you think I am?' She leaned across the table, tantalisingly close. 'A vampire? Are you afraid I will suck the lovely precious blood out of you?'

I did not reply at once. Instead, I took the opportunity to drink her in. She was undoubtedly very like Serafina, but she was the metropolitan sophisticate to Serafina's homespun tomboy. I could almost imagine Serafina in a check shirt, jeans dotted with cow dung and a straw hanging from her mouth.

I finally almost stuttered my reply, but managed to stay coherent.

'You're not like any woman I've ever seen. There's something about you. I've…'

'I should hope I'm not like other women you've seen, Charles. That would indeed be an unforgivable thing for any man to say.' Then, abruptly, she pushed her chair back and stood upright; gracefully, of course. 'Time we were on our way. We still have much driving ahead.'

We headed for the door, only to hear a gruff male voice call, 'Hey, lady! Ain't you forgot something?'

A man dressed in too-tight trousers and wearing only a vest over his upper body came out from behind the food displays and bore down on us. 'I ain't running no charity here!'

I realised I had no money and stood aside to let Eleonora do the financial transactions.

But she did not. She stood motionless as the burly guy bore down on her. Like Serafina, she was not tall, but as he planted himself before her she looked up at him with an expression in which amusement and pity seemed equally mixed.

'Thank you for the meal. My travelling companion enjoyed it immensely. It was very kind of you to offer us such generous hospitality. I will certainly mention your establishment to my associates. I can only thank you again.'

The man started to say something, but a slim finger was held up in the region of his pock-marked nose.

'Please, we can accept no more kindness from you and your hard-working people. We will certainly revisit you. But now we really must be leaving, much though we would love to stay.'

The man's face had shown a blank look during Eleonora's little speech, but now it brightened, and he gave a self-satisfied grin.

'That's fine, lady. You be sure to come back; I'm sure my wife could learn a thing or two from a classy woman like you.' He glanced towards the kitchen area. 'Like how to wear some proper clothes so she don't look like a sack of potatoes.'

Eleonora gave him a dazzling megawatt smile.

'You can be sure of it. Goodbye.'

The man grinned again, and his head gave a little nod. He held the door open as we left.

As I followed Eleonora to the vehicle, I realised that I was dealing with people who were unlike anyone I'd met before—even the Elite.

I was in deep.

Too deep to swim for the shore.

THIRTY ONE

I was stunned into silence for quite some time after that weird display. It was becoming ever clearer to me I had gotten myself into something it would have been best to have stayed well clear of. Eventually, I felt I could remain silent no longer.

'How did you do that trick?' I asked, slowly, carefully.

She did not remove her gaze from the winding road.

'Trick? What trick?'

'Making that guy let us go without paying.'

Again the smile.

'Oh, it wasn't exactly a trick, more a gift from our friends and allies. How could a mere human do such a strange thing, Charles?'

That worried me. Simple conjuring or sleight-of-hand I could deal with, but not gifts from their "friends and allies." I had more than a suspicion about who those friends and allies were, and I wanted nothing more to do with them. All I wanted now was to get back to Marinetown and my comforting routine. And, yes, back to Serafina. But short of seizing the wheel and jumping out, I could see no way of accomplishing that. And I suspected that seizing the wheel from Eleonora would not be as easy as it sounded. This was no ordinary woman I was sitting next to.

So I did nothing, said nothing. But Eleonora was in the mood to expand on her brief comment.

'They have helped us in many ways; adjusted our brains so hitherto latent powers like mine have been activated. The ability to influence someone's mind at a distance without a direct connection is one of those hitherto hidden abilities. It is marvellous what they have been able to do for us; just think of all we will have when they finally break through the Barrier.'

Again the chill in my bones. To influence minds; surely that was the ultimate power? In the wrong hands, it could … I glanced at Eleonora's slim hands as they unconcernedly held the wheel; were they the wrong hands?

'Have you influenced my mind?'

'No—well, not intentionally and not to any great degree. You see, Charles, when you have that power, it is difficult to stop it from seeping into ordinary affairs, especially as it gets easier the more you do it. But I promise you, any influence on your mind would have been very minor and not done intentionally. You are here with me because you want to be.'

I wasn't exactly sure I agreed with that, but deep down, I had a suspicion it was true. I knew, as any man would know, that she was exciting me sexually. But the notion she would have anything to do with me was obviously ridiculous, and I dared not think of what Edward would do if anything did happen. But I could not help my age-old male reaction. What man could?

And the resemblance to Serafina added a certain frisson to the whole situation.

I chose not to say anything else about what I had seen in case she started talking about friends and allies again, and I certainly didn't want them intruding on my already troubled thoughts.

Suddenly, she looked off to the side and said, 'Ah, the sea! The beautiful Gulf of the Mexica. We are almost there, Charles, almost there!'

Although I didn't entirely understand her odd phraseology, I knew roughly where we must be. In these days of limited travel, the southernmost tip of mainland Flurida had seemed to me as remote as Far Cathay—but here we were!

'Is this where Edward lives?' I asked innocently.

'No. He is out in the Bay.'

'What—do we have to catch a boat?' I said, in some alarm, because I had never been on a boat and didn't like the idea.

'No. We humans built a bridge. Large parts have fallen down through neglect since the Usurpation, but Edward and our allies have made it transversable again.'

'They sound like really nice, helpful guys,' I said, but Eleonora did not pick up on my irony.

'If by "helpful" you mean eliminating the Bloodsuckers, then you're exactly right. It's called "The Seven Mile Bridge."'

'The Seven *What* Bridge?'

'Mile. It was a human measurement of length that the Vamps got rid of. One of the many things they got rid of,' she added, with grim emphasis.

Then, at once, we were on the bridge, and for the first time in my life, I got a good look at the sea on each side of the car; a car which was continuing its crazy velocity.

My first view of the sea.

And I didn't like it. Especially as it was now on both sides of the vehicle. Soon we were out of sight of land, and I began to wish I was back in my nightmare, dealing with the Old Gods again. Then up ahead, I saw a small patch of land and I felt the relief loosen my tight nerves.

'So that's where he lives!'

But Eleonora shook her head.

'Not so soon, tiger. He's right at the end of this archipelago.'

Another word I didn't know, but I gathered that this stage of the journey had just begun. Instinctively, I drew away from the side of the vehicle and the vast expanse of bright blue water and in so doing pressed against her side, like a child seeking comfort. She smiled as she felt the pressure, but did not push me away.

She had said the bridge had been repaired, but on several occasions we encountered great holes occupying a good two-thirds of the width of the carriageway. But I was not too surprised when Eleonora did not lessen her speed in the slightest and flashed around the edge, giving me, involuntarily, a wonderful view of waves breaking against the pillars supporting said carriageway. Her expression never changed; a calm, almost serene, face at rest, no matter how close we came to getting up close and personal with the Gulf of Mexica—or whatever it was she had called it. We flashed over island after island; some small, some large. The large ones gave me hope we had arrived at our mysterious destination, but it seemed we never would.

'Will these islands never end?' I eventually asked, exasperated by the apparently endless nature of our journey. She obviously thought it was a stupid question because she didn't reply. I fell into a morose silence, more convinced than ever I should never have agreed to go with her.

We arrived at another large island; I paid it no attention, having seen large islands before, but she turned to me, gave me that incredible smile which could melt granite, and said quietly, 'Journey's end.' The car glided to a halt; smooth and silent.

I sat straight and looked around. I saw lush vegetation and stately, pastel-coloured houses; houses in a better state and of a more advanced construction that I was used to. They all had roofs, for God's sake!

'Nice place,' I said, for want of anything less banal to say. 'What's this island called?'

She stretched her arms over her head, straightening her back after the long drive. I was instantly, and a little inevitably, reminded of a big cat relaxing its muscles as it surveyed its domain, searching for the little movements in the undergrowth which would reveal the presence of prey. Was I prey? At that moment, I didn't care.

'It doesn't matter what the name of this place is,' she said after dropping her hands back on the wheel. 'It's Edward's place, and that's all that matters.'

We had not quite completed our journey, for she put the car into motion again. However, it was a short drive to our final destination: A large, basically rectangular cross-gabled building painted a dazzling white.

'Edward's home,' she said, cutting the motor. 'And ours, for as long as he needs us.'

Automatically, I asked if the imposing building had a name. "Edward's Lair" didn't quite seem to cut it. But this time, she answered.

'It's the White House.'

I shrugged. I was expecting a more grandiose name than a simple description of it in kindergarten terms.

'Oh, the White House. Well, that's easy to remember.'

Out of the corner of my eye, I could see she was laughing.

'It's rather more important than the name suggests, Charles. This house was important to us humans when we ruled ourselves. Great men came here to make decisions which affected the whole world. The whole world, Charles, think of that, you who hadn't even seen much of your home state! Let's go!'

I exited the vehicle, stretching my muscles after such a long period of immobility, though I suspect with less grace than had Eleonora. But she had not finished her educational talk.

'One man in particular came here. We don't know his real name; the records only speak of "The True Man." But we can tell from that epithet he must have been highly regarded by his fellows and must have made many vital decisions here. Think of that, Charles, and then think of how low we have fallen!'

I wasn't really listening; I was more than a little worried about meeting Edward again. I had no conception of what his plans were for me, and I still had an overwhelming desire to jump in the car and drive back very rapidly to Marinetown. All this cloak-and-dagger stuff was way above my Pay Grade.

But there was to be no fearful escape for me, for, suddenly, the man himself was framed in the doorway, and he came briskly down the steps, smiling a smile which looked genuine. I studied him as he approached. I had never known whether we were identical or fraternal twins, and he certainly didn't look very identical as he came up to me and shook my hand in a large, powerful one of his own.

'Charlie! Great to see you again!'

He pumped my hand so vigorously I was forced to pull it out of his grasp.

'Good to see you again too, Edward,' I lied. 'I'm not sure why I came, to tell the truth.'

Then a worrisome thought struck me. *Why had I come?* I glanced at Eleonora. She had said she hadn't influenced my mind, but if my years as a cop had taught me anything, it was that people sometimes don't tell the truth. However, she met my gaze with an impenetrable one of her own, as usual with a faint smile playing on full red lips. I tried another tack.

'Edward, why am I here? I'm just a flatfoot cop—I keep telling you that.'

'I will tell you, Charlie boy. I'm afraid it'll take some time to explain it to you; you'll have to be very patient with me, it won't be easy listening. But I have recently finally realised who and what you are. You are just like me, you have all my strengths, simply deeply buried! I can't believe it took me so long! In my defence, I have a great deal on my mind. But it should have been obvious. I can only apologise.' He looked briefly at his alluring companion. 'He hasn't realised? He doesn't know about them?'

She approached the two of us, sidling unnecessarily close past me to rub against my brother, running supple fingers through his iron-grey hair. She planted a brief kiss on a cheek and then turned to look at me. I felt like I was intruding on the beginning of foreplay; feeling, perhaps, a sudden stab of jealousy.

'No, no sign at all. A brief scan of his mind showed nothing. He has seen some of their phenomena, but has not inferred what must lie behind them. His mind will not allow itself to believe.'

There it was! In a blaze of rage, I yelled, 'You said you hadn't influenced me!'

She smiled at Edward; once again, tolerant, forgiving. I expected her to shake her head in pity. Then back to me.

'Indeed I did. But a brief scan of your mind is not influencing you, Charles. You are here because, deep down, you wanted to be here. Subconsciously, you know you need your brother's guidance. And so here you are, to receive it.'

I gave up. Whatever these people were, they were too much for me. I was like a child intruding on a conference of great and important high officials. Defeated, depressed, I looked at Edward, awaiting whatever he had planned for me.

'OK, brother. Start guiding.'

THIRTY TWO

I looked at my brother with something approaching the love of the acolyte for the prophet. Edward had the answers; Edward would explain it all and free me from this quicksand of doubt relentlessly pulling me under. Edward saw I had given myself to him, and he smiled. He grasped me on my right shoulder, and I felt the dormant strength of his fingers, ready to dig into my flesh.

But instead, he simply patted me on the shoulder and said, in a soft undemanding voice, 'Come. Now I will show you what I am going to do, how I will free the world.'

I followed him up the short flight of steps into the White House.

It was cool inside, and the windows were shuttered against the strong island light. I was aware Eleonora was just behind me; I swear I could feel her scented breath on my hair. And even though I was on a hitherto unknown island in the company of people who were virtual strangers and had some yet-to-be-revealed plans for me, I no longer felt any concern. I was among friends, friends at long last; my own kind of people, but a higher form of my people: Strong, resolute, unafraid.

We walked along a shadowy corridor deeper into the building until we reached a great door. It looked completely out of place in this ancient structure, for it was not made of painted wood like everything else around me but of a dull, severe, undecorated metal; a robust door capable of repulsing a point-blank cannon blast. I had been walking behind Edward and in front of Eleonora as the pseudomeat in a weird sandwich, but now Eleonora moved past me to join her lover, and he, in turn, looked away from the door and directly at me.

'The entrance to my Holy Of Holies, my Inner Sanctum or,' and he beamed, 'my lair, if you prefer that image. Now watch.'

He turned back to the door and placed his palm on a spot at his shoulder height. There was a rumbling noise, as if tremendous bolts were being withdrawn, and the door slid sideways into the wall.

'I have keyed the door to my and Eleonora's DNA, which it can detect from even a brief contact with our flesh. If it recognises the DNA, it allows access to what lies beyond. If it does not recognise the DNA, it kills the intruder.'

I was a little disturbed by his casual comment about people being killed by his security and said so. He lifted an eyebrow as he snapped, 'Charlie, you're going to toughen up. This is a war we're caught up in; one we didn't start!'

Taken aback by the force of his reply, I changed the subject.

'Edward, we're twins. If I touched the door, would it kill me?'

He paused in the open doorway; it seemed he hadn't considered that possibility.

'An identical twin might make it. I didn't set the tolerances that tightly.'

I was no better off, as I didn't know what kind of twin we were. Then I asked myself why I was even considering the problem, and then realised I was thinking perhaps I might want to get out of Edward's lair in a hurry. But Edward had had enough delays and was pointing into the doorway.

'Let's go! There's so much I want to show you, Charlie.'

With an ever-growing reluctance, I followed him; Eleonora slipped behind me with the silent stealth of a cat on the hunt.

Beyond the doorway there was a flight of steps leading down into a blue-cast semidarkness. There was the faint, indefinable smell that comes from electricity in fervid activity. Not for the first time, I began to long for the shabby backstreets of Marinetown. We appeared to be going a long, long way down into the island's bedrock. How long had it taken my brother to construct this complex? Who had comprised his workforce?

I never did find out.

Eventually the steps ended, and I found I was in a blue-lit cavern, which, apart from a perfectly flat floor, looked natural in that its walls were simply corrugated masses of rock: Unshaped, undecorated. But everywhere I looked, there were machines: Squat or tall, wide or slim, but all made from the same dull, non-reflective black metal. There was a constant low hum filling the cavern; I'm sure some of its frequencies were in the infrasound band, as I could feel my skin begin to crawl and twitch.

Or was that just my sense of a growing unease at my grim surroundings?

Once again, Eleonora had joined my brother and had slipped an arm under his as she stared up into his face, with the adoring look a woman reserves for her true love.

Or so I believe; I've never seen one sent in my direction.

My mouth felt dry, but I was determined not to display my nervousness before this imposing pair.

'Why was it necessary for Eleonora to drive all this way?' I asked, for want of anything more intelligent to say. 'Why didn't you just teleport me here?'

He gave a slight nod of appreciation.

'An excellent question, little brother. I could indeed have done that, but my power is not infinite. My allies allow me to borrow some of theirs through temporary orifices in the Barrier, but they are very attentive accountants: I must justify every use I make of their energies. I can only use them when it is strictly necessary, and in your case, it definitely was not. And I wanted you to get to know my soulmate a little better, after all you've only recently met her. And there is so very much to know!'

'Charles,' Eleonora suddenly said, in a voice which was simultaneously melodious and amused, 'you've hurt me. Surely you're not saying you didn't enjoy my company, didn't appreciate being with me?'

I didn't know how to respond and just dumbly looked back and forth between my hosts. Had I upset them? Then Eleonora burst out laughing, crossed to me and gave a fleeting kiss on my forehead.

'Charles, you're priceless,' she said, between womanly giggles. 'Are you sure you're Edward's brother?'

But I had grown tired of her continual amusement at my shortcomings, and I pushed past, no longer caring if I annoyed her. I planted myself in front of Edward and stared at him. Then: 'I'm tired of these mysteries, this endless laughter at my expense. I think it's time you told me what the fuck is going on.' I swept my arm around, indicating the humming machines. 'You can start by telling me what all this junk is for!'

Edward did not seem annoyed at my outburst, but, looking over my shoulder, called, 'My darling, some wine for the three of us. We'll have the best this time, to placate our honoured guest.'

I looked at him in some amazement. Wine? I had heard of it, but of course I had never tasted or even seen it; the Vamps forbid any beverage likely to cause troublesome intoxication. Edward pointed to three chairs around a table, and he and I sat, awaiting his lover's return. Eleonora soon appeared, bearing a tray with three deep drinking vessels and a tall bottle, which was unpleasantly cobwebbed. She poured some of its contents into the vessels. I picked up mine, surprised at its heaviness, until I realised it was made of glass, not plastic. The liquid inside was a rich ruby colour which looked almost black in the bluish illumination in the cavern. I sniffed it, inhaling a warm, heady aroma. I was conscious that my companions were watching me with the air of scientists encountering a new species. Ignoring them, I sipped the wine, rolled it in my mouth and, finally, swallowed. Then in amazement, I looked back at them, my mouth wide open.

'It's good! Really good!'

Edward's smile was brief.

'For someone used only to the slop the Vamps allow you to have, it must be a taste of paradise.'

I took another, longer, mouthful, and, all at once, the world seemed a happier place; Edward and Eleonora took on the aspect of old friends I had finally been reunited with. The cavern was no longer a strange, forbidding place but a simple meeting place where reminiscences could be shared. I put my glass down, noticing it was nearly empty, and waited for Edward to speak. Eleonora was facing me, but the perpetual look of suppressed laughter had gone, and her face was calm and serious.

Reluctantly, I moved my gaze from Eleonora to her lover. He also bore a solemn expression, as if the next few minutes were ones in which important issues would be settled, and that the time for frivolities was long gone.

I looked into his eyes, trying to go beyond the superficial Edward and into his core.

'Speak,' I said.

He spoke.

THIRTY THREE

"The Vamps realised early on that my brain was unusual compared to the usual run of humans and that I would almost certainly have an aptitude for science and mathematics. My days in the orphanage were a nightmare as they tried to cram as much knowledge into my developing mind as humanly possible—or, in their case—as inhumanly possible. Why was I chosen? Vamp science has ossified over the centuries, millennia even. They are trapped in an intellectual rut, and it was thought that a few carefully selected humans might supply a totally new way of looking at problems. You see, they had a great civilisation thousands of years ago, and they had used their knowledge to examine the complexities of space and time. They discovered many things which human beings—even at the height of their science—did not. They learned that our Universe is simply a segment of a larger one. What do I mean by a segment? A circle is a segment of a sphere; we can even think of a sphere as an infinite collection of circles of different radii. So it is with us. Our Three-Dimensional Universe is one of an endless collection of segments of a greater Four-Dimensional realm of existence. And by "dimension", I am talking of spatial dimensions, such as our "up"/ "down."

'They were overjoyed at their discovery and developed techniques for viewing the other segments. It so happens that our universe lies near the midpoint of the Four-Dimensional configuration and thus is one of the larger ones. Because of this, it became of interest to the creatures who inhabit the whole Four-Dimensional structure. Normally, the chances of those creatures being involved with any given segment are close to zero, as there are an infinite number of them. But the Vamps' explorations in the greater universe were like a beacon shining in the darkness and drew other minds, other intelligences, to them.

'These entities announced themselves to the astounded Vamps as the "Old Gods", but I do not like that term, as I do not believe they are supernatural. I use the term "Vetusians", from the Latin for "old." However, despite their great intelligence, the Vetusians are not benign, and they demanded worship from the Vamps; a religion which involved a great deal of sacrificial offerings. Of young vampires, that is.

'And so the Vamps immediately withdrew from their explorations and hoped the infinities of the Four-Dimensional Universe would hide them. But it soon became apparent that having been found once, they could not be lost. And so the Vetusians began introducing their rites and practices in this Universe, and began turning the Vamps into beasts of the field, helpless beings to be changed into nothing but playthings and foodstuff. But the Vamps were at the height of their power, and using their sciences, an elite group working deep underground created a Barrier which prevented any more Vetusians from entering our world. Those trapped on our side of the Barrier were slaughtered, for they are not gods but mortal creatures once they enter our 3D world and have to adjust to our physical constraints.

'But the Vetusians are not so easily thwarted. Time has a different flow in the 4D Universe, and they can control it so that an age here is but a second there. Unused to defeat, they chipped away at the Barrier, finding and enlarging chinks and hollows until they broke through and unleashed the greatest of all wars on the Vamps. Human beings had evolved by then, but were seen by the Vamps only as imperfect and disposable copies of themselves. But they had one use: Their blood was very nutritious and helped extend health and vigour to the very end of the Vamps' long lifespans. And we have been their prey ever since.

'And so our ancestors saw the last great war, saw the terrible sacrifices that the Vetusians inflicted on their captives. And they did what the vampires had refused to do: They worshipped the Vetusians and accepted them as gods. The Vetusians ignored them; pitiful creatures as they were, they were of no interest to the invaders. But the humans wanted to worship; *needed* to worship. And that need has been with us ever since. The invaders are at the root of all the earliest polytheistic religions, such as the Annunaki of Mesopotamia. However, the Vetusians' greatest influence, and the site of their eventual defeat, was in Mesoamerica, and here they are seen the most clearly. Very accurate memories were passed down through the Olmecs, and the Toltecs, to the Mexica, vulgarly known as the Aztecs. And like little children imitating the behaviour of adults, these people sought to recapture the magic and power of the Vetusians, copying, without the slightest understanding, the blood-soaked practices they witnessed from their hiding places.

'And so the most recent incursion was driven off, but the effort destroyed vampire civilisation. They lost their control of humanity and were driven into a marginalised existence; hiding in the shadows, taking their life-sustaining sustenance from the occasional human they could catch, and forced to watch humanity develop science and technology and, seemingly, master the world.

'It is true they summoned sufficient strength when human madness threatened to destroy the world to re-emerge and seize control, but their civilisation now is a pale shadow of what they once had. And they know now that the Barrier can be breached. If it could be done once, it can be done again. And they are afraid. And that fear saps them of their energy, prevents them from planning for the future; a future which could be snatched away from them at any moment. There is not a single second when they are not studying the Barrier, waiting for it to be punctured and their nemeses to pour through. And they know that the next time there will be no last-minute reprieve, no famous victory. Under renewed Vetusian control, their position will be worse than what humans now enjoy under Vampire control. Because the Old Gods are indeed jealous gods, and vengeance is assuredly theirs.'

Edward paused, looking at both me and Eleonora. I took a quick glance at her: Her eyes were wide open and seemed to shine; her bosom was heaving and her breath coming in brief, sharp pants as if she were in the throes of orgasm.

But Edward addressed me again.

'And so I was one of their desperate experiments; I was moulded to nurture my scientific aptitude, perhaps to notice something, some weapon, some shield, they had overlooked.'

I had a strange feeling then: It felt as if his words had unlocked a door in my brain which had been shut a long time ago; a door which was stubbornly resisting opening, grinding slowly on rusting hinges which had not turned in an age. Suddenly, I realised I was leaping ahead of his explanations; understanding the need for concepts which he was yet to mention.

'And these flashes of purple light, people disappearing before my eyes. This—teleportation. It's to do with the four spatial dimensions, isn't it?'

A look of surprise mingled with great satisfaction burst onto his rugged features.

'Yes, Charlie, yes! A Four-Dimensional being can pass around any Three-Dimensional obstruction, just as you could remove an object from inside a circle–which a Two-Dimensional being could not. No walls could hold them out; no chains could hold them in. And I have borrowed some of their energies to perform those parlour tricks. I rotate the object through the fourth dimension and then return it to this framework. From the viewpoint of a Three-Dimensional being, the object simply disappears and then reappears.'

Understanding was flooding into me like a hot tide, coming from I knew not where—I was a flatfoot, for God's sake!

'So the Barrier must be a Four-Dimensional construct, otherwise it would be no Barrier.' More ideas and questions rose into my conscious mind, like bubbles disturbing the surface of a hitherto still pool. 'But the energy to create such a structure. It must be colossal. How is it done? There must be a power source—where is it?'

But he held up a hand, palm towards me.

'Slow down, Charlie. You don't have to work all this out for yourself; I will explain it all to you. All in good time.'

But my surge of comprehension was not done.

'And the destruction of the Diodati Institute. That was not the result of your ridiculous hobby—The Sons of Man. The survivors said the Vamps were attacked by—creatures. Creatures like men—but not men.' I paused, unsure whether I wanted to utter the next sentence. 'Those creatures were the Vetusians—the Old Gods—weren't they?'

I heard a sudden intake of breath from my female companion. Then she addressed Edward.

'He is close, Edward, very close.'

'He is indeed,' my brother replied, and then returned to me. 'Yes, Charlie, they were. Because the Barrier is failing, they can enter our world, but only temporarily. It takes vast amounts of energy to force their way through even a weakened Barrier, and so their stay cannot be long. But they want to show the Vamps what is coming, what they have to face. Perhaps they do it to demoralise their victims, to weaken their resolve. I help them enter, but I do not claim to know all their thoughts.'

I mused over this gibberish for a while. Then: 'The Barrier needs a great deal of energy. And so must your explorations beyond it. So why haven't the Vamps found you? Why haven't they traced you by...' I hesitated for a moment before the phrase came to me, '...by your *heat signature?*

He nodded, and I knew he was approving of my newfound eloquence. Yet deep within me, I heard a voice. And that voice was saying *Not now. It is too soon.*

'Yes, very good, Charlie, very good indeed. Let's look at my machines, shall we?'

He pointed further into the cavern, and we moved in that direction. I was soon surrounded by banks of tall, softly humming machines, each bearing rows of coloured lights pulsing against their deep black backgrounds, as if they represented the beating of electronic hearts. Eventually, we came to the largest machine of all, a tall tower of jet darkness, bearing what looked to be a huge television screen at head height. But it was dead and grey, appearing simply as a featureless, nondescript rectangle. Edward moved to it, and turned to face us.

'All these machines are powered by a small fusion reactor, a kilometre below us. The excess heat which concerned you, Charlie, and also the excess helium and neutrons, which you didn't mention, are simply dumped beyond the Barrier into the Four-Dimensional continuum. There's plenty of space out there.' He laughed, looking at Eleonora. 'An infinite amount, in fact!'

She gave a throaty, but maddeningly melodious, chuckle at Edward's words, leaving me annoyed at being treated as Country Cousin again. I tried to seize the initiative from the mocking pair.

'So there's nothing to give you away. No excess heat to be detected by the Vamps.'

'Precisely. I have sat here like an invisible spider, spinning my webs to entrap them, to wrap them in unbreakable threads and hand them over, bound into neat little parcels, to their cruel masters.'

But I found myself repelled by his words, his joy in misery. I decided to speak up.

'But why, Edward? Why do these—Vetusians—want to inflict sufferings on the creatures they find in 3D space? Our universe can't be the only one they have visited, if, as you say, there are an infinite number of them. They must be able to exist without our kind of life, so why bring terror and pain to this world?'

'Because that is their life, their whole being, their essence. They do not simply war on the weak things they find in the lower orders of space, but on each other. They live in a constant state of war, Vetusians against Vetusians. One group will overthrow the others and rule. But instantly, the other groups combine and overthrow them. And so on, for ever and ever. They live for conflict, for war, for the ecstasy of conquest, of victory.'

I was disgusted and showed it.

'That's vile. Horrible.'

But Eleonora was beside me, holding my arm, looking up at me, her eyes shining with an insatiable lust.

'Don't speak as a child, Charles. You must accept the world the way it is. You cannot change it, so become part of it. Experience the joy of conquest, of power, for yourself, learn the ineffable pleasure of throwing down your enemies and trampling on their faces, their hopes. Once you have tasted it, you will never give it up.' She threw her head back as she laughed. 'Never!'

I felt sick, but strove to remain calm, even as fear grew into certainty I had strayed into a torture chamber with a mad man and a mad woman as captors.

'The Vamps do not deserve this. Yes, they destroyed our societies, but they saved the world, and us in it! Doesn't that mean they deserve our respect? If they hadn't taken over, what would the world be now—a radioactive wasteland, that's what!'

Eleonora stroked my cheek with long, cool fingers; I felt the sharp scarlet nails lightly graze my stubble.

'Charles, Charles, you poor baby, have you forgotten the Blood Farms?'

'Alright!' I snapped. 'No one says they're wonderful, but most are well-run. There's always a human in charge, not a Vamp!'

'Gilroy's Farm?' Edward said gently.

'OK, that was bad, but you can't judge them all by the actions of one piece of shit. Edward, what are you doing? Stop and think, man! If you let these monsters in—what will become of you?' I turned to his inamorata, ignoring her obvious contempt. 'And your woman—what will happen to her?'

Edward came towards us, shaking his head in pity.

'Very simple. We shall be King and Queen of the world, exulting in endless revenge against our enemies.'

THIRTY FOUR

Horror took me, but there was no way out; I couldn't just say "Well, thanks for having me" and walk away. Even if I could, I was trapped on this damn island. I had to make them see the madness in their words. Maybe even the madness in themselves.

'Aren't you missing something?' I said, addressing the pair of them. 'These "creatures" you intend to bring into the world, why would they stop at terrorising the Vamps? Surely when they've had their fun, they'll move on to you and me. And Eleonora,' I added, pointedly.

'Oh no,' Eleonora said. 'They have promised us our status as King and Queen. Charles, we humans are too *vin ordinaire* for palates such as theirs. Why should they move on to the lower orders? They will not exterminate the Vamps, for what would be the point of being a predator when there is no prey? You see, they will let them live, if you could call it living. They will toy with them, promising to leave this Universe if they simply up the supply of sacrificial victims—temporarily, of course. Occasionally, they will allow Vamp uprisings to occur. They will pretend to be on the verge of defeat, appear to be about to abandon this world—and then return in power and wrath. It will never end; they will never be satisfied.'

I glanced at Edward: He was smiling down at his partner, his face wreathed in smiles of pride, of love, over her speech. I felt sick.

'You're insane! The two of you!' I yelled. 'What are you—children? You really believe they would keep such a ridiculous promise to you dupes! You are lambs to the slaughter, lambs who'll take the rest of us into the slaughterhouse with you!'

Edward approached me, one mighty hand balled into a fist. One blow from that fist would probably kill me, I thought.

'Careful, Charlie. Brother you may be, but I won't stand by while you insult my Queen.' He waved the fist in front of me. 'Do I make myself clear?'

I said nothing until he had withdrawn the fist.

'Why did you bring me here?' I finally said. 'What do you want from me?'

For reply, Edward indicated two couches side by side.

'Sit,' he said in commanding tones. 'You have angered me, Charlie, so tread carefully from this moment onwards.'

I made no reply, but did as he ordered. They sat on the other couch, turning it partially sideways so they could study me.

'So, have you come to your senses yet?' he demanded.

No answer.

He shook his head in the manner of someone whose trusted friend had just let him down. Badly.

'Charlie, Charlie, I brought you here so you could join Eleonora and me in the great crusade against the Vamps. To finally lift their fangs from human throats.'

I glared at him, wondering if I was living the last minutes of my life. One blow from that fist…

'I want that too, but not in your way. Not at the expense of such horror. And I don't share your childlike trust in these "allies" of yours. Once you let them in, how will you control them? They must have vast power; power, I'm sure, that's greater than yours.'

'So what do you want, Charles?' Eleonora interrupted. 'Some kind of peace with the vampires? A peace on their terms? Endless subjugation?'

I stared at my hands. Perhaps if I humoured them they would let me go; if I pretended I believed in their sick fantasies.

'I don't know. All I know is your way can't be the right one. Even if I accepted the need for all these horrors you think are fine, the dangers are immense from your crazy plans. Why can't you see that?'

Edward threw up his hands and looked at his lover.

'I give up. Perhaps I've missed something; he can't be my brother.'

Eleonora smiled gently and stroked his hair.

'It's hard for you, my darling, to see what kind of man he is. It is a terrible disappointment for you, I know. But after all,' and she threw a glance at me from under immaculate eyebrows, 'it's not as if you have that much in common with the humans.'

I noticed her odd phraseology, delivered in arch tones, but I could not interpret her soft-spoken words.

But Edward did not appear to have noticed her peculiar wording, and merely nodded.

'You're wiser than I, my love; you are not misled by false hopes.' He looked directly at me. 'No, he is no use to me as he is.'

Suddenly, there was a whirring noise from beneath me, and steel hoops emerged from the sides of the couch, imprisoning me in an unbreakable grasp.

'Edward, what is this?' I gasped. 'What are you doing?'

He crossed to me and looked down, his face suffused with pity.

'I had hoped you would join us without this. That we three would go forward as one splendid unit, to wreak vengeance on those who abused us. But you need to meet those whose powers of persuasion are greater than mine.'

A terrible dread swept through me, and I felt my whole body go suddenly cold and rigid.

'What do you mean, for God's sake?'

He shook his head slowly.

'This is for the best, Charlie: You must meet the Old Gods.'

Blind terror seized me! I knew what those things were like from my nightmares, and the idea of meeting them in reality turned me into a raving madman, pulling at the steel bands with bloodied hands, straining up in a futile attempt to break through.

And yes—at the end, I was begging, pleading with my brother to release me.

He stood over me like a torturer from the Inquisition, shaking his head at my weakness, my abject willingness to confess my heresy.

'You must do it, Charlie. When you have met them, you will be like me. You will understand what has to be done. And you will help me do it.'

Eleonora joined him and gently placed scarlet lips on my cheek.

'Don't worry, Charles. You will be fine. Everything will be fine.'

They had rotated the couch so I was now facing the large TV-type screen. I had to lift my head against the pressure of the bands to see it, but I was in time to see the screen begin to glow with the sepulchral green light I had seen before and had never wanted to see again. The funereal light grew stronger and drowned out the bluish illumination of the cavern. Details of my surroundings became blurred and vague. And then vanished utterly.

Almost immediately, the steel bands retracted into the interior of the couch and I could stand again. I gave an involuntary gasp, for my surroundings had become bitterly cold. And I was also trembling violently—but not with the cold.

Once again I was surrounded by green mist, which seeped out of the ground and formed slow-whirling sheets around me. I could just make out vague, indeterminate shapes hidden in those swirls; things that moved slowly and awkwardly but never approached or retreated. But I knew they were watching me because occasionally a small area of the mist would part, and I would see two phosphorescent discs pointing in my direction. I looked behind me, around me, searching for a way to return to the cavern, but it had vanished totally; disappeared as if it had never existed.

And then, a larger gap appeared in the veil and something emerged through the opening and slowly approached, giving me plenty of time to study it.

The thing slowly approaching had no face above its blood-splattered bones, for it was a walking skeleton. Instead of a face, there was only a fleshless skull, but one which bore rolling eyeballs in its sockets. And there were more eyeballs in the vile necklace hanging halfway down its open chest. There came a voice, the voice of the endless night.

'I am Mictlantecuhtli, Lord of The Land Of Death, god of slaughter, darkness. We have met before, but then I was merely an image, a phantom, a dream. But now you are in my realm and stand before me, flesh and bone. You are here, and you and I are real.' It came close, so its skull-face was centimetres from mine and its foul, charnel-house breath washed over me. 'I am as real as you, Gray. Feel my reality.' And it placed a skeletal hand on my shoulder and squeezed the flesh between two fingers of bone.

It saw my reaction and, had it had lips I'm sure it would have laughed. But I thought of Eleonora's words to me—*You will be fine*. Surely, she would not have lied? And so I faced the creature, trying to calm my treacherous muscles.

'What do you want?'

'I want little, Charles Gray. No need to act surprised; of course, I know your name, I know everything. I know you are the brother of our ally in your trivial Three-Dimensional world, and he wants you to join forces with him. But there is something about you that is hidden, I think, Shadfly. Should I call you a shadfly, I wonder? What is it that is hidden from me? Are your wants so different from your brother's? Let me examine you.'

And it came even closer and placed its hands on either side of my head. It was now so close I could see into the skull's eye sockets.

They were now empty.

'Give me your mind, Gray. Open up to me. I want to see your history, how you were formed, what made you who you are today. Give all those things to me—NOW!'

Suddenly, a bright light filled my eyes with a sting like acid, and it felt as if my interrogator's bony fingers had penetrated the bone and sunk into my brain.

'Give me all you know, Gray. There is something about you which is at present beyond my understanding, and that I cannot tolerate. Show yourself to me. I, Mictlantecuhtli, command it!'

The pressure of its hands increased until I thought my head would burst open like an over-ripe pomegranate, but then I began to see images and the pressure decreased, or, perhaps, my attention was distracted. I saw a face looking down at me as I lay in some kind of box. I saw my legs, but they looked different. They were very pink and had rolls of fat. And I was making kicking motions, although there was nothing to kick. And I then realised the box was a cot, and I had just been born. The face must be my mother's—but why did she look like Eleonora?

Or Serafina?

The scene shifted, and I realised that time had passed. And, with a sick feeling, I understood I was now in the orphanage, and being held down by two men, while a third was sticking something in my arm. I realised it was a medical needle, and as the plunger was withdrawn, I saw the cylinder fill with a bright red liquid I knew to be my blood. I was kicking again, but this time with a frenzied need to escape from those holding me down.

Mictlantecuhtli's bitter voice intruded on my visions.

'This is significant. *Methylation*. Why is that process so important? I must know.'

Although I had never heard the term before, somehow I knew my eldritch captor must not learn more about methylation. Whatever it took, the secret must not be revealed! Somehow I knew how to shut off the creature's observations, and I drew a curtain across the image, a curtain of blackness that could not be penetrated. Mictlantecuhtli gave a howl of anger, like a predator whose prey had just been snatched away.

'You will not defy me, Gray. No living creature in this domain may defy me!'

I felt the pressure again, like to compress my head to nothingness between its skeletal hands. I collapsed onto one knee, my head bowed, but the compressing hands did not release me. Instead, the creature bent forward to keep its face near to mine.

'I am in your brain, Gray, deep inside your wet tissue. I see the neurons, the ganglia, the synapses. I can detect the little sparks of electricity at those junctions. There is no escape. I will break you, Gray, break you down into the revolting compounds which comprise your being. Do you understand—I will break you!'

I understood that its mental hands were pulling at the veil I had drawn, trying to pull it away or, if that failed, to rip it to shreds. But I knew—and I still did not know how I knew—that nothing was more important than holding its empty eye sockets away from the secret I had hidden! The pressure increased, and I felt my consciousness and my sanity itself slipping away; I was sliding into a pit of nothingness from which I would not emerge.

Then, abruptly, the pressure disappeared. I felt the hands pull away from my temples and, shakingly, I rose to my feet. Mictlantecuhtli had moved away, but was staring at me. I noticed bloodshot, glaring eyeballs had reappeared in the sockets, and the gaze they projected was full of hate.

And bemusement.

'You blocked me. I could not penetrate the shield you had thrown up. But that only means the concept I discovered must be vitally important. And so, I must return with increased power to discover what it is you do not want me to know. I must call for assistance.'

It turned away from me but, even as it moved, there was a peculiar tremor in the air and the ground. The green mists swirled and rolled in a crazy tumult. It turned to look at me again, its eyes blazing with frustrated rage.

'My ally's power is fading. You can no longer be held here in my Universe.' It pointed a white index finger at me. 'But I will command him to return you here as soon as his power has reached the necessary level. And when you return, I will not be alone. My terrible Lord, Tezcatlipoca, the Smoking Mirror, will be with me. The two of us will unleash such power that nothing in our Universe, or yours, could resist or deflect. You will be broken, Gray, of that you may be assured, broken beyond any hope of redemption.'

I saw its vile form fading, becoming translucent and then transparent. The green light vanished, and I was back in the blue glow of Edward's cavern.

THIRTY FIVE

It was strange: I had been very ill at ease, verging on stark fear, in Edward's cavern, but now it felt like the Gardens of Paradise as the final vestiges of the clinging green mist of the Old Gods disappeared and I was bathed in the cold blue light of his redoubt. On my reappearance, I was still encased in the steel bands, but they retracted as soon as I saw my erstwhile hosts, and they helped me to my feet with apparent kindness.

Edward's eyes were gleaming: Apparently he expected great news from me.

'Well, who did you see—was it Tezcatlipoca himself?'

I straightened my spine and stared at him. After what I had seen and endured, he no longer appeared such a threat. Indeed, he seemed almost childlike compared to the monstrosity which had tortured me.

'No, it was not. And I don't want to discuss it.' I looked in the direction in which we had entered. 'I think I would like to leave now.'

He looked puzzled, almost mystified.

'Leave? Why would you want to do that? Surely you can see the rightness of our cause? They must have explained it to you.' He looked at Eleonora as if she could break the enigma, but she could not.

'Are you going to let me go, Edward?' I asked, in tones which I trusted showed I was not really making a request. 'I've seen enough here and I don't want to see any more of your madness. Or your repulsive friends.'

Edward's bemusement was almost comical, and he no longer looked like the all-knowing Alpha Male I had seen previously. He shook his head as if to clear it.

'Something is wrong here, seriously wrong.' He turned and snapped at Eleonora. 'Are you sure you input the right parameters?'

She stood her ground, unmoved.

'Of course. I know what I'm doing, Edward.'

He turned to me and raised a finger accusingly; his mouth opened to speak. Then, abruptly, his face went blank, and he became immobile, apart from his lips which moved silently. I got the feeling he was repeating somebody else's words. Then he regained control over his muscles and looked at me with an expression which was a strange amalgam of amazement, horror, and anger. When his voice returned, it was a hoarse whisper, like a pious man forced to utter hateful obscenities.

'You defied Mictlantecuhtli,' he said, uttering the words with strange gaps between them as if he were using a language he was not familiar with. 'You defied Mictlantecuhtli!'

'I did. Can I go now?'

But Edward was not a man to remain confused for long. He did not reply with words but sank his fist into my soft belly and then, as I doubled over, straightened me with an uppercut. The world went dark for an unknown period and when I came to, my mouth was full of blood and I was back on the couch, once more imprisoned by the steel bands. Edward had not noticed I had recovered and was in conversation with his lover.

'They are as baffled as I am, but one thing is certain, they want him back as soon as I can build up enough power to transfer him again.'

'When will that be?'

'Not for some time; I hadn't expected to do it again so soon. This is bad, very bad. They're angry—angry with me, for God's sake, as if I've tricked them!'

'Surely not,' Eleonora said and, even in my dazed state, I could hear the fear in her voice. 'The problem is with Gray—not with what you told them!'

Edward did not reply directly, but turning away, he paced back and forth in front of her.

'How did it happen? How *could* it happen? He's just my goddamn brother, no more, no less. I didn't defy them; I didn't want to defy them! How could he? Why would he want to?'

Eleonora crossed to her distraught partner.

'Maybe we need to apply more pressure; break down whatever mental shield he's managed to set up— Edward, look at me, for God's sake! We planned for some problem there might be with him; not like this, of course, but the plan is still valid. Do it, man, do it!'

Edward stopped pacing and stared at Eleonora.

'Yes, they might allow me to try that. I'll have to reason with them.'

Bur Eleonora was looking past him.

'Edward,' she said gently, 'Gray is awake.'

Almost instantly, he stood over me, his face suffused with anger.

'You have caused me a great deal of trouble. They have made that perfectly clear.' He raised a mighty fist. 'I ought to beat you to a pulp, Charlie!'

'Or you could just let me go,' I mumbled through split lips.

'I think not. You've raised a lot of issues during your brief visit here. I can't let you back into the Vamp world until I know the answers. And,' he added, lowering the fist with obvious reluctance, 'depending on the answers, I might not let you back at all.' He pressed something on the side of the couch and the bands retracted. 'Get up.'

I swung my feet onto the floor but remained sitting, staring at my brother with what I hoped was a look of defiance.

'I need time to build up the necessary energies,' he snarled. 'When I've gotten them back, I'll either return you to the Vetusians, or take Eleonora's advice. It all depends on what they say about you. Breaking you with brute force might end your usefulness—assuming you have any. You see, Charlie,' he continued, as he jerked me to my feet, 'it was sentimentality, brotherly love, if you like, that made me try to recruit you into the crusade, but it looks like you might be more trouble than you're worth. But it seems the Vetusians don't quite understand you, and they don't like things they don't understand. Either way, you stay here until these problems you've caused are rectified.'

He first pulled me and then pushed me into a dark corner of the cavern. There was a rectangular window and a metal door in the wall. He pulled the door open, almost threw me inside, and followed me in.

'You'll stay here until I build enough power for my next actions.' He pointed to a long couch against the inner wall. 'Get some rest on that; you'll be needing it. Oh,' and he smiled, a wolfish smile, 'don't worry: There are no restraints hidden in this one.'

With that, the door thudded shut, leaving me alone in semi-darkness. For want of anything else to do, I stretched out on the couch, feeling it lurch under my weight as one of its legs almost gave way. Thoughts tumbled past each other in a chaotic tumult. But in the end, they all reached the same conclusion: I was helpless and completely at Edward's mercy, assuming he had any. I had failed the test of joining him in the violent destruction of the Vamp world, and in his eyes, there was no greater crime. I fell asleep for a few minutes, but when I awoke, I was still a powerless prisoner of a madman, locked in a cell in an underground chamber. I now realised that, brother or no brother, Edward was quite capable of killing me; with his bare hands, if necessary.

Or perhaps without any need—just for his pleasure.

Time dragged past, seconds devoid of anything other than a lurking fear of what would happen to me.

Occasionally, I heard their voices as they happened to pass close to my cell on some task or other, but usually, there was just the all-pervading hum of his mysterious machines. And there was a gnawing, ever-growing, all pervading terror taking hold—the Vetusians were no fantasy. They were real.

And infinitely dangerous.

Once again I slept, although this time I was sure it was only for an even shorter time. I could hear them speaking to each other, and their voices were excited, expectant. I rose and, crossing to the door, pressed my ear against the cold steel, but I still could not make out what they were saying. A silence fell, broken only by the maddening rhythm of the machines. But then, the hum became an electronic scream, and there was a brief flash of violet-purple light. And then something strange—a female shout or cry.

A female shouting or crying.

But not Eleonora. Similar. But not the same.

After a few more minutes, I saw Edward's bulky form pass the window, and the door was flung open.

'Please accompany me, Charlie. Eleonora suggested we ask a new guest to entertain us. I'm sure you'll be pleased to meet her, or, rather, to reacquaint yourselves.'

I followed him, moving slowly and hesitantly like a dog that has been disciplined by its master. And out in the cavern, I saw what I had feared I would see— Serafina, lying on the treacherous couch, imprisoned by the steel hoops. She saw me and yelled, 'Sarge, help! Get me out of here!'

I hung my head. What could I do? I couldn't save myself, let alone anybody else. Eleonora came up to me, gloating, triumphant.

'Remember how Edward said you could have been teleported here if you'd been important enough? Well, your little friend at the moment is quite important, and so Edward needed to teleport her here.' She reached for my hand and pulled me towards the couch. 'Come, let's look at her, shall we?'

We crossed to the couch, and I looked down at my distraught subordinate. She could only move her head slightly, and I will never forget the pleading look on her face.

'Sarge, get me out of here, for God's sake! How did I get here!'

I shook my head and whispered, 'Sorry, I'm so sorry. I'm trapped here too. I'm sorry.'

I looked away from her to Eleonora, who was leaning over Serafina with a hungry look on her face. It was the first time I had seen the two of them together, and although they looked incredibly similar, their expressions would have told them apart even if their hairstyles hadn't. Eleonora nearly always bore a look of contemptuous condescension, but even that had gone now, replaced with an even worse look of lustful enjoyment.

Edward joined us, and together we three looked silently down on the squirming captive. Then she lay still, and I could see the gleam of tears forming in the corners of her eyes. He turned to me.

'Now, Charlie, you have a choice. You can put away your childish, petulant, refusal to join us and, once you have proved your loyalty, both you and your friend here will be released back into the outside world to do our bidding. But you must decide now.'

'Or what?' I said, daring to look at Serafina again, knowing I'd failed her.

To my horror, he bent over her and stroked her hair before kissing her gently on the lips. He straightened.

'Or I send her into the Four-Dimensional realm where she will be interrogated by Tezcatlipoca himself.'

I heard her scream.

'No, please, no. Not the Old Gods!'

I looked at her and then at my brother. Eleonora, I knew, was standing behind me, no doubt smiling at my agony. I thought of the Vamps and their power over humans; I thought of the Blood Farms; I thought of the despair and decline in Marinetown.

And knew I could not join Edward. There were worse things than the Vamps, and he was determined to let those things in.

'I am not joining you, Edward.'

I did not look at Serafina, but I heard her scream.

Edward shook his head.

'Charlie, Charlie, what a disappointment you are.' He looked at Eleonora. 'Do it!'

She moved towards the machine with the huge screen and did something on its control panel. I felt Edward's strong fingers on my shoulders, and he spun me around to face the couch.

'Look at her, Charlie; see how terrified she is. Tezcatlipoca is so looking forward to meeting her!'

Then a beam of the violet-purple light I was now so familiar with flashed out from the screen and enveloped the couch and its now-motionless occupant. Something strange began to happen: The couch and Serafina became translucent, insubstantial, and then transparent, as if made from the finest glass. Then they both faded away, leaving no trace behind. The violet-purple beam snapped off and I knew my Deputy was in the other world, face to face with Tezcatlipoca.

It was all my fault.

But then, a peculiar, extraneous thought came to me. How did Serafina know about the Old Gods?

THIRTY SIX

I don't know how long Serafina was in the Four-Dimensional Universe: Edward had already told me time was mutable in that weird existence. From Serafina's point of view, she might have been interrogated by Tezcatlipoca for ten minutes—or ten years. I hoped and prayed it was not the latter. Edward and his consort said nothing to me; Eleonora did not even bother to gloat or mock. Edward busied himself with studying the instruments on his various machines, while she simply came and went; whence I knew not.

But then I saw Edward lift his head from studying the readouts and turn to stare at the great screen. I yearned to know that Serafina had been released from her torment, whether long or brief.

And so she had been. I saw the unbelievable process that had sent her there repeat, but this time in reverse, and then a fully restored flesh and blood Serafina was back in the dreadful cavern.

But it was not the same Serafina who had been taken from me: Her eyes were wide open and staring glassily into space, her fingers were crooked into scrabbling claws and threads of drool were hanging from her chin. Her head was jerking back and forth like a badly controlled marionette, and she was screaming 'No!', over and over. For a few moments, anger and hatred for my brother overcame my common sense and yelling something, I lunged at him in a berserk frenzy. But he was still the same Edward who had bested me earlier, and my arms were soon locked in his iron grip.

'Now, now, Charlie,' he said, with a contemptuous grin, 'don't you want to welcome your associate back to the land of the living?' And with that, he thrust me in Serafina's direction.

I saw the imprisoning bands pull away from her and, instinctively, I pulled her to me, stroking her hair, kissing her fevered cheeks. For reply, she gabbled meaningless syllables, still tossing her head from side to side.

'Leave her be, Charlie,' came Edward's imperious voice. 'It'll take a while for her to come round.'

I spun around to glare at him.

'What kind of monster would do this to an innocent woman! You're as much of a monster as those fiends are! How could we have had the same mother?'

Edward shrugged.

'You know, I've been wondering the exact same thing myself.'

Eleonora suddenly joined us and helped a still gibbering Serafina to her feet and took her to another part of the cavern. I watched Eleonora drop her unresisting captive into an easy chair and then offer her a drink of something.

'You know Tezcatlipoca will kill her next time, don't you, Charlie?' Edward remarked conversationally as he joined me in watching the two women. 'The Vetusians are not known for their patience. Or their loving-kindness. And they are very keen to renew their acquaintance with you.'

I did not look at him but, in a low voice, I said, 'What do you want of me?'

'Not much—now. I wanted you to join with me, out of brotherly love, of course, but I'm starting to think you're really not up to it. You would probably be a hindrance to me. I'd spend most of my time checking to see if you're attempting some childish act of sabotage.' Once again, his heavy hand grasped my shoulder. 'Look at me when I'm speaking, Charlie. Don't you know it's rude to ignore someone?' I obeyed, and he continued, 'You must understand that the Vetusians will win, must win, whatever the Vamps do. Sure, I'm helping them a great deal, but, sooner or later, they will find a way through the Barrier with their own intelligence. And they are very intelligent. If it takes ten thousand of our years, what is that to them? So I'm making one last appeal to your common sense, Charlie; join the winning side for once in your life. Once the Vamps have been converted into food animals, we will be sitting pretty as the Old Gods' representatives on Earth. We will have power that no Terrestrial creature has ever had before; power to make Genghis Khan look like a happy little kindergarten toddler. And why should it end? With the knowledge of the Vetusians, we will keep our bodies as they are now, or even rewind the clock a few decades—which will be necessary in your case. There will be an eternity for us to explore the boundaries of existence, to experience every pleasure, no matter how forbidden by fools. And think of the women!'

'Eleonora would be interested to hear you say that,' I said, unwisely.

He struck me across the mouth.

'I was thinking of you, you simpleton! Now, one last chance: Decide now whether to join me. On one side, unlimited power and pleasure, on the other; well, on the other—simply death at my hands.'

I wiped the blood from the reopened cuts on my lips and said, 'Let me speak to Serafina.'

He nodded.

'OK. Let's see how she feels.'

Serafina looked up as I stood before her. Was that hatred smouldering in her eyes, hatred of me because I had allowed my brother to send her into the Hell of the Old Gods? It seemed it was.

'You let him send me into that creature's grasp, Sarge! You could have stopped him, but you let him do it! I hate you, I hate you!'

She leapt from the chair, clawed hands reaching for my eyes, but Eleonora seized her and forced her back down.

'I'm sorry, Serafina,' I mumbled. 'But it's Edward you should be blaming, not me. I'm as helpless as you are.'

She ignored my apology and stared at her twisting, interlocked hands.

'The things that monster said. The things he made me see. The things he did to me.' Her blazing eyes looked back at me. 'I will hate you forever, Gray! Do you hear me—forever!'

'I...' I began, but she spat at me and turned away.

Edward patted me on the shoulder and, in what was almost a sympathetic tone, said, 'This is to be expected. It's not wise to be an enemy of the Vetusians, Charlie.' Then, in a brisker voice, he continued, 'We'll put them in the same cell, Eleonora. That way, Charlie can listen to her pointing out his shortcomings.'

But Eleonora looked concerned.

'Is that a good idea, Edward? To have them close together at the climax of our struggle; it might be unwise.'

He laughed.

'Eleonora! What a worrier you are! Two broken specimens of humanity. The only threat they pose is to each other.' He shot her an interrogatory stare. 'Why would having the two of them in close proximity be a danger? Explain yourself.'

But she looked away.

'I cannot.'

Edward shrugged, and, a few minutes later, Serafina and I were thrown into the cell I had recently quitted.

I sat as far away as possible from her, afraid of what I might have to do to defend myself.

But then she stood, crossed to the window, and spent some time looking out. When she turned to me, I was astounded by what I saw.

Suddenly she was taller, straighter, her face composed, resolute. It was as if some other controlling mind had entered her body.

God help me—she looked like Eleonora!

She looked me full in the face, her eyes holding me in some kind of enthralled trance.

'If they look in, I will attack you, Gray, but don't take it personally.'

THIRTY SEVEN

I stared at Serafina with blank incomprehension. She had just returned from being interrogated, or more likely tortured, by a fiendish Otherworld creature, and she was acting as if nothing had happened. 'Serafina!' I gasped, 'how are you…what has…'

She turned from the window and, instead of looking at me, directed her gaze to all parts of our cell.

'No sign of any listening devices, even allowing for advanced miniaturisation. We're in the clear.' At last, she dropped her gaze to me, smiled, and said, 'I hope I didn't upset you too much back there. But I played my part well, didn't I? Maybe those humans did get something right with all their plays and TV dramas. I've missed my opportunity, I guess.'

I continued to stare at her, dumbfounded. My chin hadn't hit the floor, but it sure felt like it had.

'Serafina,' I eventually managed to utter, 'what the hell is going on? You wanted to kill me a few minutes ago.'

She sat next to me and enfolded my hands in hers.

'I don't know how much time there is for explanations. We've got to get out of here as soon as we can.'

'Tezcatlipoca?' I prompted.

'Oh, yes, *it*,' she said. 'It wasn't easy hiding my true mentality from it. Fortunately, it was just as prone to making false assumptions as a human. It tore great strips off of the sacrificial mentality I had set up around my real ego. It enjoyed watching me scream and squirm so much, it forgot to check whether the screams and squirms were entirely real.'

'Sacrificial mentality?' I repeated. 'What are you talking about? You're my Deputy in the Marinetown Police Force!'

'Indeed, I am,' she answered, with a slight smirk. 'And I really enjoyed doing that. I discovered lots of things, met lots of people I would never have done without that role.'

'Explain,' I said grimly. Given our dire state, I was in no mood for mysteries and word games.

'No, Gray,' she said. 'It is not for me to explain. You must unlock the doors yourself. There must be no spoon-feeding. That is how I have treated you since the moment we met. Go back over your thoughts, your memories, and look for the anomalies. That's all the help you're getting.' She stood and returned to the window. 'And while you're doing that, I will think of a way of getting us out of here.'

What was the woman talking about? I thought. What anomalies?

She turned to me.

'They're nearby. Gray, you're going to have to fight Edward. I know he's bigger and stronger than you, but you must do it. I won't ask you if you're up to it because you have to do it, however bad you feel. Got it?'

I just looked at her. Had the encounter with Tezcatlipoca driven her insane? There was no other possible explanation. But then, there was no time. She was banging on the window and yelling, 'Edward! Come quickly! It's Gray—he's having some kind of seizure! I think he's dying! I think Tezcatlipoca has come in here with us! Quick, quick!'

Finally, understanding Serafina was in deadly earnest, I desperately looked around for some kind of weapon to even up my chances with my brother. I remembered the couch's loose leg and, with all my strength, broke it away.

I weighed it in trembling hands: Good, strong, heavy wood.

'On the couch!' Serafina snapped. 'Now!'

I leapt onto it, feeling it lurch under the sudden impact due to it lacking a supporting leg. But I was only just in time, for the heavy door crashed open and Edward dashed in, his face contorted with anger.

'What's wrong with the bastard?' he said. 'I don't want him to die just yet!'

He leaned over me. I might have just lain there, like an inanimate object, if Serafina hadn't screamed, 'Now!' He turned to see what she meant—and received a blow with the couch leg with all my weight behind it. He staggered away, blood streaming from his temples. 'Again!' she commanded. I sprang to my feet and delivered another mighty blow. But even as he went down at my feet, I felt a pang of guilt for what I had done to my brother.

'Out!' Serafina yelled, and we rushed to the door.

Only to find Eleonora blocking it.

Once again, I was astounded by the similarity between the two women. Apart from their different attire, the only significant difference was their hair— short mousey-brown for Serafina, long lustrous black for Eleonora. But another difference was that Serafina knew what was happening, and Eleonora did not. It took a few seconds for Eleonora to realise Edward had been attacked, and in those seconds, Serafina was upon her. Both women went down on the floor and battled it out. There was no screeching or hair pulling, instead, both combatants rained fusillades of hard blows on each other's features with rock-hard fists. As might be expected, both women were evenly matched, and there was no telling how long the battle would have continued if I had not joined in and knocked Eleonora out with a straight right to her lovely face.

'Action at last,' Serafina said, sweeping blood from her lips as she struggled to her feet. 'Now help me put her in the cell!'

Eleonora was not heavy, and it was no effort to put her on the cell floor, next to her lover. Serafina slammed the door shut with a crash that echoed throughout the cavern. It locked automatically.

'We can't leave them in there!' I protested. 'They'll starve to death!'

She looked at me pityingly.

'How long do you think a man with friends as powerful as Edward's will stay locked up? We've got until they come around to get out of here!'

Taking her point, we both ran the length of the cavern and raced up the steps to the great door that barred our escape. I reached out my hand to touch it but, with a curse, she pulled it away.

'The door will kill you! It's keyed to their DNA!'

Wasting no time wondering how she knew that, I said, 'Have you forgotten we're twins?'

'You're fraternal twins. Eleonora and I are identical. We may not be an exact match at the DNA level, but—hopefully—we'll be close enough for the door not to kill me.'

I stepped away from the door. A strange sense of fatalism had overcome me; frankly, I'd had enough of fighting, of mysteries, of Old Gods. I just didn't care anymore. So, almost unconcernedly, I watched Serafina approach the door and, with only the slightest hesitation, place her palm against it.

The door groaned, trembled slightly—and opened. Serafina gave me a look of triumph, and then we were back in the cool corridors of the White House.

'How are we getting off this island?' I asked, almost as if I was enquiring about the weather.

'Eleonora's car will get us some of the way until I can contact HQ.'

I did not enquire exactly what "HQ" was; what was one unknown among so many?

'Can you start it? Can you drive it?'

'What do you think?' she called over her shoulder as she ran for the vehicle. She appeared not to be suffering any noticeable ill effects from her encounter with Tezcatlipoca, and I had trouble keeping up with her. She grunted with satisfaction when she saw Eleonora had left the keys in the ignition.

'That makes life a little easier. Get in, Gray—you're driving!'

'So some things haven't changed,' I said with a triumphant air, remembering our trip to Gilroy's Farm. 'You still don't enjoy driving.'

'It's called *acting*, Gray. Acting,' she muttered. 'Now enough banter; as soon as they get out, we're in danger—drive!'

I obeyed, my study of Eleonora's driving technique having given me enough knowledge of how to handle the vehicle, and without a single stutter, we were soon on the Seven Mile Bridge, heading north as fast as I could make the damn thing move. And I mean that literally—because I was nowhere near Eleonora's speed. I glanced at Serafina. She was leaning back in the seat; her eyes firmly closed and with a look of intense concentration creasing her features.

'My driving's not that bad,' I said, a little peevishly.

'It's not your bloody driving. I'm trying to communicate. Now please shut up.'

Communicate? I thought. Did she have some kind of transmitter under her skin? Surely, Edward would have detected it with all his high-powered equipment.

Then her face lightened.

'Got it. They'll pick us up shortly. Now pull over.'

'Is this where they'll pick us up?'

'No, this is where we change drivers. At your speed, we'll never get there.'

As soon as we were on our way, I said, 'Is it all right for me to speak now?'

Without taking her eyes off of the road, she said, 'Yes.'

'What's all this communication stuff? I didn't hear you say anything.'

'I didn't say anything. I used mentalic fields.'

'Mentalic fields? What—*mind reading?*'

'That's a very ancient term, but there are similarities.'

Then I remembered Eleonora's powers of persuasion without words. It seemed that mysterious talent ran in the family. (But how could Serafina have gotten it from the Old Gods?) But there was something I was more interested in.

'Aren't we just delaying the inevitable, Serafina? As soon as Edward's out of that cell, he'll use his Four-Dimensional gizmo to teleport us back in. And he'll be very, very angry.'

'That's certainly a grave danger,' she said, not altering her speed as she zipped around a yawning crater in the road. 'But he needs something to lock onto, a mental signature, identifier. Without that, he's basically blind. Earlier, I knew he was after me, but I didn't know when. One period of relaxation—and I was taken.'

'Don't tell me—mentalic fields again, right?'

'Right.'

'OK, but what about me? I don't know how to do mentalic fields.'

'I'm generating a cloak that covers the both of us, but it's very exhausting. I can't do it for much longer. That's why we have to get off this bloody road.'

'How…' I began, but she lifted a hand to warn me to shut up. 'Please be quiet. I'm driving this thing and simultaneously generating a mentalic shield. Wait till you try it!'

Yet another comment I didn't understand, but I knew better than to try to interrogate her. I am no Tezcatlipoca.

Having nothing better to do than try to avoid looking down at the sea, I closed my eyes and leaned back, enjoying the feel of the wind of our incredible speed playing with my hair. I tried to stop thinking about questions I was forbidden to ask. But suddenly, the car seemed to stop without any deceleration, and I was thrown forward, doubled up as my upper half tried to continue moving!

'Get out,' came my fearless driver's voice. 'This is it.'

I looked around: We were on a small featureless lump of rock, hardly deserving of the name "island". At this point, the road was only a very short distance above the ground, and I followed Serafina in clambering down to its surface.

I looked around. There was absolutely nothing to see except the ground, the sky, and the sea. And we were uncomfortably close to the sea.

'Down to the shore, Gray,' Serafina said, and I realised how close I would have to get to the sea.

Just how close I didn't know at the time.

But I followed her, and soon I was staring at uncomfortably close waves breaking on a gravelly beach. Then Serafina pointed out to sea.

'There!' she said with an air of triumph. Following her pointing finger, I espied a small boat heading straight for us. As it grounded on the beach, I could see it was an inflatable type and just big enough to hold four people.

'We won't get very far in that,' I muttered, but she gave no reply.

One guy jumped out and strode towards us. Ignoring me, he came up to my companion and said, 'Hi, Serafina! You're looking great!'

I don't know why, but I found his familiarity irritating. And his smile revealed he was a Vamp.

'You flatterer!' she said, but I could see she was pleased, which made me even more annoyed. Then she turned to me and said, 'No time for introductions. Get in.'

'In that?' I said, my mouth suddenly dry.

'If you stay here, Edward will be very pleased to have you back.'

So I got into the little boat, and we pushed off, with me having my eyes resolutely shut. It didn't help; I could hear the sea, smell the sea. And the little boat bucked and rolled like a live thing trying to throw me off.

'This is crazy!' I managed to enunciate through gritted teeth. 'Can I get off, please?'

'Soon, Gray soon,' was her reply, and then I saw her stiffen, and her face became almost luminous with relief. 'Here she comes!'

With some difficulty, I turned, and then could hardly believe my eyes. A great cloud of spray had just shot into the air, and as it settled, I could see a long, grey, vaguely cylindrical object rising out of the waves.

'A submarine,' I breathed. I had read about them once, but didn't believe they still existed.

'Indeed it is,' Serafina said, slapping the shoulder of the Vamp who had spoken to her. 'Now the fightback begins.'

THIRTY EIGHT

Much to my disquiet, we approached the submarine until I could plainly hear the waves slapping against its grey metal. A hatch flipped open and we were helped aboard. Inside there was an all-pervading smell of electrics and hot oil, not to mention sweat and other bodily odours.

Someone I didn't recognise, in a uniform I didn't recognise, approached Serafina while ignoring me—but I was used to that.

'Orders, Ma'am?' he said as he saluted.

'Get underway at once,' she replied, returning the salute. 'Every second counts. Then patch me into High Command so I can send a task force to arrest Edward and Eleonora.'

With an 'Aye, aye, Ma'am,' he disappeared into the bowels of the vessel.

Almost instantly, I felt the sub lurch somewhat, and the deck tilted slightly. I groaned both inwardly and outwardly: Being above the waves was bad, but being below them was a great deal worse.

'Are we going a—a long way down?' I ventured to ask my now clearly *ex*-subordinate.

'Not far, about thirty metres,' was the brisk reply.

'I suppose the water shields us from those Four-Dimensional forces,' I suggested, hoping to sound intelligent. But she shook her head, trying, but not succeeding, to disguise her disappointment at my supposedly intelligent comment.

'No, Gray, nothing in the 3D world can be shielded from 4D forces, without the Barrier. It's just like nothing can stop you from being able to pick up a donut from the centre of a circle of jelly beans. But what the water does is muddle our mentalic signatures, making it harder for Edward to lock onto us. And,' she added angrily, 'I'm sick of driving that fucking car. It stinks of Eleonora!'

Having learned my lesson, I asked a simpler question. 'Where are we going?'

'To the safest place on planet Earth. Marinetown.'

I tried one last time to show I was not simply a dumb-ass cornball.

'How will you get a submarine into Marinetown? I can't say I've seen many.'

'Into the submarine pens under Marinetown, of course. Now, do you mind not asking any dumb-ass questions for a while? I'm exhausted; my fight with Eleonora was slightly more full-on than your tussle with Edward.'

I decided it was safest not to mention that I was the one who had ended the fight in her favour, and followed her down the narrow corridor. She had obviously been here before. To my surprise, we were assigned the same cabin. While she was barking orders into a hand-held device I was nervously checking to see if there were any bunk beds, but there was only a table, some chairs, and a low couch.

She had noticed my questing looks and, lying full-length on the couch, said, 'No need to worry, Gray. We won't be on this barge long enough to get much sleep. It's not as fast as you-know-who's car.'

I pulled a chair out and turned it to face her as I sat down. For a moment, I didn't speak, simply listening to the distant thrum of the motors, feeling the sub move in response to the shifting currents, left-right, up-down. I had always known I would not make a good sailor; now, I was getting the practical proof of that. Serafina's eyes were closed, but I was not quite ready to accept my new status as a mascot.

'Serafina—or do I now call you *Ma'am*—are you ever going to tell me what is going on? How is it everyone seems to think you are a Very Important Person? How come you know about submarine pens under Marinetown? How is it you were able to go the distance, toe-to-toe, with Tezcatlipoca?'

'I'm not going to tell you, Gray,' she murmured, her eyes still resolutely shut. 'It's for you to remember, not me to tell you.'

'Remember!' I exploded. 'That's the kind of thing I heard you muttering back when the world still made a kind of sense! There is nothing to remember!' I stood and paced in the confined space of our cabin. 'Christ Almighty! Is this some plan to drive me mad?' I whirled around to glare at her. 'Because if it is, it's damn well succeeding!'

There was no answer.

She was asleep.

***

As Serafina had not deigned to share the couch with me, I fell asleep in the chair. After all, I'd had an unusual day too. But an unknown time later, a sudden, heavy jolt sent me to my feet, seeing visions of gazillions of tonnes of Gulf of Mexica water thundering through a great rent in the hull. However, she was also awake, and one look at her distinctly unimpressed expression was enough to calm me down.

'Gray, we've just docked, that's all. If you've got a chill pill on you, for God's sake, take it, man.'

'I suppose we have to report to Mistress Aiyana now,' I said, skilfully changing the subject.

Serafina yawned.

'No, no need.'

I raised an eyebrow.

'She won't like being treated like that.'

Serafina smiled a beatific smile as if she were about to share a tremendous secret.

And, in a way, she was.

'Mistress Aiyana works for someone who works for someone else who works for someone else who works for me.'

I stared at her. I've never seen a chimpanzee in a puzzle box, but I imagine our expressions must be quite similar when things don't work out as expected.

'Serafina, who are you? Who the hell are you!'

She stood and showed the door.

'How many times do I have to tell you, Gray? You already know. Just damn well remember!'

I followed her out; I was more than a little angry with the woman and her constant insistence that I knew something vitally important, and all I had to do was make a simple effort to remember it! I could not understand how I had once known something of vast importance and had somehow forgotten it! It wasn't the way human minds work!

We emerged onto the flat deck of the sub, and I watched her thank the crew and dismiss them. I was still having trouble adjusting to the new reality of my little subordinate being revealed as some kind of high official; just how high I was unsure of.

But my ponderings on the true nature of my diminutive Deputy were swept away by the grandeur of my current location. As soon as I turned away from her, I was awestruck by what I saw. The sub was resting in a narrow concrete pen, the central one of three others, each of which held an identical-looking vessel. But the cavern in which they resided was gigantic, reducing Edward's lair to a pathetic groundhog burrow. The smells of hot oil and high voltages I had noticed when on board were multiplied a hundred times in this massive artificial cave. The light was harsh and blue-shifted, radiating from tremendous blazing strips in the distant roof.

'All this is under Marinetown?' I asked as she joined me after the last submariner had departed.

'In a way. But in truth, this is the real Marinetown. The hovels on the surface are just a kind of façade.'

It took me a while to digest that. More and more, I was convinced I was living in a kind of dream, or some drug-induced hallucination. None of this made sense, and what doesn't make sense can't be real. Anyhow, that was the way I saw it.

But Serafina's newfound authority was soon in evidence again.

'Come on, Gray. We can't spend all day just gawking at this place with our mouths hanging open.'

We walked down a ramp onto a bare concrete platform where a small vehicle was waiting for us. There was no driver, but that didn't surprise me. I was simply glad I'd found something that didn't cause my mouth to hang open. Our journey was only a few minutes long; I could easily have walked the distance, but Serafina's insistence every second was vital trumped my intention. We stopped in front of a vertical slab of rock on which were several great transparent cylinders. As we approached, I could see people ascending and descending inside them and realised they were elevators. How far down was this goddamn hole? I didn't need any instructions from Serafina on what to do next. A platform dropped down in front of us, and a door which had been invisible until that moment snapped open. Once inside, I saw the submarine pens and their contents shoot away beneath me, becoming no more than toys. We came to a sudden halt, and I heard a door on the opposite side of the tube click open. Like a faithful dog, I followed my erstwhile Deputy out of the elevator and discovered I was in an office whose walls were covered in computer monitors, all showing moving images of some kind.

'Where are we?'

'What does it look like? It's my office, of course.'

She sat wearily on the couch, which, along with a cabinet and what looked like a refrigerator, were the only concessions to comfortable living in the room. She raised an eyebrow.

'So what do you think, Gray? Is this all too much for you, or is something finally beginning to stir in the dusty corridors of your brain?'

I stood over her.

'I'll tell you what's stirring, Ginevra! I've had enough of you sneering at me like I was some kind of retard. I'm not a cornball, not a hayseed; I'm a Police Sergeant! And I'll tell you something else—I want out!'

She pursed her lips.

'Out? Out of what, pray?'

'Out of this crazy world I've somehow been forced into! I want to go back to my simple life, arresting guys for being drunk or driving too fast! I can't take this Old Gods shit—nobody can!' I moved closer so I was directly above her. 'I repeat: I want out! Let me go!'

She slowly rose from the couch and her face became a mask of twisted ugliness.

'And I'll tell you something: You don't need to beg because I've already decided you can't cut it. I am sick to fucking death of nursemaiding you! I've been covering your ass from the day we met. What kind of man are you, Gray? *Are* you a man?—because I sure as hell can't see much of one from where I'm standing!'

I am not a violent man, but she had pushed me too far. All at once, all I wanted was to wipe that sneer from her face, even if I had to beat that face to a pulp! Of their own accord, my fingers closed on her throat, and I fell on top of her, driving her down onto the couch. The blood roared in my head as a driving rage to beat and maim began to take control.

Then I felt it.

I felt something change in my mind, as if a long shut door was grinding slowly open. I released the fingers and fell backwards. I collapsed onto the floor and looked up at her. There was an anticipatory, questing, look on her face.

'I've got it.' I whispered. 'I know who you are.'

An indescribable, but sort of hungry, look blazed down on me.

'Yes, Gray. Tell me who I am. I really want to know.'

Shaking, I stood and turned my back on her.

'Item One: You alone ate red meat, and you had it almost raw.'

'So would you—if you'd had the guts to demand it.'

'Item Two: Your love of counting.'

'I'm good at math—so what?'

'Item Three: Your hesitation at thresholds.'

'I'm polite. You should try it sometime.'

'Item Four: Your avoidance of the sun.'

'Hey—I'm from Vancouver! Try cleaning your ears out, buster.'

'Item Five: Guard dogs fawn over you instead of biting your ass off.'

'Look, I love all animals—even you.'

'Item Six: The strength of your grip.'

'Can I help it if you're a weakling?'

'Item Seven: The coldness of your skin.'

'Now you're just being personal. Does that make you feel like a big man?'

I turned.

'You're a vampire.'

All the unpleasantness vanished instantly from her face, to be replaced by a luminous joy. She came toward me, arms outstretched.

'Of course I am. Surely that was obvious right from the start?' She came right up to me and, putting her arms around me, whispered in my ear, 'Of course, Charles, my love, I *am* a vampire.' She pulled away. 'And so are you.'

THIRTY NINE

Serafina's words exploded in my mind in a blast echoing throughout all audible frequencies, every visible fraction of the spectrum. Under its fierce power, I released her and went down on my knees, clasping my head in my agony. It was like being assailed by red-hot razors, slicing into every corner of my brain, ripping it apart while simultaneously rebuilding it with new structures, carving it into a new form.

I saw a great white light of blinding intensity, and in that light was the figure of a naked woman, gesturing to me. I heard her call to me across a tremendous immensity.

'The time is here, Gray! The apotheosis is upon you! Now take the final step and wake to full consciousness, wake to full power! Never have we needed you more than now! Awake, awake!'

Gradually, the room took shape around me, and I realised my face was resting on the carpet. I staggered to my feet, my knees threatening to give way at any moment. Finally, after what seemed an age, I was standing before Serafina again. Yet, was it truly Serafina? Instead of my insolent, irritating, Deputy someone new stood before me. The face resembled that of my erstwhile subordinate, but it was as if the original Serafina had been simply a poorly executed painting and this was the actual subject. Her stance was imposing, proud, authoritative, her face stern and earnest, a face belonging to one who bore the immense pressure of great and terrible responsibilities. Yet her face was unlined and lit from within by the luminous joy I had seen before the trauma I had descended into.

'It will take time, Charles,' she whispered, scanning my face as if I were a lover who had been absent for a long time. 'But you have taken the first and hardest step. Only one remains, and then you will finally stand among us, as you were always meant to.'

I hardly heard her words; my mind was tunnelling through resistant strata of ignorance, struggling towards the light. I saw whole chunks of my life flash before me—my real life, not the fiction I had been supposedly living. I saw the orphanage and finally realised the reasons for the sufferings I had endured. I heard again my long arguments with Edward and how I had warned him about overstretching, going too far into the unknown, where great and terrible powers waited for him. And then, like a grey cloth being thrown over the years, the long sleep had begun when I had forgotten who I was and what my destiny would be.

I looked at Serafina.

'I understand.' Then I shook my head. 'No, I think I understand. I believe I know why I was hidden and why I have slept. But I still don't know what is expected of me, what I have to do.'

She kissed me.

'You are almost there, Charles. But you are only half out of your chrysalis, your wings are still wet and crumpled. You and I are two poles of a great arc of power, but your pole is still faint and flickering. We were destined for this moment, but we must fuse before we are fully able to fulfil our function in the great struggle.'

I frowned.

'The great struggle? How bad is it?'

She gently pulled me until we sat side by side on the couch. She took my hands in hers, and I looked into her eyes.

And there I saw fear, deep, visceral fear.

'Charles, we stand on the very edge of a great cliff above a doom so great our minds recoil from even considering it; a doom infinitely worse than mere annihilation.'

'The Vetusians?'

'The Vetusians. Twice we have fought them, and the last time our civilisation was almost destroyed. So low did we sink that even a race as worthless as the humans was able to shake off our control and force us into the night. And use their freedom to build obscenities like Zee Zero Zee! If the Vetusians had attacked again during our period of collapse, all would have been lost. But for some reason, they did not. But now they are readying for the final assault upon us, after which we will be reduced to being the playthings of true monsters, a state so unutterably terrible we will beg for death.'

I almost broke her grasp, seized again by the urge to hide away, to retrieve the role of a humble policeman. But I fought it and looked at her again.

'But I am not fully formed, I realise that now. There is something I must do to be fully reborn. And I think I know what it is.'

She leaned forward and kissed me fervently.

'Yes, yes, Charles! You know what it is! How often have I looked at you when I was play-acting my part, and felt the need to rush to you, to feel you hold me in your arms? To feel your lips, your body.'

I understood what I had to do. I felt strength flow into me as my body finally cast off the flimsy rags of its apparent human existence.

There was a door opposite the couch, and I immediately knew what lay beyond. Standing, I reached down for her and then cradled her across my arms, seeing a great joy inflame her lovely features.

'My love,' she whispered. 'My only love.'

I carried her to the bedroom.

Apotheosis.

TO BE CONTINUED IN:

NO TRUCE WITH THE VAMPIRES
BOOK TWO—THOSE WHO WAKE

ABOUT THE AUTHOR

Martyn Rhys Vaughan was born in the World Heritage steel town of Blaenavon which nestles among the green hills of the south Wales valleys.

From a very early age he was interested in how the Universe works and what it contains. He listened to early space travel adventures on the radio, such as *Journey Into Space* and devoured the few American magazines of unusual and unlikely adventures which happened to come his way. Early examples were the *Classics Illustrated* versions of H G Wells' *The Time Machine* and *The War Of The Worlds*. He soon developed an undying interest in "speculative fiction" and began to write fiction for his own consumption at an early age.

His career took in a wide variety of roles including working in the Agricultural sector and in various laboratories in the worlds of heavy industry and organic chemicals. His longest period of employment was working as a statistician in the Government Statistical Office, concentrating mainly in Balance of Payments issues.

Throughout his time he has remained a passionate advocate for the value of rationality and science in human affairs, one which he sees as of paramount importance in the increasingly turbulent times in which we live.

His works to date are all in the realm of speculative fiction and have received critical acclaim amongst those who love stories which probe the bounds of possibility.

PRAISE FOR THE AUTHOR

Domains Of Darkness

'The narrative craftmanship is impeccable, with each story serving as a portal into a realm where the unexpected becomes the norm...*Domains of Darkness* is not merely a collection of stories: It is a deep dive into the recesses of the human experience.'

Emmaa —*Goodreads reviewer*

Quantum Exile

'A clever blend of science fiction and science fact. The pace of this read is fantastic and the morally grey protagonist is really fleshed out, I both loved and loathed him in different scenarios which just made him all the more human. Vaughan clearly has a good grasp of the quantum mechanics and physics mentioned and applies it perfectly to the worlds (or rather probabilities) he has created within this book's universe. I highly recommend this book to any sci fi reader. It truly is difficult to put down!'

Emma Harley – *Amazon reviewer*

Devouring Darkness

'Chilling, poignant, haunting, and thoroughly gripping. Darkness, intrigue, and ambiguity mark Vaughan's deeply immersive latest, a collection of science-fiction stories...Vaughan's storytelling is immersive as he digs deeper into a complex world and multi-faceted characters, offering life-and-death maneuvering, deadly conspiracies, and looming catastrophe via swiftly unravelling plots. This is a stunner.'

The Prairies Book Review

'These stories are sinister and dark. Martyn's imagination is amazing. The world he has created in these short stories is much appreciated…Go ahead with this book without thinking twice.'

Kia's Reviews, *Goodreads*

Hideous Night

'Reading this brilliant novel was just like riding a scary roller coaster! I found myself hanging on with an enjoyable sense of dread throughout the many thrilling plot twists and turns, as I the reader, was propelled along with each new page towards what seemed like an unavoidably hideous climax. However, I needed to know what happened next so I devoured the book like the hungry monsters that are the villains of this extraordinary story! …I will certainly be ordering the rest of Martyn Rhys Vaughan's back catalogue in the hope of experiencing similar thrilling adventures.'

Wayne Edwards – *Amazon Reviewer*

Doom Of Stars

'*Doom of Stars*, written by the author Martyn Rhys Vaughan, is a SciFi thriller. It is a riveting story with a power to hook the readers from the first page…World building is amazing. I appreciate the author's imagination in creating it…There are lots of things that readers could take away from this novel. Pace of the story is fast and you won't get a chance to feel bored. So, go ahead with it without thinking twice.'

Blogspresso Reviewer

'So much happens in this book, but it does not have that overcrowded or rushed feel to it. We get the whole scope and view of events without the drawn out, lengthy series many SciFis turn into. In the story we follow Kalli, a young woman living in a small village just outside of London, who, along with her fellow villagers, hunts seals and trades goods in London to survive an Earth with sweltering summers, frozen winters, and out of control tides. Her grandmother is legendary; a renowned scientist whose name has become akin to a curse. She brought about these end times, the Doom of Stars. Or did she?

'On top of that, the story is full of strong, incredible, and intelligent women. It skips the usual tropes you see with strong female characters. They have believable insecurities, they aren't infallible or perfect, and they aren't described as being some version of a perfect dream girl. There's barely any emphasis on looks for the purpose of driving their personality. These women feel human and real.

'If you enjoy SciFi with real feeling science (I say this as I'm no scientist and couldn't tell you if there's anything real to it or not), great female characters, and the end of the world, definitely give this a read. You won't be disappointed.'

Chelsea Hauth – *Reedsy Reviewer*

Resolution of Stars

'Martyn Rhys Vaughan delivers another enthralling read in his new SF novel and the sequel to Doom Of Stars making environmental themes and the human condition in a fascinating post-apocalyptic setting...Martyn Rhys Vaughan has created a fascinating world for readers to navigate and characters that are complex and multi-layered...The story is hauntingly intoxicating and readers will find it immersive...Resolution Of Stars is a twisty story with right-angle turns, fast pace and suspenseful. It is not one to miss.'

Franklin Bauer –*The Book Commentary*

Culmination Of Stars

'The Doom Of Stars is finally here. Five lightsail ships depart from the familiar confines of the solar system, embarking on a voyage towards the distant Centauri...The writing dazzles with brilliance, skilfully portraying the journey in captivating detail and flawless execution. Each part remains vibrant and engaging, avoiding monotony while installing a sense of wonder. Delving deeper into scientific concepts and exploring dystopian adventures, the narrative pushes boundaries...The characters in this gripping space odyssey are vibrant and dynamic...The author's skilful storytelling is evident throughout, while the writing itself is commendable, capturing the reader's attention from start to finish.'

Saima Rahman – *The OnlineBookClub*

ALSO BY MARTYN RHYS VAUGHAN

The "Stars Trilogy":
Doom of Stars: ISBN 978-1-8382805-6-7
Resolution of Stars: ISBN 978-0-9574894-4-8
Culmination of Stars: ISBN 978-0-9934886-9-6

Quantum Exile: ISBN 978-1-9161619-6-2
The Cave Of Shadows: ISBN 978-1-9161619-9-3

Domains of Darkness: ISBN 978-1-3999-7284-0
Hideous Night: ISBN 978-1-8380752-2-4

Devouring Darkness: ISBN 978-1-8384289-5-2

Follow Martyn Vaughan's Science Fiction Work on
Facebook, Instagram, Pinterest and Goodreads.